Broken Land Dreams

David Forbes

Everything is a living being, even time, even words. Joy Harjo

We must assume our existence as broadly as we in any way can; everything, even the unheard-of, must be possible in it. That is at bottom the only courage that is demanded of us: to have courage for the most strange, the most singular and the most inexplicable that we may encounter. Rilke

I have spread my dreams under your feet; Tread softly because you tread on my dreams. Yeats

Table of Contents

Note to the Reader from Maya, Jacob's Wife: What You Need to Know First Before Reading

This is Jacob's story. I read it after I returned from having to take a break from him. Please don't expect a conventional linear narrative. Part I is the background in which he first tells you what he broods about, why I left him, and what I told him he needs to recover from. In Part II, which is most of the book, he then tells you how he sets forth on his surreal pandemic journey and what he did to face and recover from himself. Along the way, with the help of others, he had to work to save Brooklyn from the right-wing Ratocracy and earn back my trust.

While the structure in Part II loosely follows Dante's journey through Hell and Purgatory to try to reach Heaven, Jacob's restless, imaginative mind mirrors the broken land of Brooklyn and beyond. The fragments of dreams, poems, lyrics, reflections, and social commentary he inserts illuminate his interior and outer world. Yet in his dream-infused quest for personal growth, love, and fierce compassion for all, he manages to weave together the disparate parts into a visionary tapestry.

Did Jacob the dreamer recover from being a self-absorbed kvetch to a more relatable, caring mensch? I invite you to see for yourself.

Maya T., R.N.

I

CHAPTER ONE

On the Terminal Moraine: New Notes from the Underground and Above

I live in Brooklyn on and below the Terminal Moraine, a long ridge of glacial debris shoved into a massive pile.

I'm a brooding, grumpy, white male lefty boomer from the sixties, a remaindered knock-off of Dostoevsky's Underground Man, with a senior reduced-fare pass to the Underground and a Brooklyn attitude. I was a high school social worker, retired just last year.

My wife, Maya—my heart—separated from me a month ago. Well, maybe more. We argued a lot. She said she could no longer put up with my self-absorbed sadness, my inner loneliness, my yearning for things to be other than they are. Okay, and my ruthless criticism and irritability at everything—including, of course, at her. So, she left to stay with her divorced sister, Jill, a doula, upstate during the pandemic quarantine. Maya's an OB/GYN nurse administrator in a city hospital and could work online. She said I needed to get my shit together.

Just before she left, I overheard her talking to Jill in the bedroom on the speakerphone.

"Can I stay with you for a while?"

"Sure. What's going on?"

"It's Jacob, I feel I've lost him. I've lost myself too. I feel alone even when he's around. He's gotten worse since he retired."

"I'm sorry. Look, you know you need to take care of yourself, it can't be all about him."

"Right. Thanks."

"You're welcome up here anytime, sis, love ya."

That night, Maya put down her cup of honey vanilla chamomile tea. She looked me straight in the eye and told me she was leaving.

"Jacob," she said, "You need to recover from yourself. You spend too much time brooding about how unhappy you are and being angry at things. You've become so self-absorbed I feel like you're not here with me anymore." She took a sip of her tea.

"If you can make some major changes," she continued, "then we'll see about reconciling."

Maya doesn't answer my texts. Jill's phone just rings.

I am alone for now.

The pandemic time warp magnifies this sense of endless now. The mindfulness marketing peddlers think you can capture and stay in the now, which is a myth. The now is like liquid mercury, ungraspable. It's not an object or a self-evident fact, it has to be interpreted. Stories surround and connect to every now, including other nows from the past.

I asked myself about the present: how wide it was, how deep it was, how much was mine to keep. —Kurt Vonnegut, Slaughterhouse Five

Despite their pseudo-wisdom, in a perverse way the mindfulness marketing peddlers are right: When you're in pain it's always now.

Phantom Limb
To lose a lover
is like gaining
a phantom limb

Alone in bed
you feel her stomach
on your cheeks

or feel your cheeks
between her thighs
You taste her mouth

These are all
synaptic lapses

In a safe dark room
you nurse this
phantom heart
Whose visions of love
are mortal as flesh

My Life Alone on the Terminal Moraine

Since Maya left, I spend even more time on the Terminal Moraine pondering mysterious, troublesome, and unjust things from our high-story window above and the subway below. I brood about the sky. Eastern Parkway. Brooklyn. Manhattan. The Underground. The American Dream. My life. The Terminal Moraine itself.

Some of these thoughts lead to questions I call Xen Kohens, a riff off Zen Koans. Zen Koans are Buddhist mind busters with no rational answers. They are designed to lead to enlightenment through further meditation, to get you to go beyond thought itself. Just as often they lead to more endless pondering and dreaming.

This sort of morose brooding and anger at what is puzzling and unjust is what drives Maya mad. They rob me of my time with her. I'm not present. So much for meditation.

The Terminal Moraine

What are those feeble Jews doing? ... from this heap of rubble can they bring the stones back to life? —Nehemiah 4:2

Thousands of years ago a huge wall of ice taller than any skyscraper came down and covered New York. The glacier's arrival in Brooklyn was its terminus and turning point. Its retreat north marked the end of the ice age itself. As it receded, it dumped and scattered boulders, rocks, soil, and sediment in a line thirty miles long. The moraine still lies under the city, an invisible thread that links three boroughs. The giant rock hills in Central Park, the boulders in the Brooklyn Botanic Garden, itself on the moraine, testify to what it left behind.

A New York Times journalist says the scattered fragments of the moraine offer mute testimony to the power of vanished ice.

Can the moraine speak?

Two artists imagine its voice. In spring 2021 they created a sound installation, "Terminal Moraine," in the Brooklyn Botanic Garden.

... auditory representations of tree growth and glacial ice recession are simulated by algorithms: Cells expand and branch with an element of uncertainty while crystalline structures gradually break apart. The resulting sonic dialog expresses change on the border between the deep history of this place and whatever comes next. — Ben Rubin and Brian House

Some think the name *Brooklyn* is Dutch for Broken Land. It's named, though, for Breukelen, a town in Holland, and the Dutch word also means *marsh land*. The myth persists, though. In some ways, Brooklyn today is indeed a broken land, its people fractioned and divided, split off from each other and from within. Eliot's *Waste Land* redux: *A heap of broken images.*

The terminal moraine itself fractions Brooklyn.

The terminal moraine is thus Brooklyn's continental divide, cleaving the borough into two distinct halves: a hilly Manhattan-oriented northern hemisphere, and a broad, low-slung southern hemisphere close in spirit to Long Island's south shore ... this ancient glacial binary—terminal moraine and outwash plain—has played a vital role in Brooklyn's growth and development, and remains a key to understanding the borough today. —Thomas J. Campanella, *Brooklyn: The Once and Future City*

Most people in New York don't know they live on a terminal moraine. They don't know they're like strewn boulders themselves, erratics, linked along a glacial ridge. Broken parts of a broken land.

In this, my own story, I collect bits of others' thoughts and poems, scattered about.

These fragments I have shored against my ruins —T.S. Eliot, *"The Waste Land"*

Can I restore fragments of a forgotten whole? Can we?

Some people I see don't even know they're alive. They carry around dead ideas about things, like the value of money. Money is more alive to them than they are. Money is dead labor, Marx said, it lives only by sucking living labor like a vampire.

Some walk around New York like zombies sucked dry by vampire capital.

I walk through rooms of the dead, streets of the dead, cities of the dead; men without eyes, men without voices; men with manufactured feelings and standard reactions; men with newspaper brains, television souls and high school ideas. —Charles Bukowski

They walk all over the Earth. Yet the Earth is alive. The moraine is alive. The city is alive.

The cold [building] *stone is natural, almost living: it absorbs water, warms under the sun, and sloughs its skin in rain. Like us, stone is affected by time, its outer layer softened and its veins made more prominent.* —Alexandra Horowitz, *On Looking: A Walker's Guide to the Art of Observation*

The Skyway

From our high story window, I stare at the sky above the city, trying to read it for signs, or just waiting for one. I scan it for the future. I look for a skyway that leads out of the greed and self-centeredness on the ground, toward the light. Instead, I see and hear deafening low-flying choppers that carry wealthy Wall Street commuters to JFK and self-centered rich types fleeing to the Hamptons across Brooklyn. Their menacing growl creates a war zone effect. I see dazed seagulls, geese, and other disoriented birds flying about, confused by the daily up-and-down temperatures from climate change.

The Xen Kohen I Keep Meditating On

As for the birds, I meditate at times on a line from a Dylan song that has stayed with me since I was a teen. In it his friends in prison ask him: how good (how good) does it feel to be free? Dylan replies with his own Xen Kohen: "Are birds free from the chains of the skyway?"

Are they?

Eastern Parkway

Eastern Parkway, on which I live, runs along the crest of the moraine and is one of the highest points in Brooklyn. It's one of Walt Whitman's "ample hills": stand up, beautiful hills of Brooklyn! Olmstead designed it as America's first parkway, a long tree-lined road meant for pleasure.

Since the pandemic, though, it's become less a pleasure road and more a dangerous crowded superhighway. The city has done little to make it safer.

The edges are friendly to people, but the road itself has devolved into six-lane highway. Using it requires constant vigilance, a feeling of precarity that is at odds with any of the remotely pleasurable emotions that its original vision aimed to invoke. — Diana Budds

On Eastern Parkway most days and nights, I hear the frequent whine of sirens—ambulance, fire, and police.

*Far off the banshee wail of police or fire sirens rose and fell, never for very long completely silent... A city no worse than others, a city rich and vigorous and full of pride, a city lost and beaten and full of emptiness. —*Raymond Chandler, *The Long Good-Bye*

The Parkway links Hasidic and Orthodox Jews, African American and Caribbean people, other working families trying to get by, young white professionals, alienated leftist boomers like me, and some hipsters. Some days, I long to escape.

Brooklyn

From my perch above the moraine, I see clumps of Brooklyn buildings and rooftops stretched out below. They are outmoded remnants of an earlier form of privatized life. The idea was that everyone was free to rent living spaces from those who owned them. They were to have demeaning, meaningless jobs during the day and return home at night to listen to the radio or watch TV. At least they could control and invest in their children, projections of their own broken land dreams.

These dead forms of life live on. Some people now get to "own" their residence — i.e., buy it back with interest from the real owners, the banks, as if that's a form of freedom. Others are homeless, troubled men, quite a few of them Black, who are free to roam and sleep on sidewalks or in subway stations or dangerous shelters.

Private pain, loneliness, everyone out for themselves: the sad way it is for many.

Some segregated Black and Brown Brooklyn neighborhoods are more impoverished, destitute, and dangerous than others. They are food deserts with poor services, inadequate health care, and crappy schools, held in place by racist real estate and banking practices. Since the sixties, white flight, racial tensions, loss of manufacturing, and gentrification have accelerated the divisions.

I'm going to tell you something
It's a simple fact of life.
If you're a young man in East New York,
Here's a simple fact of life:
If they don't shoot you with a gun,
They'll cut you with a knife.
—Fragment from "Dread" by Cornelius Eady

Brooklyn we go hard, we go hard... —Jay-Z

Many of the new ugly skyscrapers in downtown Brooklyn and Manhattan that mar my view stand empty. They are owned by absentee Saudi, Chinese, and Russian billionaires, beyond the reach of the countless New Yorkers who are just scraping by. There are few choices in a city with little to no affordable housing. Newer immigrants—Chinese, Pakistanis, West Indians, Russians, Central Americans—land in certain areas and perpetuate a segregated, fractured Brooklyn.

Before the hipsters and gentrifiers and real estate developers came, Brooklyn was once a gritty, ignored, working-class outsider, squatting just across from Manhattan, the center of the universe, on the other side of the bridge.

In a broken land, sweet Brooklyn nostalgia remains a popular unifying meme, mostly for white ethnics—Jews, Italians, Irish from the outwash plain. I hear some people reminisce about eating, laughing, arguing, hanging out together, listening to the Dodgers on the radio, playing skelly and stoopball and jacks and hopscotch and ringolevio, knowing the corner candy store guy and he knowing you, having an egg cream, helping the old lady in 3C with her groceries. Not for nuttin. Don't tell me. Getouttaheah. Fuhgeddaboudit.

Fragment from "Backyard" by Diane Di Prima:
O Brooklyn! Brooklyn!
where fences crumbled under the weight of rambling roses
and naked plaster women bent eternally white over birdbaths
the icicles on the chains of the swings tore my fingers
& the creaking tomato plants tore my heart as they wrapped their
roots around fish heads rotting beneath them
& the phonograph too creaked Caruso come down from the skies

Is it homesickness for an idealized, vanished past? Or a yearning for a common future? Does Francie's Tree of Heaven still grow in Brooklyn?

Where Everybody Knows Your Name: Unlike many, I was not a Cheers fan. You can only find a community of people who share your troubles in a bar with drunks and people with the emotional capacity of ten-year-olds? The song is popular, though, because it expresses what many lack and long for. It's what I lack and long for.

Another Xen Kohen: Can we create a place like the one in the song, and how do we all get there?

Manhattan

From my high-floor window I have an overview of the Manhattan skyline, from One World Trade Center to Midtown and beyond. At night the Empire State Building does occasional light shows like a hippie stoner. On Valentine's Day it simulates a pulsating red heartbeat: lub dub, lub dub. I see the Williamsburg, an ugly 1903 bridge that by night looks almost glamorous. I note the disappearance of other bridges, blocked by new high rises that sprout up every few months: the Manhattan barely flashes a slip of a span. The orange beads of the Queensboro have faded in number.

No sign from here of the most beautiful of all, Roebling's Brooklyn Bridge. You can almost sense its presence. When you see it through the lenses of the poets (Crane, Mayakovsky, Moore) or artists (Dufy, O'Keefe, Stella, Warhol) it becomes more apparent how it merges timeless love with stone and steel.

What path must one take to see the ordinary, fractured world in a new light, as one transcendent, timeless, living form?

Fragment from the cosmic poem The Bridge by Hart Crane:
So to thine Everpresence, beyond time,
Like spears ensanguined of one tolling star
That bleeds infinity—the orphic strings,
Sidereal phalanxes, leap and converge:
—One Song, one Bridge of Fire!

From our bedroom window on clear winter days at dawn and dusk the sun ignites the spires of Midtown and Long Island City into blinding pillars of fire. Before daybreak I sometimes hear a Muslim call to prayer from a nearby mosque. In the fall and winter, I awake to see if the new, thin high-rise building in lower Manhattan will catch the first rays of the sun while others around it remain dark. When it does it glows orange as if lit from within. It's a sibling of the monolith in *2001*, a mute luminous tower planted by aliens amid the urban detritus. I check to see if it's sending out signal beams to a higher planetary civilization, to guide us to the next stage of evolution. It too is being eclipsed from view by new overpriced, high-rise monoliths in downtown Brooklyn that stand empty, devoid of life.

Uptown on the edge of the river I can see the enormous new complex at Hudson Yards. The buildings loom over the city, stalking it like Stay Puft monsters from a lousy *Ghostbusters* remake. They were designed after 9/11, the fall of the World Trade Center buildings, to prop up and showcase the power and glory of Our System, monuments to undying zombie consumer capitalism. When you visit the buildings, you discover their insides are hollow, soulless. The complex, a twenty-first-century version of the Crystal Palace, regards you with indifference and contempt. It displays useless overpriced crap nobody wants and few can afford.

A monstrous sculpture at the site is The Vessel, also known as The Stairway to Nowhere and one that art critics compare to a rats' nest. The structure later reopened but the top deck has been permanently closed since four people jumped from there to their death.

Although I can't see it from here, I am haunted by dreams about Stairways to Nowhere and rats' nests.

From here, though, you can observe the other buildings standing around clumped together like big galoots trying to look cool at a party that's already winding down. The party's over, all the beautiful people have gone home with somebody else. They are at the edge of a system teetering on the brink of the future, ready to topple again this time for good.

Sadness Underground

I ride the subway for hours under the moraine, beneath this heap of rubble, below this waste land. I take underworld journeys often fraught with peril, like those of Odysseus, Demeter, Orpheus, and Dante. I'm seeking Tiresias, Hades, and Virgil to see what I can learn from them.

New Yorkers know the subway is our own version of hell. A tweet from somebody in *amNewYork* said: If you haven't built an entire personality out of hating the subway, are you really a New Yorker?

On my underground journey I see people in pain: homeless beggars, angry ranters, sad-eyed children, the anxious wage-enslaved heading to work, desperate immigrants. I see self-centered covidiots in crowded subway cars who refuse to wear a mask.

I'm cursed with cosmic vision. I see shit others can't. I see into people's hearts and minds. I see the past and future. I see timelessness in time.

Can I see the world through the eyes of all sentient beings? I wish.

Fragment from "Riding the D–Train" by Enid Dame
Notice your fellow riders:
the Asian girl chewing a toothpick,
the boy drawing trees on his hand,
the man in a business suit
whose shoes don't match.

Everything is important:
that thin girl, for instance,
in flowered dress, golden high heels.
How did her eyes get scarred?
Why is that old man crying?
Why does that woman carry
a cat in her pocket book?

Don't underestimate
any of it.
Anything you don't see
Will come back to haunt you.

The Broken American Dream

I grieve for the American Dream. Like generations before them, young people today have been force-fed the myth that success must come from inside you and if you fail it must be your fault. Many are trying to shake off the toxic debris that settles on and infects them: consumerism, self-centeredness, anxiety, loneliness, meanness, competitiveness, abuse, racism, sexist/homophobic crap.

They know the American Dream is dying, yet they still hope. They know the fallaciousness of the system that says if you work hard and follow the rules you get rewarded. They know capitalism is designed for the rich who can game the system and get to keep the goods for themselves. There is more competition for fewer rewards. They become neck-deep in college debt. They are forced to become brands and try to sell themselves. There is little sense of a decent, secure future, one with a healthy planet. Through no choice of their own they have joined the precariat. They know something is wrong and some are working together to try to change things for the better. The world is shifting, how is not yet clear.

And what about the many adults who bought into the belief their kids will always do as well or better than they? They see the income gap widening, the minority corporate elite getting richer, though many wrongly blame others, not the greedy corporate system.

One of My Broken Land Dreams: Homesick for the Future

Fragment from the cosmic poem "Antidotes to Fear of Death" by Rebecca Elson:

Sometimes as an antidote
To fear of death,
I eat the stars.
Those nights, lying on my back,
I suck them from the quenching dark
Til they are all, all inside me,
Pepper hot and sharp.
Sometimes, instead, I stir myself
Into a universe still young,
Still warm as blood:
No outer space, just space,
The light of all the not yet stars
Drifting like a bright mist,

And all of us, and everything
Already there
But unconstrained by form.

For a long time, I used to go to bed late. I was no Proust. I was a Dionysian in an Apollonian world. My circadian rhythms were nocturnal, geared to the light of the moon. When I finally went to bed, I couldn't sleep. I would lie awake and stare at the patterns coming from the car lights on the street below. At one time or another I saw some of my heroes projected on the ceiling: Joe Hill, Woody Guthrie, Walt Whitman, Paul Robeson. These guys were my soul mates. They'd wink or scowl at me depending on who showed up. They often told me everything would be all right, to stop worrying, do the right thing, enjoy life.

I would lie supine for hours. I would lie in the space between molecules formed long ago in a galaxy far away. I would fill the space between the notes of Vaughan Williams' *Fantasia on a Theme by Thomas Tallis.* I'd dwell between the characters in an Edward Hopper painting. I'd meditate in the gaps between my spinal vertebrae. Sometimes I turned on my desktop screensaver. It's a moving picture of Jacob's Ladder, the one painted by William Blake, with angels ascending and descending. It made a good nightlight, and soon I would fall asleep.

What is the trait you most deplore in yourself?

My insatiable appetite for social change, because it keeps me in a sleepless state. —"Q&A: Harry Belafonte," *The Guardian,* May 18, 2012

It was then I dreamed. Sometimes I did dream of angels, like Jacob. As a child I danced with a girl angel in the attic of my grandparents' summer house. Some dreams would be about grandiose schemes in the world, like Joseph. In one I gave away free stuff to needy people.

My dreams, like Dylan said to his landlord, are beyond my control. Some are lucid dreams, some are windows into another dimension.

Fragment from "Ode to Walt Whitman" by Federico García Lorca:
Nueva York de cieno,
Nueva York de alambres y de muerte.
¿Qué ángel llevas en la mejilla?

Ah filthy New York,
New York of cables and death.
What angel do you carry, concealed in your cheek?

In a recurring dream New York appears as a magical place. There is no HIV or COVID virus. No homeless. No slums. No poverty. No crime. No billionaires. No helicopters. No Trump.

The dream is like a children's book I once saw about a young boy who moved to New York from a small town. He described the city to his friend back home. The pictures made it look like a wonderful place, a big, happy, safe, exciting community.

In my dream, in all of New York, there are gardens and parks all over. People swim in the East River. They ride at the speed of sound in motionless subway cars filled with hanging plants and smile from within. The subways of course are free, paid for by having taxed all the billionaires out of being billionaires. (They even became happy too, like Scrooge on Christmas morning.) The sun powers everything. People dance in the streets. Every other neighborhood corner has a theater where people make art and music. People laugh and eat together in restaurants with astounding food from all over the world. They live in love. They argue in love. They suffer in love. They lose themselves in love. Rumi said: *When you lose yourself in this love, you will find everything*. Everybody has what they need. Every pore in their body tingles with joy.

After this dream I would often wake up in a cold sweat.

My life is a Terminal Moraine

My life is a Terminal Moraine. It's terminal, it's a heap of fragments held together by an invisible thread. The thread runs through time, up and down and sideways, and through space, above ground and below. It runs through me. I'm surveying the moraine. Is it sacred ground? Is anything? I'm surveying my life. I'm trying to figure out my place on the moraine, to get Maya back, to help the Earth, to help others, to help and heal myself— whatever a self is—before I go underground for good. And yeah, if you haven't yet figured out the metaphor, everyone is on a terminal moraine. Or under one. No shit.

Cosmic fragment from *A Walker in the City* by Alfred Kazin: Opening the great trunk of forgotten time

I could never walk across Roebling's bridge ... or stop in front of the garbage cans at Fulton and Cranberry Streets in Brooklyn at the place where Whitman had himself printed Leaves of Grass, without thinking that I had at last opened the great trunk of forgotten time in New York in which I, too, I thought, would someday find the source of my unrest.

CHAPTER TWO

What Maya Says I Need to Recover From

I'm in recovery from being a self-indulgent, kvetchy, grumpy, alienated, straight white male, a secular Jewish lefty feminist, anti-racist, intellectual, boomer, broodhist cosmic radical with a suburban childhood.

It's not easy being one, let alone saying it.

Especially now. It's not exactly trending. It's not easy to explain or write about what it is. It's easy, though, to slip into a walking cliché of myself. Novelist Ben Lerner, another straight white Brooklyn Jewish guy with glasses, gets it. Conscious of his own clichéd status, he wants to own it first: "People say, 'Oh, here's another Brooklyn novel by a guy with glasses.'" To make matters worse I can't discuss it since nobody gives a flying crap about my privileged syndrome and they think I want pity—see, right there you think I was trying to gain your sympathy. Any time I speak about it I'm self-implicated.

I'm going to cop to this as a way to transcend it. Katy Waldman in *The New Yorker* calls it the "reflexivity trap." She says that writers who profess a fault think that absolves them of that fault. She criticizes writers who regard this self-awareness as a finishing line, not a starting point. They think that since they now own their faults they can just go on as they are. I go further, though. I not only cop to my faults, I am *aware* I'm copping to my faults. And that's not my finishing line, it's my starting point. As some politically hip yakademics put it, I'm mindfully *navigating my positionality*. I'm mindfully *deconstructing myself*. So there.

Like Maya says, I need to recover from this stuff. That is, let go of it, work through it, so I can be present with Maya. Or I lose her. In a bad way, I lose myself.

Recovery From My Tribal Traits and Relatives

I emerged during the postwar era from the Great Primal Swamp called Manhattan. I was one of a number of ugly pink organisms, throbbing and screaming with rage, that was to find its way on to land and later to the suburbs. At that time, suburbia was the highest form of human life to which white people aspired. That is how I envision us more fortunate baby boomers: crawling away from the starting line into the bright future of fifties America. What happened along the way is called the sixties, which is another story.

As a first-born male Jew, I quickly acquired a lot of baggage. I was named after a great-grandfather, Jacob, who died in bed getting it on with his fourth wife. Not a bad way to go. More than his name, I may have inherited his legacy, if not yet his mode of death, love of women as a fatal flaw. Soon after I was circumcised according to the laws of Moses. I don't think Moses had to be grandfathered in under his own law. I wasn't so lucky. It hurt like hell, believe me. I remember. Don't let the rabbi tell you otherwise. I even remember they had good pastrami afterward, which of course I couldn't eat because I had no teeth. Okay, so don't eat meat. Save the planet. What did I know, I was eight days old.

Recovery From Surplus Sensitivity Disorder and Toxic Masculinity

A person who has not been completely alienated, who has remained sensitive and able to feel, who has not lost the sense of dignity, who is not yet "for sale," who can still suffer over the suffering of others, who has not acquired fully the having mode of existence—briefly, a person who has remained a person and not become a thing—cannot help feeling lonely, powerless, isolated in present-day society. —Erich Fromm, *The Art of Being*

I inherited sensitivity to pain and unjust suffering (is there any just suffering? Should there be?) Another trait is having a memory like an elephant trap. I remember all those pains and wrongs. People's moods and emotional agendas distract the hell out of me. I have Surplus Sensitivity Disorder. (It's akin to the *hyperempathy* suffered by Octavia Butler's Afrofuturist character Lauren Olamina.)

As a child I absorbed feelings through my pores and couldn't filter them out. If my mother suffered from a depressing thought, I suffered as if it were mine. If someone in the next room called someone stupid, my lower lip quivered and my body shook. When the Rosenbergs were executed, I felt the electricity through my own body. When my father put Tchaikovsky's violin concerto on the phonograph, I would cry inconsolably.

Nowadays the popular meme for this is *a highly sensitive person.* Today it's a recognized, common, acceptable syndrome. Everyone claims to be one on the internet, so who the hell am I to think I'm unique and complain. (According to private coach Preston Ni in *Psychology Today*, "Highly sensitive people often 'feel too much' and 'feel too deep.'")

Hey, you say that like it's a bad thing.

In this society, it is. In Lauren Olamina's world as well, hyperempathy is dangerous to feel others' pain.

Fragment from *Parable of the Sower* by Octavia Butler:

But if everyone could feel everyone else's pain ... who would cause anyone unnecessary pain? I've never thought of my problem as something that might do some good before, but with the way things are, I think it would help. I wish I could give it to people. Failing that, I wish I could find other people who have it, and live among them.

I still suffer when I pass homeless people lying on the street and subway platforms, and when I see and read about the shit being done to all kinds of people here and around the world.

Since the pandemic, though, some of my surplus sensitivity has metastasized into sheer grumpiness by the everyday selfishness and uncaring bullshit in the world. If I see a car speeding down the Eastern Parkway service road, I yell at the driver to slow down, asshole. If I notice people picnicking in the Brooklyn Botanic Garden against the rules, I will track down a guard and tell him. I report every loud helicopter to the city, and every building I see spewing toxic black smoke. Like Holden Caulfield said, it's futile to try to scrub all the Fuck Yous off all the walls in the world to try to protect kids. You're on a fool's errand, but you do it anyway.

The world doesn't change. The grumpiness stays. Maya feels the brunt of it when I withdraw and sulk on the sofa. The day before she left I vaguely remember she wanted to share pictures of her cousin's granddaughter and I was lost in my own head. So much for sensitivity.

Coach Ni says in order to "manage" being a highly sensitive person you should "utilize emotional immunity and sensory immunity strategies."

Sure, man. Helpful corporate jargon—manage it by yourself, utilize immunity strategies, it goes away.

As a child I was way ahead of him. Back then I knew something had to be done. I began to construct a hard-shell case around me that would buffer me from the pain and sadness of the world, or so I thought. I learned to act cool and impassive, like the proper American male. I was good enough at it, people even thought I was cold and indifferent to things and others. Of course, I ingested some other crap from the male-dominant culture—wanting to be super rational and competitive. To go, and get, my own way.

Today the exaggerated messed-up version of the male-dominant culture is called *toxic masculinity*. Guys are cut off from their own feelings, they're afraid facing them will make them vulnerable—turn them into "pussies"—i.e., women or gays. They think they have to be tough-ass warriors all the time. Men are on a path to pathology by hurting themselves and others. Some are beyond redemption. The not-so-big secret anymore, though, is that many harbor feelings of insecurity. They feel threatened by The Other, whom they fear will overtake them—and take them over. Some may even be sensitive about stuff inside. They're told they need to shed their armor and express their feelings. Many don't how to do that nor feel they can afford to.

Got that? Too sensitive? Just toughen up, utilize sensory immunity strategies. Too tough? Just be more vulnerable, sensitive, feel more, show more. I think too much about this. I must drive Maya just as crazy as I do myself by obsessing over each strategy.

Does this culture encourage healthy masculinity and oppose a toxic one? Does it help guys figure out this stuff and grow up to be noble, compassionate mensches? Yeah, and I'm George Clooney's twin and have more dough than Bill Gates.

And guess what else, smartass corporatized coach guy and anyone else who doesn't get it: embodied feelings are social and relational. They're part of you but they're not just private things inside your head. They link us with others and bind us together. They tell you when something is wrong in our fractured lives and relationships and crappy culture and that something needs to change in both us and the world.

Recovery From Surplus *Shpilkes* Syndrome

I have a related condition: Surplus *Shpilkes* Syndrome. It's a new diagnosis for an old ailment. Before the pandemic my friend Morty and I came up with it at one of our breakfasts at Valeska's, a Ukrainian joint in the East Village. We'd kvetch about relationships, music, and Seinfeld-type nothing over scrambled eggs, kasha with gravy, and challah toast. We discovered we have excess angst about everything and gave it a name to normalize it on our terms. Because we live in a self-centered society it's still always about me, like the parallel play toddlers do when placed side-by-side:

Jacob: So whaddya think, will the waitress remember to bring the gravy for the kasha?
Morty: I dunno. [wipes forehead] Will they refill my coffee fuh free or do I have to pay fuh moah?"
Jacob: Yeah, and will I remember to add money to the meter to avoid a ticket? [looks anxiously toward street]
Morty: *Beat.* Maybe I should call my wife and see what she needs me to pick up. [looks anxiously toward cellphone on table]

Since the pandemic, though, it's become the new normal. Now everyone has Surplus *Shpilkes* Syndrome. Will that guy who just sneezed six feet away give me the fucking virus? Was he really more than six feet away? Did I remember to not touch my cellphone with the gloved hand that grabbed the grocery cart?

The American Psychiatric Association is considering my petition to add Surplus *Shpilkes* Syndrome as a new mental disorder in the next Diagnostic and Statistical Manual. They said it looks promising. Sure, let's reduce existential angst to an individual mental pathology. Let's ignore it signals something wrong is happening here. Let's ignore the lack of public spaces and communal rituals that could help us heal ourselves and each other. It's the American Way.

Recovery from a Childhood in Red and Black and White

Dialogue from the movie *Trumbo* (2015, screenplay by John McNamara):

NIKI (Trumbo's daughter): Am I [a Communist]?
DALTON TRUMBO: Well, why don't we give you the official test. Mom makes you your favorite lunch...
NIKI: Ham and cheese.

DALTON TRUMBO: Ham and cheese. And at school, you see someone with no lunch at all. What do you do?
NIKI: Share.
DALTON TRUMBO: Share? You don't tell them to just go get a job?
NIKI: No.
DALTON TRUMBO: Ooh. You offer them a loan at six percent, ooh, that's very clever.
NIKI: Dad.
DALTON TRUMBO: Ah, then you just ignore them.
NIKI: No.
DALTON TRUMBO: Well, well … you little commie.

I used to think that to count as a *red-diaper baby* you had to have at least one parent who was a member of "the party" while you were growing up. Even though I hadn't, some friends who ought to know insisted I'm still one. Why? Because thanks to McCarthyism, the question always is, are you now, or *have you ever been*? Well, before I was born one of my parents *had been*, and once you were, you always are. Which means the offspring too are flavored red.

When I look at my childhood the moniker fits. We played Paul Robeson, Pete Seeger, the Weavers, and other lefty folk records over and over. I could recite by heart all the words to Pete's "Talkin' Union." Each week I would read my parents' subscription to *I.F. Stone's Weekly*. From the bookshelf I read and reread Howard Fast's *Spartacus,* seething with passion and restrained rage, a book he had to self-publish during the McCarthy era.

I learned about the Lincoln Brigade. They became my heroes—many of them Jewish boys from City College, some of whom my mother knew—who went off to fight the fascists in the Spanish Civil War. Many did not return. I learned about the victimized Scottsboro "Boys" and the martyred Rosenbergs. Other heroes I discovered and read about were the regular Jews of the Warsaw Ghetto and the partisans in the Polish forest during World War II. They knew they would probably die. But they decided to learn how to hold and shoot a gun and make and throw Molotov cocktails and take down as many fucking Nazis with them as they could, and they did. So there.

As a child and teen in the suburbs I often felt like a visitor from another time and planet. I hated the pressured sameness and sterility.

In high school, to escape my suburban-bubble life, I would go down to Greenwich Village by myself to hear counterculture performances that flaunted and celebrated sensuality: the Fugs, The Mothers of Invention, Paul Butterfield, and readings by poets like Allen Ginsburg. I went to the local art house movie theater that showed foreign, mostly British films, and saw *Morgan, The Knack, The Loneliness of the Long Distance Runner,* and *Zorba the Greek,* among others, all black-and-white flicks that matched my mood. I read Bellow's *Herzog,* Hesse's *Steppenwolf* and Joyce's *A Portrait of the Artist as a Young Man,* Camus's essays, and poems like *The Waste Land* and *The Bridge,* along with the critical essays that helped explain them. I played guitar in my room and memorized the harmonica breaks on Dylan's albums along with all the lyrics to *A Hard Rain's Gonna Fall* and other of his songs. At a backyard party I wrote and sang a parody in the style of Woody, Pete, and Dylan, "The Talkin' Goldwater Blues."

In the spring of 1967, my high school friend and I went down to the massive anti-war demonstration in the Sheep Meadow in Central Park. I still recall the responsive chant that enthralled me, that seemed to go on forever, led by a Black man near where we stood. It gave me a brief sense of solidarity with people I didn't know and didn't get to know: "Are you going? *Hell no!* To Viet-nam? *Hell no!* We ain't going! *Hell no!* To Vietnam! *Hell no!* Black people! *Hell no*! White People! *Hell no!* Are you going? *Hell no!* We ain't going! *Hell no!*

Some tribal quirks I did inherit: Love of beautiful shiksas. Craving for Zabar's pickled herring in sour cream. A desire, like the Marx Brothers, to dismantle everyday WASP power hierarchies and create happy anarchy everywhere. A belief in cosmic communism: the Earth "belongs" to everyone. *They shall not build, and another inhabit; they shall not plant, and another eat.* —Isaiah 66:22. Why people don't get that is beyond me.

Ones I did not get: being good at chess, bridge, and pinochle. A head for business. Wanting to be a doctor or lawyer.

Some of my cousins fortunately got those, so they're not lost to the goyim.

Recovery from My Parents

When my parents were young, they worked in unionized jobs and identified with the working class, the poor and oppressed. They hated injustice and racism and fought for fairness for all. After the war, though, when they met, their upper-middle-class aspirations got the better of them. Like everyone else they wanted a good life for themselves and a happy childhood for their children, better than their own. As Jews they now had membership perks that came with their postwar acceptance into the wealthier white people's club. Most of the antisemitism they'd experienced as kids went underground, at least for the time being. They could move into Stuyvesant Town in Manhattan, a new apartment enclave that didn't allow Black people. I lived there until I was five. My father, a World War II veteran, could get a GI loan for a mortgage on a house in the suburbs. Only white guys could get a GI loan. Can you believe that shit? So, like many others, they scouted places outside the city, in disturbia, for a "good" school system.

Sure enough, my folks settled on an upper-middle-class, white-only community in Westchester. It had some old-moneyed WASPs in stucco and Tudor mansions who let them in, along with plenty of other up-and-coming Jews from the city who bought up the new quarter-acre tracts with split-level houses.

Despite their new respectable status, my folks were still progressives and internationalists at heart. Part of their old selves was not suppressed, just kept on the down low. I was able to absorb the moral demand to work for social justice for all, to hate racism, and feel for the downtrodden and the underdog. To an extent that inoculated me against the bland, white-bread, materialist suburban milieu that tried to paper over history, including my own.

My mother was a restless spiritual seeker throughout her life. In his own more philosophical way, my father was as well. That spirituality, explicit or implicit, undergirded their political sense of injustice about the world and wanting to heal it. Both were in healing professions and had a sense of compassion for all. Another postwar cultural trend, though, was the move away from public and political matters to more personal and inner concerns. My mother followed suit. She shifted from politically active public social work to private-practice psychotherapy. She also began intensive studies of the Kabbalah and Eastern spiritual traditions with other shrinks. In my own life, like my role models the prophets, the political, the moral, the emotional, and the spiritual are inseparable.

Recovery from Being an Unconscious White Guy in a Racist Society

Dialogue from the cosmic punk movie *Repo Man* (1984, written and directed by Alex Cox):

DUKE: [wounded after a botched robbery] *The lights are growing dim, Otto. I know a life of crime has led me to this sorry fate, and yet I blame society. Society made me what I am.*
OTTO: That's bullshit. You're a white suburban punk just like me.
DUKE: Yeah, but it still hurts [dies].

Otto's point to his wounded friend Duke is that we're not victims, we're not supposed to hurt, and if we do, or even die, so what. It's not about us. We're supposed to be privileged white guys. That stuff about scared, whiney white guys losing their power and status and feeling victimized, too damn bad. Work on and get over your own shit.

Yeah, but it still hurts.

Why? Because being a white guy in a white system doesn't erase personal pain. It doesn't shield us from worry and fear and self-doubt, getting sad and depressed, drinking too much, getting addicted to pain killers, suicide, having a crappy job, a crummy relationship, and a messed up or broken childhood and family.

How do we reduce everyone's pain and go toward something better? In *Repo Man*, Otto escapes his dead empty suburban existence by—well, I won't give away the ending. For the rest of us, we all need to make a better society *for all*—not a racist oligarchy that benefits the few, run by rich corporate zombies with their love of money who want to commodify everything.

Recovery from Being a Broodhist Cosmic Radical

Fragment from *Notes from Underground* by Fyodor Dostoevsky:

I swear, gentlemen, that to be too conscious is an illness—a real thorough-going illness. For man's everyday needs, it would have been quite enough to have the ordinary human consciousness...

You might want to know about the broodhist cosmic radical part of my recovering self. I brood on meditating. I meditate on brooding. I ponder the imponderable. I'm a perpetual recovering broodhist.

Meditating connects with the cosmic radical stuff. *To be too conscious is an illness.* How do you escape the reflexivity trap? I'm stuck seeking both the relative and absolute, the immanent and the transcendent. The ordinary and paradise. They're both right here at the same time and place; in Buddhist terms, Samsara and Nirvana. Where's Leonard Cohen's *Suzanne* when I need her? *She shows you where to look amidst the garbage and the flowers.* I'm trying to figure out how they go together, how to live with both at once.

History is full of horror and violence and injustice. You know the James Joyce/Stephen Dedalus quote, *History* is *a nightmare from which I am trying to awake.* Yet it's the one place we have to work out our shit and make things right. *The pandemic is a nightmare from which I am trying to awake.*

You try to stay in the nightmare while knowing you're awake. You remain aware you're dreaming at the same time you're dreaming. That's lucid dreaming. I do that at times. Mindfulness practice is like that, you witness yourself.

Is that enlightened consciousness, awakening? In lucid dreaming, in mindfulness, there's still a duality, a splitting off. You see yourself.

Can we go further?

But, well…

Camus wrote: *There is no love of life without despair of life.* I got that second part down. Rilke's advice is: *Let everything happen to you: beauty and terror.* How do you do that? Who the hell wants to?

I'm stuck thinking we have to help the universe evolve in both historical and timeless ways. Buddha and Jesus and Marx and the other prophets with cosmic vision who fight to make the world a just place.

To those of us who study history not merely as a warning reminder of man's [sic] *follies and crimes, but also as an encouraging remembrance of generative souls, the past ceases to be a depressing chamber of horrors; it becomes a celestial city, a spacious country of the mind, wherein a thousand saints, statesmen, inventors, scientists, poets, artists, musicians, lovers, and philosophers still live and speak, teach and carve and sing … let it be our pride that we ourselves may put meaning into our lives, and sometimes a significance that transcends death. —Will Durant, The Lessons of History*

I Want It All

I want it all, the absolute and relative world, nirvana and samsara, changeless change and social justice change.

Sometimes, though, we can meditate and be still and feel the cosmic presence. Right here amidst the overstuffed garbage bins near the forest pool in Prospect Park (well, it's the dog pond). *She shows you where to look amidst the garbage and the flowers.* Since the pandemic, the city cut the budget for park sanitation pickup. The garbage bins are also part of the cosmic presence.

From A *Still Forest Pool* by Achaan Chah:
Try to be mindful, and let things take their course.
Then your mind will become still in any surroundings, like a still forest pool.

Maybe you can experience the absolute and still engage in the relative world and fight for what's right.

The ability to be fully present yet not controlled by conditions creates a stable mental and emotional foundation even in the midst of turmoil. —Peter Levitt, "Introduction to The Essential Dogen"

After you sit and meditate by the Prospect Park dog pond, call the city hotline, 311, about the lack of garbage pickup. Then go have a beer and a slice, takeout only.

Recovery from the JuBu Blues

Jews tend to dwell on the borders of society, like aborigines squatting outside the gates. Marx had a good metaphor for it: Jews live in the pores of Polish society. I envision these tiny Jews in the pores of a Pole's face, in the skin but not of it.

To take it further, I dwell on the border of my own border-dwelling tribe—in writer Isaac Deutscher's term, a non-Jewish Jew. I join an honorable non-tribe of non-religious, internationalist, and revolutionary Jews he names (I'm not saying I'm anywhere near as smart, though): Spinoza, Heine, Marx, Luxemburg, Trotsky, and Freud. You could argue that, like Deutscher and myself, Bernie Sanders and David Graeber are recent versions.

So you think I'm another JuBu, a historically situated Jew who'd rather be an ahistorical Buddhist, a timeless Buddhist who's still some sort of historically situated Jew…?

As far as being religious, I'm not into either. Here ya go. I was in an old-timey acoustic band once, the Good Old Boychiks. I wrote some verses of some mountain music for y'all, Catskills and Himalayas, that is—the "JuBu Blues." It's a takeoff of bluegrass guitar picker Doc Watson's "Deep River Blues" (you oughta see him pick it, something he himself, being blind, couldn't do).

I prayed to Buddha over you
My rebbe said that wouldn't do
Lord lord got them deep Buddhist blues

I paid my meditation dues
They said that doesn't work for Jews
Yeah Lord got them deep Buddhist blues

Met a dharma gal we began to schmooze
She said "kishkehs, chakras, you got to choose"
Oy life's tough for us deep Buddhist Jews

Here's the kind of JuBu I am: a Bundist Buddhist. Though they come at it from different angles, the common principle is *hereness.* Both the socialist Jewish Labor Bund—the secular, non-Zionist, political and cultural organization of which my paternal grandfather was a member—and Buddhists—not the commodified, stress reduction, market-mindfulness peddlers, though—subscribe to *hereness.* Not in heaven, not in Israel, not in some future utopia somewhere else, but *here,* in the historical present, where we are, as who we are, ourselves, in both nirvana and samsara, in the diaspora, together with all others, fighting for the right to be at home for all, to make a home for all, for the good of all.

To be a Jew means always being with the oppressed, and never the Oppressors. —Marek Edelman, commandant of the Bund fighting group in the Warsaw Ghetto Uprising

Some say Jews are white, so they're immune. Oh really, tell that to the Nazis and antisemites who even today spew jealous hate and harmful lies about how we control everything and who harass and murder Jews in synagogues and elsewhere in the world.

The Hereness of My Grandfathers

"I hate this world." As a moody teenager, my mother told me she once said this to her father. He answered her with a loaded question, a thing Jews do: "Do you know a better one?" That shut her up for a while. It's a pretty good response from the family breadwinner, a guy who ran a small paint and sign supply business in a storefront in Spanish Harlem: practical, material, down to earth, no-nonsense, reality based, accepting, enjoying, and dealing and being with what is, what's needed now, not what could or should be. My grandfather was a quiet, generous man who sponsored and paid for thirty-nine visas of Jewish refugees in Europe, fleeing the Nazis, to come to New York, which saved their lives. He would never hurt a fly. My mother told me, though, he once came home bruised from a scuffle after he stood up to defend an orthodox Jew with a beard who was being bullied on the subway.

My father told me that as a teen he too felt angry at the world. His father, a Sheepshead Bay, Brooklyn working stiff who pressed clothes all day with a heavy steam iron—which gave him the emphysema that killed him—said, "*Nu*, then we have to fight alongside others and change it." There's the other Jewish response, from a socialist Jewish Bundist and militant member of the Amalgamated Clothing Workers of America: resist injustice, join in solidarity with all oppressed people, imagine and fight like hell for a better, just world for everyone. My father told me that some nights his father, a *shtarker* mensch, would come home bloodied from fighting scabs who tried to break through their picket line. I learned to hate scabs and never cross a picket line. You should do the same.

Both grandfathers practiced hereness in complementary ways.

I, however, just want to be able to have a beer and pizza and watch a Yankee game without brooding or meditating about all this, about moral obligations and the universe and human history and racism and antisemitism and why love manages to exist while there's so much misery and hate in the world.

CHAPTER THREE

Recovery from Being a Leftist Feminist Boomer

I'm a Marxist surrealist feminist who is not just anti something, but pro-emancipation, pro-liberation. —Robin D.G. Kelley

This is a civilization searching for its humanity. It dehumanized others to build its civilization. Now it needs to find its own. —Gary Michael Tartakov in *Caste: The Origins of Our Discontents* by Isabel Wilkerson

I'm in recovery from the sixties and seventies, a turbulent bubble on the froth of time. The hangover continues into the twenty-first century. We radicals once thought the world was going to go our way. We thought we were going to help it along. We had a beautiful vision. We saw it with our collective third eye. We were going to help everyone, *everyone,* defeat the meaningless, deadly, daily grind of everyday corporate work, the sterile, bland, conformist suburban life, the ever-present ads, billboards, and jingles that get inside and corrode your head and sell you plastic and garbage, the government lies about the vicious war that killed thousands of people, all the stupid racist and sexist institutional and mental shit, the mind-forged manacles. (Okay, not everyone hurt the way we hurt, not everyone wanted what we wanted, not everyone could afford to dream like we did. We wanted to do it for them and with them.)

The thing the sixties did was to show us the possibilities and the responsibility that we all had. It wasn't the answer. It just gave us a glimpse of the possibility. —John Lennon

We're gonna fight fire with water. We're gonna fight racism not with racism, but with solidarity. We're not gonna fight capitalism with Black capitalism but with socialism…. We're gonna fight with all of us people getting together and having an international proletariat revolution. —Fred Hampton, deputy chair of the National Black Panther Party, who was drugged, shot, and killed in his bed during a predawn raid at his Chicago apartment by a tactical unit of the Cook County State's Attorney's Office, which had received aid from the Chicago Police Department and the FBI leading up to the attack.

In our bones, in our guts, in our hearts, in our groins, in our souls, we felt we were going to win. Fuck capitalism, fuck bullshit meaningless work, fuck the war, fuck corporate pollution, fuck racism, fuck the racist police, fuck sexism and male chauvinism, fuck homophobia, fuck the patriarchal, privatized nuclear family.

We were subversively sensuous. We had great music. We had great highs. As much as anything, for many it was a spiritual quest. For some, certain drugs showed new possibilities of consciousness, visions of freer ways to be. Everybody was gonna get together (c'mon people now) and get *it* together.

Want a feel for some of it? Watch Jefferson Airplane, "We Can Be Together" at Woodstock on YouTube, and play "Get Together" by the Youngbloods.

I'll wait.

What happened instead was the greedy racist sexist bastard zombies won. They wreaked havoc on unions, civil rights, Black and Brown people, coalitions of Black, Latino, and white radicals, students, women and feminism, LGBTQ people, reproductive rights, the environment, progressive antiracist and democratic political groups, alternative schools, communal alternatives to the privatized patriarchal family, and the ideals and visions of the counterculture, much of which they managed to co-opt and repackage in order to sell us back more crap. What's more, they broke our sense that economic and cultural justice are inseparable.

Part of the success of neoliberalism consists in how effectively it has co-opted the spirit of the 1960s…. It accomplished this by driving a wedge between social justice efforts focused on economic fairness and those emphasizing cultural identities. —Bruce Rogers-Vaughn, *Caring for Souls in a Neoliberal Age*

The older Right was and still is furious about the sixties. They can't let it go. One anti-right-wing pundit (Lucian K. Truscott IV, *Alternet*, August 30, 2020) put it this way: "*They want revenge because love is stronger than hate, and we believe in love.*"

Damn right we do. Some critic said we just got stuck playing out one of Jung's archetypes, the eternal child, who believes in the innocent myth of universal love and has never grown up. Yeah, okay, some wanted to rebel against any authority and were immature, self-centered, amoral, and childish.

But here's why that doesn't negate what we stood for and why what the critics say is bullshit. They want you to believe there is some objective standard of "grown up" we failed to meet. Oh really. Says who? Where is that written? Just what does that look like and how much does it cost?

I am convinced that most people do not grow up. We find parking spaces and honor our credit cards. We marry and dare to have children and call that growing up. I think what we do is mostly grow old. —Maya Angelou, *Letter to My Daughter*

They then think any rejection of this soulless, conformist, conventional adulthood must be less grown up. In fact, for many of us it was *more* grown up. Why is it wrong to believe in universal love?

Yeah, but it still hurts.

The loss is a double whammy. Besides the country suffering the political backlash, we ended up on our asses, dazed, wondering what the hell happened to us and our dreams. For some it's a lingering wound, a kind of post-trauma thing. Symptoms are sudden bouts of nostalgia, depressing flashbacks, hallucinatory dreams, wailing and gnashing of teeth (more dental bills), getting stoned on cannabis, and binge watching on Netflix and BritBox. General melancholy, from which we need to recover.

Today *trauma* is a hot buzzword. Trauma healing is big business. It aims to fix individuals, inside and in their brains— but not the society, itself traumatized and fractured, that itself creates the personal trauma. Standard trauma work aims to help you cope and adjust and restore yourself to some kind of balanced state, not help change the social sources of the pain.

You're supposed to return to normal, see. But there is no normal, nor can or should there be in a sick society. More so now—the bastard zombies have taken over more territory and are still in power, still causing more trauma. More so now, as the pandemic rages on and so many people are in pain and in need of personal and community and systemic healing and change.

Nobody even talks about this post-sixties post-trauma. Why start or even stop there? Nobody talks about any of those other undigested social traumas we carry around as living history.

Then there's the ever-present low-grade trauma, the enduring, lingering stench from the president, the abuser who, like COVID, refuses to go away. He's like long COVID—it never leaves the body.

Trumpism and neofascism and similar dark forces of recent years have inflicted great trauma on the American people, which has not been properly diagnosed, never mind healed. Forgetting or ignoring the pain is a maladaptive response, encouraged and enabled by leaders and other elites, which does nothing to address the underlying injury. Americans need to do some difficult collective emotional and

political work, akin to the mourning process, to reach real catharsis.
—Chauncey Devega

Don't even bring up the horrors and trauma of the Vietnam War. There's no point. Why suffer? There's no time anyway. History becomes a nebulous blur. Those in power like it that way.

It's as if you're riding on the express subway train, on the middle track that skips the local stations. You happen to glance up and catch a glimpse of one station as the train whizzes by. Wait! What the hell was happening on that platform! What are those people doing! They're maiming and killing women and children! The killers are being hurt and killed too! Before you can make any sense of what you just saw and why, it's gone.

Ah never mind. You turn back to your cellphone.

Yet the flashbacks recur. The images, the accompanying fear, the collective guilt. They light up at unpredictable times on some wall of your mind like an electric bug zapper. You want to scrub your mind clean, like Lady Macbeth washing her bloody hands.

We're the walking wounded. The wounds are open and festering. We wade in a rising cesspool of racism, greed, violence, and fear. We barely keep our balance. We stumble onto shore and end up squatting on stolen land.

Can we connect the dots and piece together the fragments? Can we unforget?

There are no recovery groups for any of this. Even if there were, I wouldn't join them. In recovery you're supposed to have a higher power. Since I don't believe in a higher power, I've had to hire one. I have a Hired Power. I submitted an ad for one in the *Brooklyn Cosmic Inquirer.*

Hey, even spirituality is a consumer good you are "free" to purchase.

You'll meet my Hired Power soon.

CHAPTER FOUR

Idiot versus Fierce Compassion

Socialworkers Anonymous: An Attempt at Conventional Recovery

I did try a recovery group once, Socialworkers Anonymous. You don't have to be an actual social worker to join, although I was, before retiring from working in a high school last year. Anyone who identifies with wanting to rescue everyone in the world, all the time, often at the expense of your own self, can qualify as a Socialworker. You know, like Holden Caulfield—he wanted to save kids from falling over the cliff, he almost fell off the damn cliff himself. I wonder how *he* made out. Hell, he would be in his nineties by now, if he made it that far.

The problem with being an addicted Socialworker, we learned from a guest speaker, a mindfulness and therapy guru from Headcase Inc. who of course had his own tapes to sell, is *idiot compassion*.

Idiot compassion is when you think you always must be the nice guy. You feel you must make things right, solve everyone's problems, make changes people aren't ready for or just plain don't want, and bring social justice to everyone, at your own expense, no matter what. You can't say no to anyone's requests, so you burn yourself out.

Yeah yeah, it has to do with the caretaker role you played as a child in your family system, the fixer. It has to do with that you yourself were fucking wounded. You didn't get what you needed; you felt you had to please your parents to get your needs met. It has to do with that you learned you weren't even allowed to feel entitled to your own needs and opinions. It has to do with not wanting to deal with your own inner life, especially the donut hole of pain, so instead you focus on others all the time.

The solution is constant mindfulness and self-affirming mantras—available on the guru/shrink's tapes. *I'm good enough. I love myself. I affirm everything about me. Breathe and let go.*

As if that's gonna solve it. It's all about me. That's like a dog chasing its own tail. Toxic positivity, too.

There. Now you know. For that workshop that'll be $50. Tapes are extra.

Early Qualification: Socialworkers Anonymous Meeting

My name is Jacob and I'm a recovering socialworker.
—Hi Jacob!
As a for-real high school social worker I wanted to rescue all the kids who were in pain, no matter what it took. I wanted to fix the entire lousy school and make it better, more socially just, twenty-four seven. I took it all personally. That was before I got burnt out, before I learned about these meetings.

I used to believe in fixing everyone, not just kids and schools. I believed you could figure out everyone's problems in a rational way. I thought that if you showed people what they were doing and gave them better choices they would do it. Like, if my parents, Cy and Thelma, were bickering I wanted them to stop so I could train them in mindful conflict resolution. When my sister Bobbi got pissed off at her kid, I wanted to step in and show her the latest mindful childrearing practice. Every time my authoritarian principal, Mr. Martinette, treated us like members of his dysfunctional family I wanted to give a workshop on mindful communication right there on the spot. And with my wife Maya— fuhgeddaboudit. We quarreled a lot. She was wrong, I was right, of course mindfully so. Try that sometime, see how far you get. Anyways, I thought if everyone learned the most, you know, emotionally smart way to solve their problems, the world would be a nice place, with no conflicts. Then I'd feel good and, okay, I'd look good too.

Thing is, it didn't work. Everyone would just keep doing what they were doing and get annoyed at me. I just ended up grinding my teeth and got sick from exhaustion.

Since I learned about idiot compassion, I know better now. I know I can't figure out other people's stuff. There's no one right way to look at a problem and fix it. I'm no longer gonna try to get it right. It's futile. I've given up trying to help anyone. It's kind of a relief. I'm just gonna focus on myself.

Thanks for listening.

I stopped going to Socialworkers Anonymous meetings after a few sessions. Who wants to hang out with people who were such a mess. It was the blind leading the blind. Besides, who am I, their social worker?

The Traum-atix

I should say I did do some good as a Brooklyn high school social worker–counselor type. In my last year, just last year in fact, I met with a group of six alienated kids who wanted to get their shit together in a wise way. They were Cami (Afro-Dominican), Dina (Palestinian), Billy (Irish-Italian), May May (Chinese), Derrick (African American), and Arielle (Jewish), of various sexual and gender identities. We meditated and talked about how personal lives are inseparable from the crap in this society. Since my last name is Traum, which happens to mean *dream*, they called themselves the Traum-atix in my honor. So, it's not that they're saying they're all *clinically traumatized victims*, understand, but they're *dreamers* who are buggin' out from this crazy society that does traumatize a lot of people. Yeah, I was one of the older counselors, and a white guy to boot, so why would they trust me? Well, I had been in the school a while and earned a good reputation among the students. I always listened and showed them respect and felt especially gratified we could connect in this group. Besides, my own anti-authoritarian inner teenager, now a bit more mature, is never far from the surface.

Since I retired, they've stayed together as seniors and are now the Post-Traum-atix. We check in with each other through texts and sometimes on Zoom. You'll meet them later.

What the hell, maybe the world needs more damn socialworkers. The world needs to recover from itself.

A Curse, A Prayer, A Xen Kohen

To all hateful, jealous, ignorant, murderous antisemites who are threatened by our right to enjoy life and live as best we can, who blame us for their own damn problems, or for the world's, or even for antisemitism itself, as if it must somehow be our own fault (and yeah, some call themselves leftists); to all greedy, self-centered, heartless, racist, capitalist, sexist, imperialist zombie bastards who oppress, colonize, exploit, and kill poor and working people (and yeah, some of you are even Jews—you're a *shondeh*), I say: Fuck You. I oppose you with every fiber of my being. The blood of my grandfathers, grandmothers, and their ancestors, the prophets and bodhisattvas, all the cosmic Jewish socialists and my other international comrades across time and space runs through me. I will never stop fighting for life itself and for a better and just and free world for all.

L'chaim. Pa'lante. Black Lives Matter. All Power to All *the People. Om Shantih.*

Muthahfuckahs.

An Anishinaabeg Prayer

Grandfather,
Look at our brokenness.

We know that in all creation
Only the human family
Has strayed from the Sacred Way.
We know that we are the ones
Who are divided
And we are the ones
Who must come back together
To walk in the Sacred Way
Grandfather,
Sacred One,
Teach us love, compassion, and honor
That we may heal the earth
And heal each other

A Broodhist Xen Kohen

One of my favorite Xen Jewish socialists, Jesus, an enlightened dude, came up with a short Xen Kohen: *Love your enemies*. Because I respect him, I brooded and meditated on those three simple words for a long time. Hell no, I first said, and most people make the same mistake. They think he means, what the hell, they're just people, you gotta love everyone. Yeah, they hate us and are trying to harm or even kill us, but they're not bad, they just didn't get enough love. So, give 'em love, be nice, and that will change them.

No way. That's idiot compassion.

After meditating on this Xen Kohen, after staring at it for years, I had an insight into it, part one. Once you realize it, it's even staring back at you in the face. He didn't say they were just people; he said they were *your enemies*. They're still *enemies*. There's nothing sentimental or idiotic about that. That means you must oppose them and fight them when necessary. That's ingenious. The dude is real—up to that point. Okay now for the hard part, part two, which is why it remains a Xen Kohen: *how* the hell do you manage to *love* people who are still your enemies in the relative world? Can broodhist meditation get you to a state—and a higher stage of awareness—some call that *fierce compassion*—so that you can *love* the people whom you *still need to oppose*?

Watch this space.

CHAPTER FIVE

The Pandemic as a Portal to My Recovery

The Pandemic is a Portal

Historically, pandemics have forced humans to break with the past and imagine their world anew. This one is no different. It is a portal, a gateway between one world and the next.

We can choose to walk through it, dragging the carcasses of our prejudice and hatred, our avarice, our data banks and dead ideas, our dead rivers and smoky skies behind us. Or we can walk through lightly, with little luggage, ready to imagine another world. And ready to fight for it. –Arundhati Roy, "The Pandemic is a Portal" April 3, 2020

The Pandemic Strikes

My life was calm. I had the underground pretty much to myself. Then the pandemic struck. People in New York began to die. Early on, Brooklyn became an epicenter of death. My underground life became the norm. With the quarantine, everyone was now underground. Everyone stayed inside, kept their distance. They'd glance up at times over their masks as they'd hurry by to give a brief furtive look to passing joggers, nannies, and service workers. Even extroverts were forced to become withdrawn and join us introverts, who now felt validated for staying in. Some introverts tweeted they'd been preparing for the quarantine and social distancing all their lives.

The ambulance sirens that plagued me with their ultra-loud whine are now just humdrum background noise as they go back and forth to hospitals. Everyone is high-strung, anxious, not knowing what the future brings. Will my wife fucking die? Will I fucking die? I don't know. Nobody knows. Tens of thousands of people have already died. They died here in New York; they've died across the country. They're still dying.

The feeling from the pandemic and lockdown now is *wabi-sabi* on steroids. An untranslatable aesthetic quality, indefinable even to the Japanese, it embraces imperfection, incompleteness, and transience of nature and human life, spiked with melancholy. With love and sadness, you sense and cherish the flawed and temporal beauty of the world, the decaying autumn leaves and the fading spring cherry blossoms, the fractured, peeling buildings, our aging wrinkled faces.

In New York, the sense of melancholy is overwhelming. The lockdown began in the spring, but the spring and the summer felt just like fall, that foreboding sense of sadness, of darkening, closing in, shutting down. In the fall the feeling of impending pandemic doom has caught up with itself. In your mind you hear some lines from Leonard Cohen's "A Street": *It's going to be September now, for many years to come / Every heart adjusting, to the strict September drum....*

This sick, racist, for-profit society has failed to overcome the pandemic. Why? Because it can't. Our society's functioning is incompatible with public health, with promoting the well-being of all. Health care and insurance are privatized. There is no national health service, no national coordinated strategy.

Self-centered assholes have had a field day. Get the federal government off my back! Fuck know-it-all scientists and elite experts! Don't tell me what to do! Fuck masks! Fuck vaccinations! Open the businesses! Party on! During the pandemic, billionaires have made enormous profits at others' expense.

Meanwhile, essential health care workers work their asses off under impossible conditions. As stand-ins for families and loved ones who could not come to the hospital, they were the only ones who could be with the dying. Many themselves have gotten sick and died.

For millions of parents and children—and especially the poor, the old, the sick, and the isolated—the quarantine has been a new form of hell. They mourn their dead and become ill themselves. Drug and alcohol addiction has increased. More report new symptoms of loneliness, sleep disruption, overeating and drinking, anxiety and depression. Apathy and numbness, missing your routine, not quite depressed, feeling meh ... a business psychologist in the *Times* labeled these zombie blues *languishing.*

The pandemic has distorted and changed our relation to time. It's vanquished any sense of hope or even a future, another perverted twist on the interminable now. It's forced us to convert conventional time into a period of mourning, not just of lives lost but of what we thought was normal.

In the beginning Manhattan felt destroyed, like the aftermath of a neutron bomb. Streets and subways were devoid of people; buildings and stations remained. In a *Times* piece, a parks administrator said Manhattan suffered from creeping *Blade Runner* syndrome—giant LED advertising screens, loud helicopters overhead shuttling wealthy employees from the suburbs, eerie empty high-rises and office buildings. Those who could afford it left for good; they and others who were told they could work from home discovered they can stay there. Many stores and restaurants went out of business, Broadway theatres and hotels closed. After a while bits of Manhattan began to open, but New York still isn't New York. Melancholy and angst, a toxic cocktail.

"In Kyoto" by Basho

In Kyoto,
hearing the cuckoo,
I long for Kyoto.

In New York, hearing the sirens, I long for New York. You're here in New York, but New York isn't here, and you miss it and are homesick and sad as hell.

The virus exposed many to the everyday racist crap already familiar to Black and Brown people. Black and Brown people have died in higher numbers. Their often-premorbid conditions, their inferior health care, their crowded living spaces, their essential service work, already marked them for death. Instead of any unified, galvanized public health attack the sociopath racist president and some dumbass right-wing governors politicized the crisis. They did nothing to stop the spread of the virus and allowed it to get worse. They committed bioterrorism. And murder.

From an obituary by Kristin Urquiza, a Latina who lost her father to the virus, in the *Arizona Republic, July 8, 2020*, which I turned into a poem:

His death is due
to the carelessness of the politicians
who continue to jeopardize
the health of brown bodies
through a clear lack of leadership
refusal to acknowledge
the severity of this crisis
and the inability

and unwillingness
to give clear and decisive direction
on how to minimize risk

A Dormant Future

The slumbering past pushes up the earth beneath Brooklyn like a rough beast ready to be reborn.

Visible traces have been uncovered of the Porte Road that ran through what is now Prospect Park down to the Gowanus Canal. The American army fled in retreat down this path between what were once large hills of the terminal moraine, in the Battle of Brooklyn, before Washington regrouped his men.

The skeletal remains of a street with forgotten shacks were discovered by aerial view and dug up and restored in Crown Heights. They were part of Weeksville, the nineteenth-century community of free Black people that is now a historic district.

Revolution and freedom for all—can they awaken from the underground?

Uprisings and revolutions are often considered to be spontaneous, but less visible long-term organizing and groundwork—or underground work—often laid the foundation. —Rebecca Solnit, Hope in the Dark: Untold Histories, Wild Possibilities

Amid the pandemic some have started to wonder about everything. I see emergent signs of a hopeful future, dormant, underground beneath the layers of the liminal present. You catch a glimpse, then they hide.

Early in the pandemic, from my window I could see Manhattan in detail, an eidetic diorama etched in silvery gray, like the magical city it could be. Why? Because the air above Manhattan turned pristine, there were few cars to drive in and about to create the lingering, poisonous, overhanging haze. More birds sang with more fervor—there were no people on the street to chase them off. The future could resemble that.

The hard working, low-wage public servants and others who staff the hospitals, food services, sanitation work, and subways were risking their lives for others. More people began to realize that care and service are valuable activities for all. That could be the future too. Not just on Valentines' Day, but each night during the early days of the quarantine, the Empire State Building flashed the red heartbeat for them: Lub dub. Lub dub. Each night at seven people would clap and cheer and bang pots out their windows in their honor. Some organized group sings. From here you couldn't see anyone doing it but you could hear them.

One internet meme, though, showed a nurse who says, "I can't eat applause!"

Fragment from "After the Pandemic, We Can't Go Back to Sleep" by David Graeber

In reality, the crisis we just experienced was waking from a dream, a confrontation with the actual reality of human life, which is that we are a collection of fragile beings taking care of one another, and that those who do the lion's share of this care work that keeps us alive are overtaxed, underpaid, and daily humiliated.... Most of the work we're currently doing is dream-work. It exists only for its own sake, or to make rich people feel good about themselves, or to make poor people feel bad about themselves....

The pandemic has exposed the system's failures. People have begun to question this sick, racist society. Millions began to quit their jobs, sick of low pay and meaningless work, a trend that became known as the Great Resignation. What does it mean to go back to normal, back to meaningless dream-work? Why do just some get to work at home? Is not having good health care for all normal? Is being bored in a large university lecture hall only to end up in massive student debt normal? Why don't, why can't we have good health care, housing, education, basic income, a clean environment, and justice for all, not as private commodities but as a human right?

Are birds free from the chains of the skyway? We are free in lockdown every day.   55

II

CHAPTER SIX

Above Brooklyn: My Recovery Begins

Come like a light in the white mackerel sky,
come like a daytime comet
with a long unnebulous train of words,
from Brooklyn, over the Brooklyn Bridge, on this fine morning,
please come flying. —Elizabeth Bishop, Fragment from "Invitation to Miss Marianne Moore"

From Paumanok starting I fly like a bird,
round and around to soar to sing the idea of all. —Walt Whitman

Fragment from *The Waste Land*
I do not know whether a man or a woman
—But who is that on the other side of you? — T.S. Eliot

Yo no soy yo
Soy este
que va ami lado sin yo verlo;
que, a veces, voy a ver;
Y que, a veces, olvido.
El que calla sereno, cuando hablo,
el que perdona, dulce, cuando odio,
el que pasea por donde no estoy,
el que quedará en pié cuando yo muera.

I am not I
I am this one
walking beside me whom I do not see,
whom at times I manage to visit,
and whom at other times I forget;
who remains calm and silent while I talk,
and forgives, gently, when I hate,
who walks where I am not,
who will remain standing when I die. —Juan Ramón Jiménez, translated by Robert Bly

One night I was flying over the rooftops of Brooklyn, like Chagall's Jew over Vitebsk. Someone else was next to me but I couldn't see whom. The red brick buildings of Bed-Stuy gleamed like shiny candy. I flew over Fort Greene and went up close to the Brooklyn Bridge. The stones of the gothic arches glowed with a strange light. The bridge kept changing iridescent colors like Warhol's screen prints of the bridge. I flew down over the Gowanus Canal, up over the Park Slope brownstones, along the terminal moraine to Crown Heights. Hasidic Jews and Black people were on the streets together, twirling and doing cartwheels. I hovered over Prospect Park. The park was a deep green, a tropical jungle with Rousseau fronds.

Above Brooklyn the air was soft and fragrant. Clouds formed marshmallow sofas. On the 9th Street ball fields I saw children holding hands in a big circle. I heard them laughing and heard wind chimes, too. I headed further into the park and the person next to me spoke and said, "*Look down.*"

I saw the Camperdown Elm near the Boathouse, its branches parallel to the ground. It was on fire but not consumed. It stood as Marianne Moore described it in her poem about the tree she helped save: its intricate pattern of branches that arch high and curve low, its fine twigs, and the last line: *our crowning curio.*

Next to it was a stack of some kind of parchment, like a *Daily News* tabloid. I swooped down and grabbed the copy below the top one. Even in a dream, New Yorkers know you never take the one on top.

Fragment from the Great American Cosmic Novel *Raintree County*, by Ross Lockridge Jr. that I first read at the formative age of 13:

...[he] felt that there was only one tree, one sacred trunk standing in the druid silence of woodlands in the middle County. Someday, perhaps he would find that tree and thus become the hero of the County, the Alexander who cut the Gordian knot, the Hercules who obtained the Golden Apples of the Hesperides, the Oedipus who solved the Riddle of the Sphinx.
The secret of the tree was blended strangely with the whole secret of his life and the mystery from which he had sprung.

The Brooklyn Cosmic Inquirer

When I awoke, I found the parchment tabloid next to me on the floor. Its banner said *The Brooklyn Cosmic Inquirer.* What the fuck? Yes, of course, what the fuck. *Buddha found enlightenment under the Bodhi tree. Jacob found the Cosmic Daily News under a tree that grows in Brooklyn.* Half awake, hoping it was still a dream, I began to browse through it.

Fragment from Sleepless City *(Brooklyn Bridge Nocturne)* by Federico García Lorca

No es sueño la vida. ¡Alerta! ¡Alerta! ¡Alerta!
Life is no dream! Beware and beware and beware!

The first thing I found on the inside page was a forgotten poem I had written years ago. It was about a billboard in Brooklyn I had seen put up by a Hasidic sect that believed their rebbe, already dead, will return as the messiah (moshiach). It even had my name in the byline:

Moon Over Moshiach
by Jacob Traum

Above Brooklyn
the parchment moon
looms large and full

Blue dusk glows
through its skull-boned
face

Over the billboard
of the bearded man
the moon broods
like a solemn
emoticon:

Pray for
the coming of
Moshiach

Below the poem was a counter response on another billboard I had filed somewhere. It had the face of one of Bed-Stuy's pride-and-joy inhabitants, June Jordan. Beneath that was her quote from a poem of hers beloved by all feminist/spiritual/lefty types, turned into a song by Sweet Honey in the Rock and a book title by Alice Walker: *We are the Ones We Have Been Waiting For.*

Some writings were just lines I had wanted to turn into T-shirts:

Your Mind: Don't Take it Personally
Your Original Face Does Not Need Botox

Other pages had fragments I had begun and abandoned years ago:

Schmucks With Bucks. *My god, there are so many of them in New York. I see and overhear them in restaurants. There are movies and TV shows about them. They get away with everything.*

Cosmic Demo Against the War in El Salvador March, 1983 *By Jacob Traum, reporter for The Brooklyn Cosmic Inquirer*

The march down 42nd Street was a fluid womb of warmth and comfort. The city was transformed into a home. The harshness of the streets, the indifferent stores, the towering, cold-gray buildings all receded and melted away. The Empire State Building winked. Grand Central Station smiled. I looked up at the multi-levels of people in the windows. The scene became a cityscape of Ralph Fasanella, the New York leftist primitivist painter, a visionary image that includes and connects everyone. The city was ours. Even the cops were forced to bend back the pressing traffic to let us pass. We chanted slogans over and over in unison. They became a mantra, an enveloping, sensuous, moral whole. You feel the force of breath moving up from your chest and through your throat into sound formed as words. Your own voice gets lost as it merges with others: Hey, hey, Uncle Sam. We remember Vietnam! No draft, no war, US out of El Salvador! The wind was bracing, the sun was punching through some nasty clouds, the bright satin banners were flapping all along the line, kids were bouncing on folks' shoulders. It was one big raggedy and spirited living thing and you were a part of it. We shouted and the buildings rose up and floated away like when Ginsberg and the antiwar protesters surrounded and levitated the Pentagon...

I was stupified. I turned the pages and found the Ads section:

- *Ego addiction app. Give your ego a massage! #Headcase Inc. Mindfulness Studio*
- *Got Surplus Shpilkes Syndrome? These chill pills guaranteed. Text #Yeshi234*
- *We will childmind your inner child. Dreydel to the Crave Daycare Center. 6 Gowanus Canal*

In the middle was my ad:

- Seeking Hired Power J. Traum Box 18, 11238

Below it in pen was written *Contact Tzadik Associates 36 Terminal Moraine BK*

What the hell was this? Plus, there is no damn street called Terminal Moraine.

CHAPTER SEVEN

I Meet My Hired Power

There was no way around it. I was about to enter some kind of Brooklyn-style Bernard Malamud magic realism story. This so-called *tzadik* who answered my ad might be an instructive African American Jewish angel like Harry Belafonte in the film version of *The Angel Levine* who tests Zero Mostel's faith— another version of the racist "Magical Negro" media trope who's always rescuing the broken white guy's ass. Or maybe it would be some kind of sad-sack Yiddish matchmaker-type *schlub* with a hidden agenda for finding love like the one from *The Magic Barrel*. I was trapped in a clichéd story of my own making.

My nerves were a mess. I went into the kitchen to make some herbal tea. I grabbed a bag of Honey Vanilla Chamomile, Maya's favorite, which I never cared for but what the hell. From the shelf I took down one of my favorite mugs that said Buddha is My Om Boy.

Before I could boil water, I saw a note lying on the counter in the same handwriting as the one below the ad. Next to it was a pair of Apple wireless teal earbuds. The note said *Put them on.* I froze, then became frantic, and looked around and checked the door. It was still locked. Nothing in the apartment was out of place.

You've seen the movie, the guy doesn't know what else to do, so he does something stupid and/or that makes no sense, like stick the earbuds in his head, which I did. Keep in mind they're not linked to anything. Sure, it's a bit like Alice who finds a bottle and drinks it just because it says *Drink me.*

The voice in the buds said *Go outside your building and turn left down the terminal moraine. Stay on the median. Wait for further instructions.* I put on my COVID mask and jacket, took the elevator downstairs, and crossed the lobby. Outside I headed left onto Eastern Parkway toward Crown Heights. I was almost run down by a millennial cyclist who had veered off the bike lane onto the walkway.

I walked a few blocks deeper into Crown Heights on the median, past the Brooklyn Museum. Black kids skipped along with their moms and Orthodox men ambled by, prayer shawl *tsitsis* flapping beneath their shirts. A Latino food delivery guy zipped past on his motorbike. Few people go out for groceries; they get stuff delivered. A subway train rumbled below the grates under the Parkway.

Stop and walk down the emergency stairs, the voice said. I stopped and looked down and around. The pavement was seamless. "What stairs?" I growled way too loud. A Black woman on the bench across from me looked up from her book. I noticed she was reading *The Fire Next Time* by James Baldwin. "Great book," I said, trying to normalize myself.

Fragment from *The Fire Next Time* by James Baldwin:
I imagine one of the reasons people cling to their hates so stubbornly is because they sense, once hate is gone, they will be forced to deal with pain.

Then I heard, *rub your eyes, close them for ten seconds, then open them.* Okay, what the hell, which was becoming my mantra. I did, and an opening in the median appeared, the emergency type trap door for passengers to escape a track fire or stalled train below. The two side doors spread apart, and I could see an iron stairway. So, this is just a Harry Potter type moment, I thought, like track 9 ¾ at Kings Cross, invisible to muggles. Or is this one of those stairways to nowhere?

Damn, is this the best I can do? I'm living a derivative daydream. Sure enough, no one around saw it happen. The woman on the bench gave me what I thought might have been the wisp of a smile and returned to reading Baldwin.

I descended the dim stairwell for what seemed like forever, with no bottom in sight. People appeared out of nowhere, moving past me going both up and down the stairs, passing each other as well. It was as if they didn't see me. I could just make them out, they wore no COVID masks, just flimsy gowns and could have been men or women. I realized they resembled the angels from Blake's painting of Jacob's Ladder on my screen saver. They couldn't wait to go down or up, whatever those meant to them. For some reason, maybe to break the absurdity of the scene, I thought of a cartoon by John Callahan. It shows a bar next to an AA meeting. From each place a guy is desperately running past the other, out of one door into the other.

Just then though I remembered two things I had read about Jacob's Ladder. It's a link between the Earth and those from a higher plane of awareness who come down to teach us wisdom. It's also a ladder for stages of spiritual evolution.

I didn't know what to think and just kept climbing down.

At last, I found myself on a platform unlike any I had seen in the subway—gleaming tracks, cushioned benches, marbled walls. On the walls were elaborate inlaid tiled murals that depicted people planting seeds and fishing. I paused to read the illuminated sign on the platform. It said this was a site of the Canarsee, a Brooklyn tribe of the Lenape. They lived here before the Dutch and English cheated them out of their land and killed many of them. "All This Ground is a Burial Site and is Therefore Sacred," the sign said, and below that: "We are still here."

Native people believe that the earth is alive, and that everything living is a part of it... Land acknowledgements should not and do not live in the past, because colonialism is ongoing ... at the end of the day, no matter where you are in the United States, you're standing on Native land. Someone's ancestors were forced off of the land where your museum or your university or your town is now, whether you acknowledge that or not. —Heather Breugl, historian and member of the Oneida Nation, interviewed by Sarah Schmidt, *Plants & Gardens*, Brooklyn Botanic Garden Members' Newsletter, Fall 2021/Winter 2022

Okay. I think the Earth is alive too, and I acknowledge with compassion the people who were here first and who were forced off the land in terrible ways, many killed. But acknowledging it alone—is that just virtue signaling? Does that mean I should feel guilty every minute, or I should tiptoe where I stand, or I shouldn't even be here at all? What should anyone who cares do next?

I noticed someone a few yards away on a bench and figured that was my Hired Power, the Malamud character. I walked toward the guy, who, whoa, wasn't wearing a mask.

Well, not a guy exactly. For sure not anyone out of any Malamud story, like the Angel Levine. No one resembling a *tzadik*, either. The person motioned for me to sit down on the bench. Plenty of New Yorkers with masks were standing on the platform around us, pacing, waiting for the next train. Right away I saw they were also translucent and never noticed us, like the angels on the stairway. We were invisible.

I couldn't figure out who I was looking at. The person, it had to be my Hired Power, wore an iridescent teal shirt and had ancient, wizened eyes, one blue, one Minerva gray, or so I thought. When I looked again, though, one was brown, the other a bright green. Their skin was silken smooth and youthful, mocha, and had an inner glow. Their hair was kinky blonde. No, wait, it changed to jet black straight; now millennial dyed purple.

"Hey Jacob! I'm glad you could meet up," the person said. Of course, I couldn't tell if I was with a man or woman. I was stuck in binary gender thinking, my bad. I'm a damn boomer, for chrissake. All we knew from gender role models growing up was John Wayne and Marilyn Monroe. Okay, just taking a piss, as the Brits say. I support transgender and nonbinary people, and I hate the way they get shit, some even murdered—and this person was blowing my mind.

"Uh yeah, thanks," I said. "Do you mind telling me what the hell is going on? Who are you? Where are we? How did you...?"

"You know who I am, your Hired Power. I answered your ad in the *Cosmic Inquirer.* This is where I meet all my Brooklyn clients, the Terminal Moraine sub-subway station. I used the *tzadik* ploy to get your attention. And I'm sorry you're disappointed I'm not the Belafonte Angel Levine. Black people always having to magically appear and save the broken, disheveled white guy's ass....

So you can read my mind, I thought.

"Yes, I can," smiled my Hired Power. "And you can tuck those earbuds in your pocket now." I'd forgotten I had them and I did so.

"So," my Hired Power continued, "I see you want references, you want to know whom I've worked with, who summoned me. From Brooklyn alone there was Walt Whitman, Dorothy Day, Jacob Lawrence, Diane Di Prima, Jackie Robinson, Richard Fariña, and Woody Guthrie. There are regular folks too, of course. Right now, the woman you saw on the bench reading James Baldwin, Marva Williams. Then there's your paternal grandfather Benjamin, the socialist, when he and your grandma lived here in Brooklyn in Sheepshead Bay in the nineteen forties...."

"Getouttaheah," I blurted in Brooklynese and tried to stall before the Hired Power moved on to my case. "Wait, did you say you worked with Richard Fariña?" I knew he grew up in Brooklyn. My college mates and I dug his novel, *Been Down So Long It Looks Like Up To Me* for its mad anarchy and rebelliousness. We also loved his creative folky tunes he sang with Mimi. That one song, how does it go...? *If there's an end to all our dreaming....*

I asked, "Why couldn't you stop him from getting on the motorcycle that killed him?"

"He let me go just after the novel was published. He was ecstatic and felt he had made it. Then he jumped on the bike. That was sad, still is."

I couldn't think of anything else to say. Damn, my Hired Power is another magical realism character, maybe a visitor from an advanced future society who can time and space trip. Probably even shape shift, too. Worked with my Bundist grandfather, though. I wish I coulda met him myself; he died right after I was born.

"You got it, Jacob. All of us from the future have the power to move through history. We've practiced and mastered Dogen's Being-Time..."

Fragment from *Hymn to Time* by Ursula Le Guin
Time is being and being
time, it is all one thing,
the shining, the seeing,
the dark abounding.

Wow, the folks from the future arrived at Dogen's Being-Time! Dogen, the thirteenth-century Zen master! Through the Gateless Gate! Not horizontal, sequential, ordinary time, past, present, and future. That's a mental construct! Instead, everything is all happening right now in a vertical column. You can go up and down from one to the other, like Jacob's Ladder. We touch all past times and all future times through *ourselves at once*. Why? Because you realize you are time itself! You are embodied time! As Borges said, *Time is the substance I am made of ... time is the fire that ravages me, but I am the fire....*

Why? Because everything and everyone that ever existed and will exist is *connected. You are interconnected with everyone and everything. Co-dependent origination—cause and effect, it all arises together.* Everything *is one continuous presencing, hereness*. The empty self—no absolute, permanent nature—is a form that is one with all empty forms. When you get to that, you yourself *are* fierce compassion for all. No separation. No duality, no barrier between self and other. You identify with and care about everyone and everything ... you see beyond the constructs of language ... you see the fluidity of the universe...

The Shapes arise! ... Shapes ever projecting other shapes... —Walt Whitman, *Song of the Axe*

... I see the Past, Present and Future existing all at once Before me. O Divine Spirit, sustain me on thy wings, That I may awake Albion from his long and cold repose... —William Blake, *I See the Four-Fold Man*

"Are you a Tralfamadorian?" I asked.

[On Tralfamadore] *All moments, past, present, and future, always have existed, always will exist. The Tralfamadorians can look at all the different moments just the way we can look at a stretch of the Rocky Mountains, for instance.... It is just an illusion we have here on Earth that one moment follows another like beads on a string and that once a moment is gone it is gone forever.* —Kurt Vonnegut, *Slaughterhouse-Five*

My Hired Power just laughed. "Well, we also evolve through history, through time, since we *are* time. Time is not just a static backdrop, it's not just an illusion, it's embodied in the material fabric of the universe, in *us*. We create more complex material from the past. Our development, and that of the universe, depends on the memory of what we have created before."

Assembly theory treats time as fundamental and material: time is the stuff out of which things in the Universe are made. Objects created by selection and evolution can be formed only through the passing of time.... If what exists now determines the future, and what exists now is larger and more information-rich than it was in the past, then the possible futures also grow larger as objects become more complex ... there is more history existing in the present from which to assemble novel future states. Treating time as a material property of the objects it creates allows novelty to be generated.... —Sara Walker and Lee Cronin, "Time is an Object," Aeon.

"So, for example, in our future we have been able to transcend and create more complex social identities. We can be a man or woman or in between, we can change our looks. It depends on whom we're with and what we feel like now. If I feel like indulging your fantasy and transform into Malamud's magical Negro angel who saves the Zero Mostel guy, I can." My Hired Power winked. "Watch."

After a blur of rainbow light, I was now facing the astounding Harry Belafonte as the Angel Levine in the movie version, wearing that cool leather jacket and a slight moustache. He gave me a big grin.

I stared in disbelief.

"Okay, I believe, I believe," I gulped. "You *are* some kind of angel. Just don't turn into the guy from *The Magic Barrel* who's always eating herring in front of everyone."

I had to collect myself and took a breath.

"So, what's your name? And could you please go back to how you were before? This is freaking me out."

The Belafonte Angel Levine shimmered in a rainbow flash of colors and changed back to the slightly feminine, sexy, ambiguous, mercurial character I had met. Whew.

I wondered if my Hired Power was a fluid version of Tiresias, who helped Odysseus and appears in Eliot's *The Waste Land*. Or even Tiresias uh, themselves, maybe the one beside me in the dream, the mysterious person whose gender I couldn't make out … or maybe a kind of futuristic, integral, nonbinary Ursula Le Guin character. I tried again. "So are you a Gethenian?"

The Gethenians do not see one another as men or women. This is almost impossible for our imaginations to accept. After all, what is the first question we ask about a newborn baby? … there is no division of humanity into strong and weak halves, protected/protective. One is respected and judged only as a human being … you cannot think of a Gethenian as "it." They are not neuters. They are potentials or integrals. —Ursula Le Guin, *The Left Hand of Darkness*

My Hired Power caught my thoughts and just winked and smiled.

I tried another angle. "Hey, can you, like, turn into my mom, so I can see her?" Even Harry Potter gets to see his dead parents, I thought. This would be even better than those cheap hologram effects. "And Maya? She doesn't want to see me."

"Sorry, Jacob, they're behind a fire wall at the moment."

I felt a pang of disappointment. I wondered if my Hired Power was going to try to appease me with Robert Thurman's Tibetan Buddhist claim that *everyone* you see and meet is your mother.

"No." My mind was being read again. "It's true we're all made from the same cosmic dust that gets recirculated every few thousand years. You know Whitman: *For every atom belonging to me as good belongs to you*. But you don't have to take Thurman literally. The point is to care about and treat everyone you meet as if they were your mother."

"Huh. Yeah," I thought, "that's good." Assuming you like your mother. At least I did. My dad too. Then I remembered the crowd scene with Jesus and *his* mom, whom he didn't even care to say hi to....

"Yup, same with Jesus," my Hired Power continued my thought. "When someone told him his mother was there, he asked and answered his own Xen Kohen: *Who is my mother*? He pointed instead to his disciples."

My jaw dropped. "He chose them over his own mom! It's kinda like Buddha who left his family. For Jesus, *all* those people are his freakin' mother," I said. "The Mary worshippers must not wanna deal with that one."

"Yes, though Mary stands for the divine feminine side, which exists in many spiritual traditions—the Shekhinah in Judaism, Quan Yin in Buddhism. She's both compassionate and open to receiving universal love. Both Jesus and Buddha said treat everyone like a mother does, with a limitless heart."

As a mother would risk her life
To protect her child, her only child,
Even so should one cultivate a limitless heart
With regard to all beings
—Karaniya Metta Sutta

"Well, you might get to meet your grandfather," my Hired Power went on. "And Maya is an open door, it'll be up to you. Okay, for your purposes here's who I am."

I sat up straight.

"I'm nonbinary, bisexual. I'm Afro-Dominican, African American, Palestinian, Italian-Irish, Asian Buddhist, and Jewish. You will meet me at different times and in different forms, even as a non-human, but you'll always know it's me. I will be using the pronouns *we, us, and our.*"

I was trying to take this all in. Okay, choice of pronouns is now a big deal—include and respect everyone.

"And my name," I leaned closer, "is Xen Kohen."

Xen Kohen. Of course, I should have known. Maybe somehow I had.

"So, you spell it with an X and a K, are you a...."

"Yes, I'm a *Kohen*, a descendent of the Temple High Priests."

"Then you're...?"

"Messianic, like Leonard Cohen's family."

"Do you always finish other...?"

"...people's sentences. Remind you of anyone?"

Yeah, I admitted to myself. I do that to Maya. It drives her nuts. I interrupt her and try to guess what she's about to say, I get it right maybe half the time. Then she forgets what she was going to say. Then we're both aggravated. I was silent.

To try to gain some equal footing I summoned my inner snarkster, but it was clear I was out of my league with uh, us.

"Okay, what's with the X. Are you woke?"

"Let's get this woke stuff straight,' Xen Kohen said. "The original meaning, coined by African Americans, is to care for and have compassion for all, to bring the truth to light against bullshit and meanness and stand and act for loving justice for everyone, period. In that sense I'm woke as fuck.

"There are two perversions of the word. The right wing has now managed to co-opt and twist it to sarcastically smear all progressive and caring and inclusive values and policies. Unfortunately, it's become the dominant trope. A few on the left play into their hands by being self-righteous, rigid, judgmental, closed off to dialogue, and dismissive of those who disagree with them. A damn shame. I like the X as a creative take on existential puzzles, same as you."

On point.

I tried again to delay my reckoning. "Well, Xen Kohen, you fit hipster Brooklyn to a tee. I hope you're caught up on your shifts at the Food Coop—I mean before they suspended them for the pandemic ... and ... I haven't hired you yet. What's your fee?"

"Not to worry," Xen Kohen said, and flashed a charming megawatt smile with teeth that would have set me back thousands with my East Side dentist. "The down payment is set. A bunch of people who know you took up a GoFundMe."

Xen Kohen took out his, *uh our*, mobile—and read the list of contributors.

"Your great-great-great aunt Ida on your mother's side, a feminist seamstress, from your family shtetl, Otynia, during the early 1800s. The gay kid you and your friends teased in junior high school, Sid Handlor, who ended up dying of AIDS. The young woman, Isabelle Vimuney, from college, whose heart you broke. An anonymous person whom I am not at liberty to disclose at this time. A few others who seem to recognize you— Paul Robeson, Joe Hill, Woody Guthrie. Here's Juan Carlos Marx, a distant Mexican cousin of Karl. Leonard Cohen, yup, my eighteenth cousin. And a future female relative from the twenty-second century named Xozha. From Red Hook."

"Jesus."

"No, he passed on you, wasn't confident you'd be a good investment."

"I just meant ... wow." My heart sank. Damn, these others believed in me but not Jesus.

"He did say he'd wait to see how you do, though," Xen Kohen said, and winked. The joke was on me.

"What about the final payment?" I asked.

"That also depends on how you do in your recovery. If you complete it, there's no fee."

"What do I have to do?"

We'll get to that. You have a lot of work since you want to become something of a wise mensch and recover from being a self-centered, kvetchy asshole."

Ouch.

"I know, but you can do it. And you know that letting go of your ego attachment means you can recover from this selfish culture that's infected you, all the better to work with others to change it," we said.

I was speechless.

"Okay," Xen Kohen continued, "let's take a quick look at your cosmic rap sheet." We held up our mobile again and swiped a few times.

"There are three categories here," Xen Kohen said, "the first one includes selfish stuff you've done in your life, like ghosting girlfriends, picking on weaker people. We'll send you to the underground to work those out. The second group is about stuff you could have done or done better, dreams, visions, actions, but you abandoned, gave up on, for various reasons—laziness, despair, lack of confidence. But not always your fault—you've grown up in a toxic epoch. You'll go to a purgatory district for work on that. After you've done those, you'll get to go to a higher place to see what might still be possible."

"So, this is out of the Dante playbook then," I said. "You're the Virgil character."

"I'll be around but not by your side, like Virgil," said Xen Cohen. "Besides, we're different, Virgil did not evolve enough to accompany Dante to the heaven realm. These are designed for you, they're not quite out of the *Divine Comedy*. But first we must do some work with a map and ladders."

At the word *work* I wanted to stall again. "Can you tell me a bit about your future society?"

"Here's a hint, it's like what Maya Angelou wrote about in *A Brave and Startling Truth*. We came to it. We managed to work it out together. As she says, we are 'neither devils nor divines.' Nondualism. Nonbinary in the most evolved sense. But we had to evolve. We had to climb the divine ladder of human consciousness, like Dante, like you will. Like everyone. We start with the lower realms of existence and move up from there—we become the caretakers of the Earth."

"Awright," I said. "So, we all made it past a lot of lousy history and dangerous climate change. But isn't that stuff about us being, how does she put it, the true wonder of this world, a bit anthropocentric?"

"No, we figured out together how to live with and on the Earth and also honor ourselves and all beings and things," Xen Kohen said. "It doesn't mean we have to oppress others and animals and exploit nature."

I always thought so too. We need to have a respectful relationship with and a responsibility to care for the Earth. But we have a lot of growing up to do, and fast. Hell, we *are* the damn Earth, but don't know it—yet.

"What else does this sort of remind me of?" I mused out loud. "*A Christmas Carol*. Spiritual—*and* psychological—*and* anti-capitalist as fuck. Time travel to the past, present, and future. Helping ol' Scrooge give up greed, gain insight, become a selfless, self-accepting mensch. That's a great cosmic magical realism story before anyone even thought of the term."

"Yes, it is," Xen Kohen said. "I helped Dickens write it. And there's some time travel for you as well."

"… and did you know," I went on, still trying to stall, "as a play it's so popular that small theater companies rely on the profits from their annual *Christmas Carol* show to fund more experimental plays during the year?" I read that in the *New York Times*, so it must be true. Yeah, right.

"Of course."

"And ... wait, did you say you helped Dickens wri...?" I was speechless again but still tried another diversionary tack. "So, how come you're not wearing a mask?"

Xen Kohen gave a slight smile and focused on me with those multicolored laser eyes. "There's no COVID down here, you can take yours off too." Which I did.

"You all just can't fix this damn virus?" I asked.

"Nope, *you all* have to work that out together."

I had to let that one go. But I kept going one more time.

"You remind me of different people," I mused, "but I can't quite...."

"For one, you know that angel you dreamed you danced with as a kid in the attic of your grandparents' summer house?"

"That was you?"

Xen Kohen flashed me the knock-out smile again. Still, there was something else familiar.... Before I could sort it out, Xen Kohen switched to the look of a *mami* ready to throw a *chancleta* at me. I sat up straight.

"Now, your first assignment," Xen Kohen said in a severe tone, "is to read Joy Harjo's *A Map to the Next World.* Meditate, and then follow its instructions. I just downloaded it onto your phone. Then we'll go over it."

I knew something about Harjo. Poet laureate of the United States. Member of the Muscogee Creek Nation, feminist, radical. Deals in myths, symbols, landscapes. Connected to the subconscious, to the Earth, attuned to Dogen's Being-Time. Highly evolved cosmic consciousness. My kind of gal—uh, well, person.

Fragment from an interview with Joy Harjo:
I feel strongly that I have a responsibility to all the sources that I am: to all past and future ancestors, to my home country, to all places that I touch down on and that are myself, to all voices, all

women, all of my tribe, all people, all earth, and beyond that to all beginnings and endings.

I was feeling exhausted. "Can you get me out of here?" I asked Xen Cohen.

"Sure, just click your heels three times…," I was about to give Xen Cohen a look that would have terrorized the Wicked Witch herself. "Just kibitzing witchoo," we said. "We'll give you a lift on our broomstick. Where do you want to go?"

I would have preferred my regular coffee shop hangout, Café Regular in Park Slope. That's Reg—oo—*lar* to you, *mes amies.* They even have a painted mural of Sartre's phrase, *L'enfer, c'est les autres.* "Hell is other people." Perfect for a grump. Since it was closed due to the pandemic, I had to go back to the apartment.

"See you soon," Xen Cohen said.

"So, what about…?" In an instant I found myself seated on my living room couch back home. How Xen Kohen transported me I had no idea. *My, people come and go so quickly here.*

CHAPTER EIGHT

A Map to the Next World

In every situation, latent possibilities are waiting to come into being. In dreamy visionary states we get glimpses of these possibilities; when these visionary images land in us, they can work through us and take form in our actions. —Joanna Macy and Chris Johnstone, *Active Hope*

I went into the kitchen and put the water on for the tea I didn't get to before. I brought it into the bedroom, set up my zafu in front of my altar, and prepared to meditate like Xen Kohen had asked me.

The altar is interspiritual. It has two small Buddha statues. A statue of the compassionate Quan Yin. Two *yahrzeit* memorial candles. A mezuzah left to me by my grandmother. A figurine of Ganesha the Hindu elephant god with the requisite rat—you need to know why there's always a damn rat beneath or alongside Ganesha. A votive Jesus candle in Spanish. A Moorish magnet from when Maya and I went to the Alhambra. An incense holder. And three postcards.

The postcards are, first, *The Penitent Magdalen*: she's holding a skull and contemplating a candle in darkness, by Georges LaTour, from the Met. Second, Rembrandt's *Philosopher in Meditation*: he's seated by a luminous window, next to a fire and a winding staircase, from the Louvre. And third, *Jacob and the Angel*, a statue by Jacob Epstein, from the Tate Britain. You can't tell if the two are wrestling, dancing, hugging, or even getting it on. Next to the altar is a coaster for a mug of tea with a cartoon image of a seated Buddha that says *Let That Shit Go.*

Yeah, I've already brooded on the smartass objections you will come up with about my altar: it's a parody of hippy trippy woo-woo pseudo-spirituality. It's a disrespectful, culturally appropriative, eclectic hodgepodge of various traditions—tacky, disparate, fragmented, and cluttered—in Yiddish, *ongepotchket.* Worse, it reeks of perennialism: the sloppy belief that every varied culture across time ahistorically shares the same underlying universal spirituality. That's right: diversity of surface, universality of depth. Take that, shallow, pomo relativists. Do I contradict myself? Very well, I contradict myself. The altar pays homage to my restless third eye. I've embraced and folded all that awareness into the whole schmeer.

As spiritual people well know, and as great scientists are now discovering, consciousness in the universe is one, and likely to be infinite in space and in time. Cosmic consciousness is the Great Spirit of indigenous belief systems, the Godhead of the Abrahamic religions, the Dharma of India and the Dao of China. Our individual consciousness is a fragment, a projection, or a fractal element of cosmic consciousness. —Ervin Laszlo, *The Way Forward*

After some tea, I had a helluva time settling my mind meditating. I focused on the sensation of my breath. I tried to watch the images from the day and all the thoughts, feelings, and judgments that kept cropping up. Instead of playing whac-a-mole with each and repressing them, you try to witness them, be with and feel them, then return to your breath as they pass through—if they do, that is—and move on.

There was the sacred Brooklyn tree, the Camperdown Elm. *The Cosmic Inquirer.* Missing Maya. What was she doing right now? The stairs down to the sub-subway station. Xen Kohen. My recovery assignments. Feeling anxious. Missing Maya ... wishing I could see her ... what were she and Jill gonna do for the holidays ... I also noticed patterns I'm stuck in—self-pity, denial of pain, self-centeredness, wanting to escape somewhere, missing Maya ... I thought of how impatient at times I'd get with her, criticize her like an insensitive smartass when I thought she should have known something that seemed apparent to me ... how she'd feel wounded and upset ... I felt pretty shitty about it....

From when your Brooklyn broke my skin and bones... —Taylor Swift, *All Too Well* (ten-minute version)

I managed to reach a moment in which I let it all go, to promise to give myself, Maya, and others forgiveness and compassion, to swear I'd start to say and do the right thing with her, with everyone....

For a while I could get behind the discursive, stormy clouds. Experience the clear light. The transcendent. Awareness itself. One thing mindfulness can do is remind ourselves what we have forgotten—our inseparability, our fluidity, our life unattached to divisive concepts, like linear time ... like the ego ... connecting to the world and everyone anew ... even compassion for everyone ... almost.

I took a deep breath and rang the bowl.

The whole *mishegoss* came flooding back. I sat there astounded and brooded. After a long while I took out my mobile and looked at the Joy Harjo poem. I began to feel sleepy and returned to the living room couch.

Fragments from *A Map to the Next World* by Joy Harjo:

In the last days of the fourth world I wished to make a map for those who would climb through the hole in the sky.

I Googled what the fourth world means in several Native American beliefs. It's the world of today, not a great place, and it's already ending. So I'm supposed to climb through a sky hole to get the hell out of here. In Hopi mythology the hole is a small tunnel or interdimensional passage to the fifth world, which sounds like a better realm. Spiritual beings will then be around to create one world and one nation under one spiritual presence. Sounds good. Beam me up.

She also says the map is not perfect and provides no escape. It's made of sand and can't be seen under ordinary light. Well, that doesn't sound too useful. Come on man, it's a metaphor.

The map warns us that forgetting the language of the land is bad news. Once we knew everything, but we have forgotten ... I hope she doesn't mean going backwards on some kind of nostalgia trip ... no, I think it's more to do with returning to a source but with awakened consciousness.... My eyes became heavy. I stretched out on the couch.

Sometimes I do better trying to sort stuff out asleep, dreaming, than awake ... like Oloff Van Kortlandt in Washington Irving's *Knickerbocker's History of New York*. As a kid I read how he envisioned where to build New Amsterdam ... in a dream he climbed a tree and saw the smoke from St. Nicholas's pipe form images of the city, "shadowed out palaces and domes and lofty spires" ... then ol' Oloff woke up and told his pals, build the city right here....

Fragment from *Knickerbocker's History of New York* by Washington Irving:
... and from that time forth the sage Van Kortlandt was held in more honor than ever, for his great talent at dreaming, and was pronounced a most useful citizen and a right good man – when he was asleep...

...I'm inside Joy Harjo's poem, standing in a desert. I see supermarkets and malls, altars of money. Children disappear in the fog, flowers of rage spring up. I have forgotten how to speak to the birds. I travel through a death membrane into the Milky Way and smell food from a camp where our relatives are cooking. I'm in the fifth world now, with no guide except my mother's singing. Courage comes from seeing the planets, courage lights up the map. I see red cliffs that contain a ladder—a ladder!—that everyone climbs up from the wreckage. The Earth speaks to us and says we might make mistakes too, just like she did. At the end the poet says, You must define your own route.

I woke up and sat up straight. There is no map, I have to make my own? So why the hell do I need a map that's not a map?

Fragments from *Only the Dead Know Brooklyn* by Thomas Wolfe:
"How'd yuh know deh was such a place," I says, "if yuh neveh been deh befoeh?"
"Oh," he says, "I got a map."
"A map?"...
"I got a map dat tells me about all dese places. I take it wit me every time I come out heah," he says.
...I says, "yuh ain't gonna get to know Brooklyn wit no map."
...How long would it take a guy wit a good map to know all deh was to know about Brooklyn!... It'd take a guy a lifetime to know Brooklyn t'roo an' t'roo. Ane even den, yuh wouldn't know it all.

How do you know there's such a place if you've never been there before? From a map. But no map can help you find the way to the fifth world. And unless you're a dead zombie, no map can even help you know Brooklyn *troo and troo.* Yeah, both would take a lifetime.
And even then, you wouldn't know it all.

A map of the world that does not include Utopia is not worth even glancing at...—Oscar Wilde, *The Soul of Man Under Socialism*

In Prospect Park

I needed some air. It was early December but crazy mild: climate change. I put on a light jacket and a mask and walked down Eastern Parkway to Prospect Park. Once inside I dipped into the meadow and followed the path along the perimeter. Many leaves were still on the trees—clashes of red, orange, yellow, even leftover green. The sun was low in the sky and produced stunning patterns of light and shadow. Some young cherry trees were in bloom, fooled by the warm spell. Nice, but maybe not a good sign for the spring. The walk rekindled the meditative mood I thought I had lost.

Fragment from *When I am Among the Trees* by Mary Oliver:
Around me the trees stir in their leaves
and call out, "Stay awhile."
The light flows from their branches.
And they call again, "It's simple," they say,
"and you too have come
into the world to do this, to go easy, to be filled
with light, and to shine."

I found a bench in the sun with no one on it and sat down. Some benches had gold leaf plaques on the back from donors dedicated to the memory of a loved one. This one said: *A donde quiera que vayas, no dejes de ser luz* ("Wherever you wish to go, may you never stop being the light").

Just as I sat back, my mobile dinged. Maybe it's Maya returning my texts. I always hoped. Instead, it was my former counseling group from the high school, the Post-Traum-atix, all six on a group thread. They were just checking in on me. They were all at home trying to get through the pandemic school year on Zoom.

Cami: *Hey Mr. T how r u*

Arielle: *We miss you!*

Billy: *What's happening Mr T*

Dina: *We hope u r OK!*

Derrick: *Zoom school is wack*

May May: *Let's zoom Mr. T.*

I texted back to the group *thanks gang*, I was happy to hear from them and was okay. I said I know it's tough doing everything online in school and wished them the best and told them I'd get back to them and zoom soon.

Many benches in the park have a partition in the middle. Since social distancing began under COVID, if a person or two is on one end of the bench most often no one will sit on the other. Not this time.

A minute after I put away my cellphone, a young Latina nanny pushing a stroller with a round-faced Black baby in a pink bonnet and stud earrings walked up and motioned to me if she could sit on the other end. I shrugged and moved closer to my end. The baby was doing a yoga–like stretch impossible for most adult yogis, grabbing her feet and lifting them as high as her face. The little show-off. The nanny sat down and pulled out her mobile, dropped down her mask, and began speaking into her phone in Spanish. "*Qué pasa, mija?*"

I lost her after that and gazed toward the meadow. Some kids were throwing a Frisbee. Others were sitting in a circle with proper distance. A couple played fetch with their dog. A jet on the flight path to LaGuardia roared overhead. Another damn helicopter flew past, low and growling.

People were adjusting to the pandemic in small ways. The sociopath president had lost the election a month ago, and we were all feeling a lot more relaxed and hopeful.

I returned to the nanny as I tried to half-listen to her Spanish, which was too fast for me. What was it like raising somebody else's kid? Was she well paid? What about her own life and family?

"Hey Jacob," the baby said. I almost jumped out of my skin. The nanny kept talking to her girlfriend.

I stared hard at the girl baby in the stroller. I recognized the voice. "Jesus, you scared the crap out of me!"

"So, what did you learn from the poem?"

"What did I learn from the...? Shit, lemme calm down a second here, will ya?"

My heart was still racing. I looked over at the nanny. "Listen!" I went *sotto voce*. "When she sees me talking to you, she'll call the cops on me. Or the men in white coats."

"Don't worry, she can't hear or even see us speaking," said Xen Kohen, now a mini occupant of that Beemer of Park Slope strollers, the Uppababy, and still practicing a ridiculous *navasana*, touching feet to face.

I looked across the meadow again and took a few breaths.

"So we've forgotten a lot of stuff," I said, "like how the Earth is our body. We've strayed, the world is on its head, it's a mess. But we don't just go back. We need a new way, a path, to get to the next level. I need to go through my own rebirth, pass through a membrane of death. It's fucking scary to go to a place unknown. It would have been nice to have the poem as a guide. But I don't need an actual map for this journey. I need a map of my own personal consciousness, toward a higher future vision."

"Yes. What else?"

"There was a ladder," I said, "you spoke about ladders before. It's in this vision. We gotta climb it."

"Yes. Your namesake Jacob saw it in a dream. Christian mystics called it the Ladder of Divine Ascent. Dante climbed it. Spiritual psychologists describe it. This journey toward the sacred every day, this healing, is not a private one. While it is your own, it's also for the sake of everyone. By embarking on this path, you broaden and expand your consciousness and that of the universe."

Watching a baby talk to you like a grown-up was as jarring as seeing the ones in those ridiculous TV ads and movies. Xen Kohen could have advised Madison Avenue and Hollywood how to do it.

Xen Kohen, *enfant terrible*, reached for a plastic dreidel on her snack tray. A dreidel? Maybe the Hasidim on Eastern Parkway were handing them out to everyone, even non-Jewish kids.

"And by the way, this transformation of consciousness occurs in the everyday, on Earth. We're not splitting up Earth, heaven, and hell as separate realms. We're talking about depth. Everything is here."

"Okay," I said. The Frisbee the nearby kids were flinging around landed at my feet. I got up and managed to toss it to the closest kid in a straight flight, which impressed the hell out of myself. I sat back down.

Xen Kohen, the baby prodigy, continued bringing her feet up to her head. "As we said, the journey is in stages. You will begin by descending first, to the lower depths, to the underworld. You will start at the bottom. We all need to go there; we need to know what evil is. That includes facing what's within our own lower self, before we can include and transcend it, before we can ascend."

"And how do those spiritual psychologists see the ladder?"

"It's about our development to become fully human," Xen Kohen said, trying to twirl the dreidel with stubby fingers. "Many traditions such as Islam have stations or stages of human consciousness. Our early stage is all about me. Some get stuck there. Most of us though move up to conventional thoughts and beliefs—what most people think and believe—tribal loyalty, conformity, us versus them. A kind of zombie functional existence. A few of us then climb up to become autonomous and can think for ourselves. At the highest rung of growth, the rare universal level, you have let go of ego-clinging. Your self dissolves and you realize your fluid union with all, with the divine."

I was struggling to take this in. I began thinking about Maya, how I missed her. What was she doing this minute? The baby Xen Kohen caught where my distracted mind was going.

"Yo!" the stroller yogi yelled, pulling at her feet like they were stretched out toffee bars. "Do you want to return to and restore your broken homeland and your own broken home? Do you want to get to your higher self? Do you want to reclaim Brooklyn and the world? Are you willing to let your ego *die*?"

What kind of questions were those? Xen Kohens.

Fragment from *Letters to a Young Poet* by Rainier Maria Rilke:
Live the questions now. Perhaps you then may gradually, without noticing, one day in the future live into the answers.

I thought of the ladder.

I took another breath. "Okay, yes to all. Now can you please stop doing that damn yoga *asana*? I'm jealous. Only a baby or super yogi can do that."

The baby Black Budai, the chubby monk of happiness, began to laugh. That got the attention of the nanny. We were through.

"*La nena está contenta!*" The nanny laughed.

"*Claro que sí!*" I had to laugh too.

I got up to go.

"Mister," the nanny stopped me. "You forgot your earbuds."

She pointed on the bench. There they were alright, this time colored crimson. Nothing surprised me. I knew the drill. I picked them up and thanked her. I glanced at the baby, whom I could see was now drinking a bottle of Earth's Best Organic Toddler Pineapple Orange Banana Smoothie. Xen Kohen put down the bottle with her pudgy hands, winked, and gave me a super smile. Nothing but the best for my Hired Power.

CHAPTER NINE

Hell Inc.

I Came to Myself Within a Dark Wood Where the Straight Way Was Lost —Dante, *The Divine Comedy, Inferno, Canto I*

Aboard the H Train

The voice of Xen Kohen in the crimson earbuds said *Return to the opening at the Terminal Moraine sub-subway station. Wait for the H train.* I left the park, headed up Eastern Parkway, and found the place on the median where the doors had appeared. Marva Williams wasn't there on the bench. I shut my eyes and the doors appeared and opened. I descended the stairs.

No one was on the platform. I sat on the same bench where I had met Xen Kohen. After about ten minutes, during which I tried to meditate, I saw the lights of a train coming out of the tunnel. As it came closer and pulled into the station, I saw it had an "H" on the front and was just one car. It stopped in front of me and the conductor, a woman wearing the blue/gray MTA uniform, opened her window as the doors opened and pointed for me to enter.

I went in and sat down. The car was dimly lit and designed with faux wicker seats made to look like a vintage train. I looked around and saw I was the only passenger. No one was in the motor cabin up front. The train began to move at a slow speed.

I was surprised when the conductor left her cabin and sat down across from me. I guessed she was Afro-Latina, in her fifties, but it was hard to tell with her mask on. She took it off and motioned for me to do the same. She had a great salt and pepper *pajón* that spilled out from beneath her cap. Her name tag said *Jizo*. In Japanese Buddhism, Jizo is the bodhisattva of hell beings, those condemned to hell by their own actions, whom Jizo vows with compassion to make their existence there less painful.

When I looked at her penetrating eyes, I knew who it was.

"This part of your journey is treacherous," Xen Kohen said. "You need a guide. I decided to accompany you."

"Thanks, I think."

We sat in silence as the train began to gain speed through the darkness. It clanked, groaned, and whooshed at a deafening level.

"Why isn't there a motor person driving this thing?" I asked.

"It's an early Tesla model of an autopilot subway car," my conductor said. "They brought in Eelong MuskRat when the MTA was defunded and laid off workers like Charon. He'd been driving the original rig for a few thousand years."

"Damn arrogant techno-union-busters," I muttered.

The train suddenly did something no train does. It dropped downward at warp speed on a sharp angle steeper than the Coney Island Cyclone. The noise was ten times the ambulance sirens on Eastern Parkway. I wrapped both arms around the pole next to the seat and held on, terrified, and looked across from me. Xen Kohen said nothing.

A Greek word from a college class on mythology entered my mind: *Katabasis. The descent to the underworld.*

Xen Kohen nodded.

For an agonizing amount of time we were in freefall. Finally, the train leveled off and slowed down. The noise lessened. My panic began to subside. To say I felt disoriented is a fat understatement.

"It's also the Winter Solstice now," Xen Kohen said, continuing to read my mind. "We've jumped ahead a few weeks. Where we're heading it's always the Winter Solstice. No turning to the light, ever."

Winter ... dormancy and darkness ... the underworld ... going within....

I looked out the window in the dark and could make out we were on a trestle crossing a churning river.

"Is this Minetta Creek," I asked, "the lost underground stream below lower Manhattan?"

Xen Kohen nodded again. "The local tribe called it the Devil's Water. The city builders tried to get rid of it for years but never could. It's since become impossible to separate it from the urban wastewater and sewage. We're crossing it at the border now."

The border Charon used to transport souls across…. "You mean it's the Styx." The river, once immortal, was now a dead sewer. Nature covered over, forgotten. We've left the world of the living and entered hell, the land of the dead. Now I knew why it was called the Devil's Water.

The conductor, Xen Kohen, my reluctant Virgil, my compassionate Jizo, locked eyes with me.

"In Japan this river is called the Sanzu, also the border between the living and the dead."

Fragment from "A Brook in the City" by Robert Frost:
...The brook was thrown
Deep in a sewer dungeon under stone
In fetid darkness still to live and run –
And all for nothing it had ever done
Except forget to go in fear perhaps.
No one would know except for ancient maps
That such a brook ran water. But I wonder
If from its being kept forever under,
The thoughts may not have risen that so keep
This new-built city from both work and sleep.

The train rumbled along at a slow pace.

"What is hell to you?" I asked.

Xen Kohen kept her eyes on me. "*What is hell?* Dostoevsky asked. *I maintain it is the suffering of the inability to love.*"

I thought about it. So, Hell is disconnection, lousy relationships, being cut off from others. Clinging to your ego as a defense. Then Sartre is wrong. Hell is not others; it's being unable to love them. Though what if you didn't get enough love to even love yourself... We're going to Hell ... or am I already there...?

The conductor continued my thoughts. "Hell is both inner and outer. When we don't get the love we need, we become broken, wounded, feel worthless, fearful. We're liable to create our own hell within—critical judgments, petty meanness, competitive greed, self-righteous anger, violent thoughts, self-delusions, toxic imaginings and desires. Others disappoint us, like we do ourselves. We cling harder to conventional, divisive ways of self-validation like approval, skin color, material possessions, social status..."

She glanced out the window.

"If we get stuck in this kind of hell it gets expressed not as healthy, loving attachments but through hurtful, deluded, lousy ones. We end up extending our lack to painful relationships in families. Then beyond, to harsh societal institutions that exploit and hurt others, and heartless, violent, racist societies. It takes on a life of its own ... which we then deny or don't even see. Media lies, thought control make it worse. We become addicted to delusions and toxic loyalty to our race, to our tribe. More fear, protective indifference to suffering, defensive violence, hurt, destructiveness. Loss of love, inside and out...."

Xen Kohen interrupted herself. "We have to stop at the border checkpoint." She motioned me over to the window and opened it. I was expecting Cerberus, the three-headed dog guarding the gates of Hell. Instead, there were three bland-looking, bald white men in identical black suits and red ties seated next to each other at one desk.

A plaque in front of each identified them. The first was the insurance underwriter of Hell Inc. The middle one was a lawyer, the senior partner of Hell Inc. Legal Services. The third was the Hell Inc. accountability coordinator. Each one busied themselves staring and typing away at their laptops for a long while and ignored us.

I took a closer look at them. Instead of hair, tiny twisting snakes coiled and uncoiled behind their shiny heads. Below the desk their legs ended in cloven hooves. Their coffee cups had logos from Meta, Google, and JP Morgan Chase.

At last, the accountability coordinator looked up but didn't bother to make eye contact.

"Fill out this form." He printed out a paper and handed it to me through the train car window.

It said, *Reason for Visit. Choose One Defense, or Any or All from the Menu Below*:

The Persephone: Escape from unhappy marriage

The Orpheus: Seek to overcome separation

The Herakles: Correct a wrong

The Odysseus: Quest for knowledge

I checked off the second, third, and fourth.

Below that was a statement releasing Hell Inc. of any liability in the event of injury or death on the premises with a space for a signature.

I signed and handed back the form. The lawyer snatched it from my hands.

"That'll be one hundred thirty-four dollars and eighty-nine cents," the insurance underwriter said.

"Did you bring your credit card?" Xen Kohen asked me.

"You didn't tell me!" I protested.

"Just pay them and we'll be on our way."

"Shit." I took out my wallet and handed over my card. "I want a receipt."

So Hell is a corporation. Damn blood-sucking capitalist bureaucrats.

"Hey, whaddya think Heaven is, hah?" the accountability coordinator huffed. "No diff'rint."

Jesus, they could read my mind too.

The accountability coordinator pushed a button on his console. It kicked in the rhythmic karaoke background from the Paul Simon song about heaven, "The Afterlife." The other two started gyrating their heads and snapping their fingers. The accountability coordinator was about to sing when the lawyer stopped him and turned to me. "We sing more than four lines, we gotta pay royalties to Simon. We ain't paying. You?"

"No way."

"Okay then, here are some lines."

Buddha and Moses and all the noses from narrow to flat

Had to stand in the line just to see the divine, what you think about that?

...You got to fill out a form first

and then you wait in the line.

"I'll paraphrase the rest." Which he did: God won't let anyone cut in. How about that, hah, no one there likes a cheat....

I was mesmerized by the beat and watching these demi-humans bop their bald heads around. We waited for the accountability coordinator to finish. The scene was insane. I had to shake myself out of it. Disgusted, I made a face.

"Do I at least get to see the boss?"

The other two turned to the lawyer. "He's busy upstairs," the lawyer smirked. "Helping his cousin pardon his treasonous associates, war criminals, spreading conspiracy lies about COVID and the election, separating immigrant children from their parents, disenfranchising voters, deregulating environmental protections, ensuring the Russians have access to the US government data banks, and inciting an insurrection against the US Congress."

There was a pause. They then turned to look at each other and laughed loud and long like deranged jackasses.

"*Carajo!*" said Xen Kohen. "We're getting the hell out of here," giving new meaning to the phrase.

The subway car moved on.

We began to pass local stations at a slow pace. I stayed at the window to get a closer look. Above each platform was a marquee that spelled out the name of the station.

As we traveled, I realized the residents were all well-off white-collar criminals, mostly white, mostly men—part of the oligarchy that benefits from the country's two-tiered, racist legal system.

Unlike poor and working-class people, they were seldom held accountable and prosecuted, and they paid few taxes. So, Hell Inc. was profiting from screwing its own, like a private prison.

The first station was *The Worst New York Landlords*. The platform had large, sharp icicles hanging from the high ceiling that kept falling onto and stabbing dozens of naked people jammed together below. Their screams were unbearable. It was payback time for these slumlords who had refused to provide safety repairs and adequate heat in their buildings and for intimidating and rent gouging their poor tenants.

"Fucking greedy bastards," I said.

"More to come," Xen Kohen replied. She looked over at the former slumlords, who glanced back at her with pleading eyes.

The next station sign said *Tobacco, Pharmaceutical, and Petrochemical Executives*. Lots of mostly white guys again, huddled together naked. The air was smoky gray and putrid, the people were up to their necks in a pool of black slime from oil spills. They did nothing but cough, choke, gasp for air, and beg for bottles of gray water just outside their reach. Some were strapped to machines that stuffed OxyContin laced with Fentanyl down their throats in honor of the thousands each year who became addicted and died from overdoses, while others are forced to swallow psychiatric drugs that turn them into emotional zombies. Big Pharma profits from overmedicating millions of children with drugs that numb their feelings, create dependency, and are based on the unproven causal theory of chemical imbalance. Other execs were forced every two minutes to inhale menthol cigarettes, easier to become addicted to and harder to quit, aggressively marketed to Black people, who have a higher rate of death from tobacco than white people. The Earth was evening the score with the corporate abusers who profited from addictive pharmaceuticals, allowed horrific climate change effects from carbon emissions while falsely claiming to move to low-carbon energy practices, and produced massive water and air pollution and oil spills.

"Death merchants. Greedy, lying, sadistic shits," I said to Xen Kohen, who looked pained. Here, too, she and the wretches seemed to acknowledge each other.

The subway car rounded a bend and pulled into the *Bank Executives* station. Naked, mostly white men—who else?—were writhing on beds of nails. Some were licking toilet bowls. They had gotten away with luring in and defrauding thousands of people during the mortgage lending scandal that led to the 2008 market collapse. They had redlined and denied mortgages to Black and Brown people, ploughed their tax breaks and subsidies into stock buybacks instead of investing in community businesses and industries, which decimated towns and cities, and laid off their own employees.

"Criminal assholes," I sneered, and turned to Xen Kohen for affirmation. Her eyes were moist, and she looked away from the scene.

We passed other stations. *Health Insurance Executives*—yeah, the usual naked folks, who rejected claims for pre-existing conditions that led to people's deaths and made huge profits off of health care, while some die for lack of it. They were strapped tight in chairs, their rotting bodies and faces mottled with thick red and purple cankers, forced to watch a video loop of dying children that alternated with a Bernie Sanders speech on how universal health care is a human right.

The *Corporate Media Executives* platform held those who wielded the means of mass thought control. They had knowingly spewed endless hate- and greed-promoting lies on TV, radio, and the internet. They practiced "greenwashing"—spending time and money to make their polluting corporations look environmentally friendly, placing the onus on the consumer, cutting costs, while doing nothing to minimize their environmental impact. They targeted children with toxic garbage ads for junk food and flooded poor Black neighborhoods with alcohol and menthol cigarette ads and billboards.

They were forced to endure loud horrendous sounds, repetitive moronic jingles, and propaganda slogans in endless overlapping loops blared through deafening mega-speakers.

In a separate corner sat executives from the giant social media companies. They had marketed to and targeted children and teens with emotionally harmful screen time social media sites and video games. They'd long known the sites were toxic and addictive, a kind of digital fentanyl, which contributed to many kids' cyberbullying, vicious comparisons, loss of social skills, depression, sexual exploitation, and suicide.

They had to sit and face video loops of angry, anguished parents screaming and blaming them for their addicted children's pain and suffering, then watching scenes of bullied and beaten teens who commit suicide.

The last station held a small but upcoming group, greedy, selfish AI (artificial intelligence) corporate executives. While some AI can be used for public good, it makes it easy for students, already pressured to succeed, to plagiarize by using AI which diminishes critical thinking and increases cheating. By crowdsourcing and recycling existing information for their own profit, AI corporations eliminate original thought, dumb people down, and allow the spread of disinformation as truth. AI generating stations negatively impact the climate through massive energy usage in marginalized communities where they are located while the corporations exploit data workers in the Global South. Elsewhere it leads to many people losing their jobs.

The punishment for these immoral execs was to stand all day and read, research, think, and write about the meaning of education and social justice and to distinguish knowledge from lies without the use of AI, which if they tried to use caused them to receive an electric shock. They were then forced to use an AI Assistant to write endless essays which over time led to loss of memory, language, and critical thinking; their brains turned to mush. The third punishment was being forced to filter despicable online material for content moderation for AI and Chat GPT that was part of the exploitation and traumatization of Global South workers.

I looked at Xen Kohen, the Latina subway conductor, the compassionate bodhisattva for those condemned to corporate hell, who was close to tears. She was getting to me. I almost felt some compassion for these turds myself.

"So," I began, "these guys seem to be at the bottom of the phylogenetic scale of moral development. They're self-centered, they only respond to reward and punishment."

My conductor looked at me. "It's true that for many of them there was no hope they would ever change," she said. "And they were criminals. They're now facing the consequences of their actions."

"And they avoided taxes, environmental regulations, living wages for employees, formed monopolies, and busted unions," I said.

"Yes," Conductor Kohen said, "they bought into a selfish system and need to be held accountable on a personal level. But this is mean-spirited. It's harsh, it's retribution, it's revenge. No chance for personal recovery; no chance for them to help change the system to prevent these horrors from continuing. Maybe some of them, not all, could have learned to take responsibility, apologized, and made amends to those they harmed. If so, they could even be forgiven. But this doesn't help anyone. In their case, down here it's too late."

Xen Kohen pulled out a tissue from her vest and dabbed her glistening eyes.

"Now think about your own feelings that kick up when you see them punished like this," Jizo Kohen said. "It's right you're *enojado*—pissed off—at what they've done. They needed to be stopped. They needed accountability. But there's also *schadenfreude*. Enjoying their suffering, getting back at them, wanting them to feel pain. That puts you at the same primal level they're at."

"So you're saying that traps me into a kind of mental hell, too, it dehumanizes them as the Other as well as myself. I'm no better."

Fragment from *Think Big* (2008) by Hell Inc. chief resident-in-waiting (Trump):
I love getting even when I get screwed by someone.... Always get even. When you are in business you need to get even with people who screw you. You need to screw them back 15 times harder. You do it not only to get the person who messed with you but also to show the others who are watching what will happen to them if they mess with you. If someone attacks you, do not hesitate. Go for the jugular.

Xen Kohen's glance told me I was on point. She said, "And that means the punishments they're getting down here in Hell Inc. are just as low and mean themselves. This place is an upside-down mirror that reflects their world; the one they benefited from when they were above. There's no change going on here."

I looked back at the last platform. I had to admit, revenge felt good—to see rich greedy bastards get the same nasty treatment they dished out. Even more so after they had taken advantage of a rotten system and gotten away with victimizing others. But I saw my own reaction was still at some primal level. For the world to evolve, it needed something better. "I guess it ain't called Hell Inc. for nothing," I said.

We rode on past empty platforms. One station was labeled *President's Enablers and Cult Followers*—those who cheered on, lied, or were silent about his lies, vicious atrocities, murderous policies, and treasonous assault on democracy. It displayed plaques with names in anticipation of the eventual arrival of these criminals in their proper place in the world order.

Sure enough, the last empty platform station was reserved for the most wounded, loveless, dangerous, destructive, lazy, ignorant, phony, grifting, criminal, traitorous, incompetent, immoral, narcissistic, pathological, hateful, sexually abusive, fascistic, racist, antisemitic, xenophobic, white supremacist of recent times—the monster of mendacity, meanness, misery, misogyny, madness, mayhem, and murder. It was a bare cell with a gold-plated toilet in the corner. Since he himself was a firm believer in revenge against anyone who opposed him I could only imagine what lay in store for him. Having compassion for him, I concluded, is possible only if I get to make it as a wise saint or a Brooklyn bodhisattva.

[Narcissistic personality disorder] *is a coping strategy in response to serious developmental trauma.... Fred Trump Sr. told the Trump boys to be killers.... Given that history, I find it quite simple and natural then to feel compassion for such a person...In this case it means to feel deep sorrow for the fact that Donald Trump got brutalized as a boy and the natural innocence of his being was (literally and figuratively) beaten the hell out of him.... Wisdom ... is to know the nature of such a being and understand that one could never ever give such a person any such power.* —Chris Dierkes

The next-to-last station we passed was the *Hell Inc., Boutique.* The train stopped to let me window shop and I glanced at the merchandise.

You could purchase mesh "masks" imprinted with the Coronavirus graphic and pictures of the president kissing Putin's ass. There were hoodies that said *GREED IS GOOD* and *ALTERNATIVE FACTS MATTER.* A prominent item was the Melaria line of unisex jackets. One had a photo of Melaria and Ihonka mudwrestling, with the president refereeing. Another jacket touted her notorious quote, *I REALLY DON'T GIVE A FLYING FUCK, WHY SHOULD YOU?* You could choose one with a picture of immigrant Mexican children in cages, the president posing with his porn star and Playboy bunny consorts, or a hospital room crammed with people on ventilators dying from COVID. A shelf displayed discounted MAHA hats—Make America Hate Again. A black military-style beret caught my eye. It had a patch of a mean, angry face of a rat frowning and baring his teeth in front of a pizza slice with a bite taken out of the corner.

The train came to a sudden halt at a station marked *Last Stop: What Fresh Hell is This?* Dorothy Parker might have been amused. Fresh my ass. The smell of rotten eggs was overpowering. Three janitors were sweeping the trash, polishing the walls and benches, and cleaning the open latrines and pissoirs. I recognized Roy Cohen, Margaret Thatcher, and the president's father, Fred Trump Sr. I knew he had been Woody Guthrie's racist slumlord when Woody lived in Coney Island —he even wrote a song about "Old Man Trump."

Of course, essential janitorial work and toilet cleaning are not demeaning jobs, nor is there anything inferior about the people who do them. You can be sure as hell, though, those shitheads thought so.

"You get off here," conductor Jizo Kohen said. "We won't be going with you. The three residents you need to meet will see you downstairs after you exit the turnstile. They embody the three poisons in Buddhism: greed, delusion, and meanness. In Buddhism they're usually represented as a pig, a rooster, and a snake, but down here they're all New York rats."

Figures, I thought, New Yorkers hate rats. They are a nuisance and seen as selfish, devious, aggressive, disease-spreading pests. Since the pandemic they've become more brazen, troublesome, and out of hand. Restaurant closings and construction of outside dining sidewalk structures have led to more street garbage. More rats are out marauding for food. During the pandemic, the city cut back the budget for garbage pickups. In the Chinese calendar, 2020 was the Year of the Rat.

"Despite themselves," she went on, "they're gonna help you if you let them." She turned to go. "We'll catch you later."

"Wait, can you tell me a bit more about them?"

Xen Kohen turned back to face me.

"All of us have been wounded in various ways over a lifetime," she continued. "The difference is what we do with it. These rats, like the other characters you passed, instead of dealing with and recovering from their ratty lives, they've indulged and acted on their lower selves and fears. They're stuck at it's-all-about-*me* and blaming others. They let their baser parts take over—racism, fear, hatred. Then they harm others and themselves. That's why they're here. It's sad."

I nodded and started to walk away.

I had not thought death had undone so many —T.S. Eliot, *The Waste Land*

"Jacob."
I brought my focus back.
"Rats live with us, they live in places where no one wants to go. They eat what we throw out. They mirror us, they mirror our darker side."
I took a breath.
"You need to go *deep*." Xen Kohen touched her head and heart at once. "*Katabasis*. This is an Inner journey to the abyss, to embrace the pain, to heal from past wounds."
I took another breath.
"It will be like a dream—at first you might not know the difference between the ordinary and a higher realm."
Xen Kohen was my conductor on the inner underground railroad.

... to enter the Inner Underground Railroad, you must first want it, then be prepared to face all the obstacles that come up.... I'm tryin to take you there, to show you that the chains you need to break are the ones inside.... Ultimate abolitionism *begins with* a clear understanding of spirit, *with seeing the dreamlike nature of reality and moving between the worlds of ultimate and conventional realities.* — Spring Washam, *The Spirit of Harriet Tubman: Awakening from the Underground*

"Okay," I said at last.

Fragment from *Sonnets to Orpheus* by Rainer Maria Rilke:
For among these winters there is one so endlessly winter that only by wintering through it will your heart survive.

"I'll be giving you the Dogen Potion when you meditate," she said, "This is a quick fix; getting to this level really requires continuous practice."

Wow, consciousness hacking ... better than that shallow mindfulness app, Headcase. Dogen again. All things are happening at once ... one big, continuous presence ... seeing the entire historical world, with its sadness, with wise compassion....

"Well, what about...?" Before I could ask her to say more, the subway car reversed itself and Conductor Kohen was gone.

I passed through the antiquated creaking wooden turnstile and saw a descending stairway ahead. On the wall my name was inscribed in mosaic tiles next to a downward pointing arrow. *How low can this place go?* I thought and headed down the stairs.

CHAPTER TEN

Pete The Pizza Rat

The ideal subject of totalitarian rule is not the convinced Nazi or the dedicated communist, but people for whom the distinction between fact and fiction, true and false, no longer exists. —Hannah Arendt, *The Origins of Totalitarianism*

As I descended, a large gray rat with a slice of pizza in his mouth scurried past me from behind. I recognized him as the Pizza Rat. Every New Yorker knows the Pizza Rat. A while back he was a YouTube sensation, the video of him racing down the subway stairs with the slice between his teeth had gone viral. The rat stopped on a stair, turned back and looked up at me, and signaled with his head to follow him.

At the bottom we landed in a sewer, a relentless maze of ankle-deep sludge. It mucked up my sneakers and chilled my feet. I had to run, high-stepping it, to stay close behind the Pizza Rat as he scampered ahead through dark, narrow tunnels lit by dim fluorescent bulbs—two lefts, a sharp right, a long passageway, a quick right and left.

At last we came to a small black, unmarked door. The Pizza Rat unlocked it, then after we entered, slammed it shut. It opened to a small, dry room, also dimly lit. It had a long ratty sofa, a beat-up chair, and a dusty, food-encrusted table. One wall was taken up by the biggest refrigerator I'd ever seen. Another displayed a smaller video screen, some newspaper clippings, and other notes. The third held a monster TV screen with a muted Hell Fux Fake News program. I could make out the panel of bottle-blonde female rat entertainers lying about how the election was stolen from The Boss.

The Pizza Rat dropped the slice onto the table, grabbed the wand lying nearby, and turned off the TV. He picked up a dirty jacket from the floor, one of the Melaria designer jackets I saw in the Hell Boutique that declared, "I REALLY DON'T GIVE A FLYING FUCK, WHY SHOULD YOU?" with the dying people on ventilators. He jumped up on the sofa, gestured to me to sit on the chair, snatched the slice back with his tiny paws, and began to chomp at it.

I was too nervous to sit for long and got up to watch on the small screen wall a video loop of the Pizza Rat running down the subway stairs, accompanied by commentary by a local reporter.

Pizza Rat is the perfect metaphor for life in New York: He is hungry, he loves dollar pizza, he hates his life and he is trying to carry something that is way too heavy down the subway stairs because the elevator is broken. It's almost too perfect. —Maxwell Strachan

On the same wall next to the small screen I looked at some clippings hung with thumbtacks. Three *New York Post* articles—who else but Ratpert Murdoch's rag would be fascinated with rats?—described recent rat events in the city during the pandemic.

The first one that caught my eye had the headline "'Brooklyn For Real': Rat Takes on Pigeon in Ruthless NYC Showdown" (9/3/20). It was accompanied by the video from the internet edition, a rat viciously attacking a wounded pigeon. A Brooklyn resident was swatting and chasing the rat away with a metal bar. The woman who took the video said, *"If you've ever been to Brooklyn or know someone from Brooklyn then you are like, 'that is Brooklyn for real.'"*

"That's me," the Pizza Rat spoke with pride, his mouth dripping with slimy cheese. "That pigeon was a chickenshit punk. 'Rats with wings,' my ass. By the way, call me Pete."

"Okay, Pete," I said, feigning respect, and continued to peruse my host's other clippings.

Another *Post* headline (8/18/20) said, "NYC Will Be Overrun by Rats if de Blasio Doesn't Curb Trash: Pols." The piece quoted the city comptroller: *"These rats are walking around waiting for a table at outdoor seating … I've seen them walking upright. They come up to me and say, 'Good morning Mr. Comptroller.' They have become part of the fabric of this city because city government has failed to get trash and sanitation under control."*

"That's me too," the Pizza Rat said. "I'm willin' to wait for a table but not too long. I figured I'll stand up and be polite to the Comptroller, he's running for mayuh, he could use a good rat to help run things."

In a third *Post* story entitled "Giant New York Rats Overtaking Central Park and the UWS" (11/21/20), a woman was traumatized by a gang of ten to fifteen rats outside the 96th Street subway stop. "You used to see the rats … on the tracks," she said. "Now they are literally part of the neighborhood. They should pay rent."

"I should pay rent?" Pete was indignant. "She's got some noive. They should pay *me*. I give people sumthin' to do and keep 'em in business. The city's Health Department has a Rat Academy for supers and tenants. We chew through expensive car engine wires. That keeps mechanics in business too. Some of them give me handsome kickbacks—they leave their garbage dumpsters open."

Higher on the wall was a mounted certificate, "2020: Year of the Rat," dedicated to "Pete" and signed by Patti Smith. It was an excerpt from her 2019 memoir, *The Year of the Monkey*, about her hopes for the upcoming year:

It is after all the Year of the Rat, a cunning survivor, and as we cautiously project the fate of the coming year, we must don the best of the resilient rat's qualities, maintaining the enthusiasm to be productive, the courage to face our adversaries, and the will to set things right.

"See? Cunning, resilient, enthusiastic. That's me. And boy, little did she know how right she was predicting 2020. The Year of the Rat! What a great rat's ass year, hah? The pandemic, millions dead, a crappy health system, fewer garbage pickups, more food for us, boy. We're thriving."

Next was a photo of Ganesha, the Hindu elephant deity, who always sits atop or near a giant rat. The short version of the story is that a demi-god angered a saint, who turned him into a lowly rat. The rat terrorized people until Ganesha brought him under control. The rat asked for forgiveness and the compassionate Ganesha allowed him to be his mount whom people would worship as well. A plaque beneath a thirteenth-century statue of Ganesha in the British Museum says, "The impossibility in the material world of an elephant riding on a rat makes the deity even more endearing since, unlike his devotees, he is not constrained by the laws of physics."

"See?" Pete said again, missing the point of the story, "the gods reward us as superior beings!"

Next to the picture of Ganesha on the rat was a story about another character familiar to New Yorkers: Scabby the Rat. He's a gigantic inflated nasty rat balloon that unions set up on the sidewalk in front of a worksite or corporate headquarters—anywhere management is screwing them over. The news clip said the Republicans were trying to prevent unions from using him in public streets. It would be easy to think Scabby was a native New Yorker since New York is rat city, it went on, but a union in Illinois created him.

Pete would have none of it.

"*I* was the inspiration for that rat balloon," Pete insisted, "da woiking people of New York love Scabby, even kids. They got my profile wrong though." His self-serving BS was starting to irritate the hell out of me. Except, I remembered, hell was not just in me, I was now in *it*.

The last two pieces on the wall were framed pictures of colorful logos for the minor league Yankee baseball team, the Staten Island Pizza Rats. A few summers ago, the Staten Island

Yankees, now defunct thanks to the pandemic, had rebranded themselves the Pizza Rats as a marketing ploy. The shirt logo is an aggressive looking rat running with a clenched fist wearing a chef's hat and an apron with the initials SI. Over his shoulder he carries a pizza slice overloaded with mooh-tzadhell'.

Just so you know, that's how we say it in Brooklyn. If you say mahtzahrella you're marked as an out-of-towner. When I hear someone in the Park Slope Food Coop ask for "mozzarella" on the loudspeaker, I immediately grab the phone myself. I pose as a member of the Coop Proper Language Committee and educate them on the Brooklyn way to say it and issue a stern warning that another violation would be punishable with not one but two makeup shifts.

The second frame on the wall displayed a photo of a Pizza Rat team baseball cap with the logo identical to the one on the black military beret in the Hell Inc. Boutique: a mean, angry face of a rat frowning and baring his teeth in front of a pizza slice with a bite taken out of the corner.

"Of course, I also modeled for those," Pete said. "They had to pay me extra, because what the hell? I had to jump on the ferry to get over there. It don't make sense, there's not even a friggin' subway on Staten Island! Great piles of garbage though! A lotta rat fans too. They voted for me; I can't help bein' so loveable and irresistible." He laughed and more pizza slithered out from his narrow jaws.

"After they chose me, a local Eye-talian fraternal group had da noive to be offended and cancelled Eye-talian heritage night at their stadium, they didn't like linking pizza wit' rats—they musta nevah hoid of me." He flashed a phony look of wounded pride.

I lost my patience—and mindfulness. "Aren't you just fake news, a creation, a myth, a product of a performance artist's shtick?" I asked. "I read that a stand-up comedian posed you with the pizza slice in your mouth as a prop and had a guy shoot it, while you ran down the subway stairs, a staged viral video."

Straightaway I regretted what I said. Pete stood up with fury and looked like, well, a cornered rat.

"Getouttaheah! That so-called artist, Zardooley or whatever, *she's* the fake news! She won't even show huh face and hides behind some freakin' mask! Here, look at this clipping." He walked me over to another part of the wall.

Zardulu, the surrealist, makes fake scenarios, like a video of the pizza rat. She releases them as real news, social media and whatever else...a slightly kitschy pagan wizard, all flowing mystical robes and masks and rat insignias.... As the surrealists believed, art comes from the unconscious, then the ideas art conveys are often built on Jungian mythological archetypes. That means art is, by its very nature, mythological, and vice versa ... Zardulu follows André Breton, who imagines a world where fantasy and reality blended together in a super reality, or surreality.... —Vox, 2017

I had to check in with my better self and appease him. "You must be right, Pete, I'm sorry. She's mixing truth with fiction and calling it art."

Still, I was haunted by a quote from this Brooklyn so-called artist, Zardulu, in another clip next to it, from the *Times* (March 29, 2016) no less. "I think creation and perpetuation of modern myths is a tragically underappreciated art form. It upsets me when I hear people refer to them as lies."

Here I was in my own story, caught up between myth and truth, dream and reality. Am I talking to a pizza rat or the artifact of a surrealist who blurs fact with fakery and calls it art? What is the difference between dreaming and being awake? Between the real and surreal? On the other hand, what's wrong with surrealism, with blending imaginative myth with futurist art as a way forward? That's different than the fake news and lies practiced by the rats above and the rats below.

Surrealism, I contend, is a vision of freedom ... it is a movement that invites dreaming, urges us to improvise and invent, and recognizes the imagination as our most powerful weapon. —Robin D.G. Kelley, *Freedom Dreams*

Pete calmed down. "Yeah. Doin' fake news, makin' truth into fiction, mixin' the two so nobody knows the difference. That's the job of us rats down here. And the Ratpublicans upstairs. *Alternate trooth!* My pal, Ratty Ghouliani, he's a master at that. He'll be here soon wit' his ghoulfriend, Ayn Ratnd, for our party we're havin' in your honor."

Pete turned to the refrigerator. "Hey, how 'bout starting out with some grub before they get here? Check out the stuff I got in the fridge. Nuttin' but the finest garbage from Brooklyn neighborhoods!

Ya know," Pete continued, "people hate us rats but we ain't bad creatures! We got feelings too! *They're* the ones that make us evil by leavin' their garbage around everywhere! We can't help ourselves! Look at all this."

Before I could take in what Pete had said, he opened the fridge and proudly showed me the shelves piled high with rancid scraps he had collected from all over the borough. Some of my favorite foods, now all garbage.

"Stuffed derma and potato kugel from da Jews in Borough Park! Jerk chicken from da Jamaicans in Crown Heights! A provolone and prosciutt' sangwich from da best Eye-talian deli in Bensonhoist!"

"Uh, no, thanks, I...."

Pete was undeterred. "Cerdo asado from Portorican Bushwick! Chow Fun from Sunset Park Chinatown! Ribs an' mac'n'cheese from Bed-Stuy! Pierogis from da Poles in Greenpernt!

"No, Pete, I...."

"...Shawrma from da Palestinians in Bay Ridge! Biriyani from Little Pakistan in Midwood! Avacado, kale an' keenwah salad from hipster Williamsboig! Blintzes from the Russkis in Brighton Beach! Nathan's hotdogs from Coney Island!"

And of course, Pete had a piled-high stack of stale pizza slices from all around the borough.

Any appetite I had vanished like—I already had the analogy—a rat offering me garbage in a sewer in hell.

"Got any ratatouille?"

Pete snake-eyed me like Clint Eastwood, then saw I was joking. "Ha, you're a wise guy. That was my Frenchy cousin Remy in that Disney movie. They paid him good. 'ey, no self-respecting rat would become a chef when there's so much great garbage to eat."

"Thanks Pete, I'm just not hungry."

"Suit ya self, but when my guests arrive, we'll be chowin' down, I hope ya join in…. Ah, here they are now…!"

CHAPTER ELEVEN

Going Deep with Pete, Ratty, and Ayn

Fragment from an article on Picasso by Karl Jung in the *Neue Züricher Zeitung*, 1932
The Nekyia [descent into hell] *is no aimless and purely destructive fall into the abyss, but a meaningful katabasis … a descent into the cave of initiation and secret knowledge … its object the restoration of the whole* [person]…

Pete got the door and Ratolfo (Ratty) Ghouliani and Ayn Ratnd entered the room. Ghouliani came up to me to shake my hand with his rat paw. He was a pale zombie double of the one upstairs, with mascara dribbling down both sides of his long face. He wore one of the hoodies from the Hell Boutique that said ALTERNATIVE FACTS MATTER. "Pleasure, Jacob." That was his first lie.

"Likewise," I rep-lied.

Ayn Ratnd was another zombie ghoul, her pancake makeup whiter than Morticia Adams. Her blood-colored mouth formed a slight sneer held in place by lip filler. I managed to touch her extended slimy paw for a second. In the other paw was her signature cigarette holder with a cigarette, unlit, thank the gods. She was wearing the Hell boutique hoodie that said GREED IS GOOD.

Pete gestured for the two guests to sit with him on the sofa. He prepared and handed them plates of some of the garbage from the fridge, took out a pitcher of some putrid liquid, and poured them into four red Solo cups.

"We order this from the Muslims," Ratty told me. "They're guest workers down here, they make and deliver it. It's called ghislin, made of pus mixed with blood of other hell residents."

I looked at him askance.

"No lie, Google it! We asked all the other tribes what people drink in Hell, they were the only ones that had something prepared. Of course we ban all Muslims at the border from permanent residence, they have their own hell. We order this batch spiked with four-star rotgut."

Pete passed me my drink. I sniffed it, stifled a wave of nausea, and set it down. "No, thanks," I said.

Pete and Ratty looked at me with mock disappointment. "Aw, we're here to celebrate your accomplishments," Pete said.

Ayn Ratnd came to my defense. "Let him be, he's doing what he wants. Bravo."

The three held up their cups for a toast. "To Jacob," they said in unison. Ratty said, "We want you to join us here as an honorary member."

"Whoa, thanks, but I...."

Pete was channel surfing on the jumbo screen and found another Hell Fux Fake News program.

"Hey Ratty, here's a report about your presser on Fux Fake News where you said the election was stolen! The one with your hair dye comin' down ya face!"

A rat reporter in bleached blonde hair, however, for some reason engaged in rare truth telling and told her viewers it was unmitigated BS. "A colorful news conference," she smirked, with bold and baseless claims. Ratty said he could "smell" crime but could provide no evidence of voter fraud or irregularities, and all claims had been thrown out in court. Even the signage on the poster behind him, "Multiple Paths to Victory," was bullshit, the Hell Fux Fake News rat reporter concluded in her report.

"It's nothing, it's what I do," Ratty beamed. *Disinformation narratives.* The other two applauded, raised their cups, "To disinformation narratives!" they said in unison, and chugged down the spiked ghislin.

"Now let's bring up one of my favorite segments for Jake, the piece on the Ayn Ratnd Conference from last year," Ratty said.

Pete found the tape and clicked it on. Another bottle-blonde from Hell Fux Fake News was reporting from San Francisco, standing inside a hotel lobby.

"I'm here at the close of the annual Ayn Ratnd Conference. The enthusiastic crowd of rich white people are pouring out now. Some highlights include the attendees laughing at activist Greta Thunberg's urge to reduce fossil fuel consumption—the environment should adapt to human needs, not the other way around, they state.

"Attendees also mocked philanthropic billionaires for conforming to societal expectations. Altruism, a keynote speaker said, is a dirty word in the Ratnd lexicon—concern with the well-being of others is perverse. A moral person, on the other hand, should only be concerned with the heroic self, he told the enthusiastic members.

"The conference closed with this tiny elite, who regard themselves as superior members of the ruling class, of which only a few can be a part, offering a rousing pledge: the Ratnd philosophy is available and applicable to everyone."

Pete and Ratty applauded, toasted Ayn Ratnd, and the three swigged down another round of ghislin.

I kept my mouth shut about the recent online novel by David Sloan Wilson, *Atlas Hugged*, a devastating critique of Ayn Ratnd's so-called philosophy, with his character, Ayn Rant. Sloan said he decided to fight fiction with fiction. Hell yes.

"Let's get down to it and watch the video," Ayn said, "I'm getting bored."

Pete flipped from the stations to a tape. The GIF red flaming letters of the title said, "Life of Jacob, Candidate for Honorary Member of Hell Inc."

I started to hyperventilate, then caught myself and slowed my breathing. Here I was, stuck with three psychopaths. Together they embodied and glorified the worst of a fractured America—racism, meanness, manipulative lies, deception, grandiose self-centeredness, greed, lack of remorse. They put down others, thinking they were superior beings, thinking that will make them feel better about their own miserable lives. They indulged in and glorified the lowest parts of humanity. Were they that far from normal?

Pete was empty, he could never get enough of anything to feed his ego—attention, food, or praise. Insecure, easily threatened, violent, conniving, bullying, and jealous and hateful of others. Ratty Ghouliani was a racist and compulsive liar who made up shit and appealed to people's worst fears, which he then manipulated for pure power. Ayn Ratnd's pathological pseudo-philosophy of greed influenced the entire nation to think that selfish individualism, winning at all costs, and gaming the market were the keys to happiness.

Now they were about to scrutinize and dissect my life. I knew I had to meditate, to check when the mind clenched and contracted, and remember Xen Kohen's words, *go deep*. I hoped to hell—shit, I was already there—I could be fully present and embrace it all without being sucked in and reacting to the garbage around me. I hoped for compassion for myself, even for my hosts, my enemies, of whom I still had to remain wary…. At the crossroads of fact and fiction, I was feeling on the edge of madness … was it psychotic or enlightened?

"We've studied many videos," Ayn Ratnd said. "You were high on my list—some great cold, unfeeling, and self-centered crap."

"Mine too," Ratty Ghouliani said. "You're a good bullshit artist when you've had to be, propping up your self-image. Like me."

Was I ever a goddam liar like this guy? Well, I've lied to myself at times, okay, to others sometimes…

I braced myself as best I could.

My mobile buzzed in my pocket. "'Scuse me for a second everyone," I said, and opened it up. It was my counseling group. *Mr. T.,* Cami said, *we hadn't heard from u & r worried.* Dina wrote, *We got this funny feeling. R U OK?* May May texted, *we're trying to practice what you taught us when we meditate—it's hard!*

I texted back *yes, thanks gang, don't worry,* and that I would get back to them. They had the funny feeling down, all right.

And yeah, some of the stuff I'd tried to teach them suddenly seemed like an unfunny joke.

I took another deep breath and returned to the rat business at hand.

"We thought you'd enjoy this tape of your parents foist," Pete said, "since you love that short story about a dream by that Brooklyn Jewish guy. You know—get this!" He turned to the other two. "This guy dreams he's in a movie theater watching a movie of his father court his mother, before he's even born. He don't like his life, so he tries to stop them from getting married in da foist place and having him as a kid, by standing up and yelling at the screen, 'Don't do it!'" Pete laughed. "Whadda freakin' dream! Tryin to control ya parents before they even had ya! In yer own dream!"

Fragment from the Cosmic Brooklyn short story *In Dreams Begin Responsibilities* by Delmore Schwartz:
...then, then with awful daring, then he asks my mother to marry him ... and my mother says: "It's all I've wanted from the moment I saw you," sobbing, and he finds all of this very difficult ... scarcely as he had thought it would be, on his long walks over Brooklyn Bridge ... and it was then that I stood up in the theatre and shouted: "Don't do it. It's not too late to change your minds, both of you. Nothing good will come of it, only remorse, hatred, scandal, and two children whose characters are monstrous."

The first segment on the screen was a black-and-white tape of my parents, before they married. It was all I could do to stay seated and keep breathing. There they were, younger than I had ever seen them. They flirted a bit but also started to bicker over a few petty things. Then they'd go back to flirting. Then bickering. It was maddening. Years later they quarreled when my younger sister Bobbi and I were growing up and made parts of our childhood a living hell.

"So," Ratty said, like the slimy prosecutor he was, "Good bullshit. You present your parents in the most idealistic light to yourself and others. Bleeding hearts for the oppressed. So then, why did they move you and your sister to an all-white community? Meanwhile, they did a lot of fighting and made your childhoods miserable. Yeah, you could say they loved each other. But what kind of love is that, hah?"

"They began to groom you," Ayn Ratnd said. "Growing up there you learned to feel superior as a white male. And their arguing made you mistrust intimate relationships. They did you a favor. You didn't want to get close, you didn't want to have to fight. After that you decided to be all about yourself when you were with women. You learned you weren't gonna be a sucker like your parents, you were gonna look out for yourself, withhold yourself. You first, just for you. Excellent."

My parents acted out of the limits of their own lives, I reminded myself. They didn't have such great childhoods themselves. Still….

The video then jumped to scenes of my early childhood. It was mind blowing to see myself at that age. I kept breathing and tried to embrace it all with—what—acceptance? Forgiveness? Self-compassion?

There I was, teasing my sister, who broke down in tears. I saw how I griped to my parents about my one assigned chore, taking out the garbage. In one scene I was arrogant and disrespectful to our Black cleaning woman. Christ, if I knew where she was now or if she was even alive, I'd go find her and apologize. Despite the values I was taught I saw I was also being groomed by those around me, my family and the community, to be an elitist little white male. Even at that age on some level I knew better.

I wondered who was holding the camera for all this. Where were they standing? Why should I think this was some objective perspective? Who edited it? I saw these questions more as ways my mind sought to avoid having to keep watching. I let them go, took some more breaths, and returned to the screen.

In the next scenes I'm in junior high school with my male classmates. We're teasing and laughing at Sid Handlor, an effeminate guy in our class. He had no muscle tone. It was winter and he kept slipping down a hill on the school grounds. Okay, we were pubescent boys, self-conscious, insecure, finding our way about our own sexuality and identity. But being mean … damn. And Sid chipped in for me to work with my Hired Power, and had died of AIDS, probably in the eighties. Now I really felt shitty. I had to talk back at the screen like the narrator in the Delmore Schwartz story and apologize to Sid. "I'm sorry, man!" I said aloud.

Ayn Ratnd snarled at me. "That guy was weak and refused to stand up for himself. You all were just expressing the truth about him and asserting your own natural dominance. Everyone gets to control their own destiny. You did the right thing."

The scene moved to my early college days, with my first girlfriend, Isabelle Vimuney. I was trying to break up with her, which I didn't know how to do with any skill or integrity. The phrase *he's just not that into you* wouldn't make it into the popular lexicon until years later—it would have named and normalized my feelings at the time, at least for myself. So, I sat there watching an awkward scene of me bullshitting her, telling her I really liked her but yadda yadda…. She's crying. Then she dries her eyes and turns and looks right into the camera. My heart jumps into my throat. She says, "Jacob, more than the breakup, it took me a long time to get over your dishonesty. But after a while I learned to forgive you." Holy crap.

"See?" Ratty Ghoulani says. "Your lying paid off. It worked. Like she says, she got over it. And you got out of it. Later you went on to a successful career as a ghoster. Here's a few great scenes."

I sat there watching myself with different women I never called after going out with them. Whoever edited that sequence knew what they were doing. It showed me at times I could be a hurtful, self-centered prevaricator. I worked to maintain my self-image as a nice guy. Great.

"Watch this next one," Pete chimed in. "Here's ol' Jake, having had a bit too much to drink, taking advantage of a woman who also had too much to drink. Didja ever call her after that? Haha! Oh yeah, here you are at that same party sneaking back into the kitchen and takin' seconds after the desserts was put away. My man!"

I said nothing. What could I say?

"Aha, here are the scenes with your wife, Maya," Ayn Ratnd smiled through her tiny, pointed teeth. We were arguing. I was being a rigid control freak. "You're doing great," Ayn Ratnd said. "Judgmental, dismissive, withholding. Your angry mood dominates and controls what goes on between you. You choose to pull away, you feel like escaping. You're in command."

I sat still, watched, absorbed and embraced all the scenes. I began to tear up, which I tried to hide from the rats. I missed Maya and was sorry as hell for my actions. How did she put up with me? I hoped she would forgive me. I was hoping she'd turn to the camera and talk to me. Jesus. I almost thought she did at one point. "Maya!" I sobbed at the screen.

The rats just laughed. Meanwhile they were drinking the spiked ghislin, like a Mad Hatter party, getting louder and nastier. From their chatter between breaks watching my video I was stunned to learn how powerful they were in the upstairs world.

CHAPTER TWELVE

Rat Power

Living under the paving stones, consuming our refuse, and incubating our diseases, the city rat is a ubiquitous part of global, urban capitalism. The revulsion rats inspire actually speaks of our closeness to them—rattus norvegicus burrows through the supposed human/nature divide. —Brian House, Urban Intonation.

They [rats] exist without permission. They are hated, hunted and persecuted. They live in quiet desperation amongst the filth. And yet they are capable of bringing entire civilisations to their knees.
—Banksy

"Hey Ratty," Pete asked, "how's your Fux Fake News media mogul uncle, Ratpert Murdoch?"

"Ah, he's doing great as ever," Ratty grinned, "has me on TV often. We got a huge audience; people eat it up. The disinformation campaign is going great, not just on Fux Fake News but on social media platforms. Bad Muslims and criminal Mexicans are invading us! The Chinese caused COVID! Climate change is a hoax! The deep state runs everything! QAnon is right! They're killing Christmas! Democrats eat babies! Soros the Jew is bankrolling the radical Democrats! White people are victims of cancel culture! They're going to take away our guns! Biden's a crook like his son! Black Lives Matter is a terrorist group! Hey, any group you want to eliminate, just say *they're* a terrorist group!"

Ratty was working himself into a frenzy, the mascara dripping down his face.

"COVID will disappear, just like the flu! Masks are bullshit! If you wear a mask, you're a pussy! They're trying to regulate you and strip away your freedom! Antifa did it! The election was stolen! Voter fraud! Our Boss cares about you! He's the untouchable messiah for the evangelical right wing! They consider him God, he's gonna save us! And Our Boss won the election! Haha, he won, that's the Big Lie! Sow doubt and repeat ad nauseum! It's going great! It's so easy to lie and keep lying! It's great for business! And we don't even have to work that hard, the regular media does a lot of our work, they continue to take Our Boss seriously! He gets lots of free publicity every time he opens his mouth! The media makes bank off him like crazy!

"Oh yeah, darling!" Ayn Ratnd was ecstatic.

"There's more! With Pete's gang we create campaigns scaring parents about transsexuals, gays, and drag performers! We've been outlawing their health treatment, bathrooms! We attack drag shows and tell parents it's to protect their kids! We tell them we're gonna protect their kids from being uncomfortable learning about the history of slavery and racial stuff and they need to ban books with disturbing topics! We're banning them like crazy! We're winning over school boards and even firing principals and teachers who try to teach this stuff! We push The Great Replacement Theory—a perfect religious right-wing conspiracy fantasy! Black people hate white people! Jews, gays, Blacks, Latinos, and Muslims, they want to take over everything and bring in murderous, Third-World immigrants! They want to destroy your way of life! Meanwhile, we tell them us put-upon white folks have to have guns! School shootings? Thoughts and prayers! Bwhaha!"

Ratty stopped and wiped his face. The mascara stayed on. "What about you, Pete?"

"'ey! My boys are mobilizing like crazy, militarizing everything," Pete laughed, the ghislin dribbling from his mouth. "Armed militants, white supreemists, hate groups, militias attacking state capitols. They're getting stronger all the time. We got some of 'em infiltrating the cops and the military. Cops keep shooting Blacks and gettin' away with it, those stoopit body cameras don't matter. We got people intimidating mask wearers everywhere. We took over the Justice Department. We got more people locked up in prison than any other country! More money goes to the military and for wars than anywhere else! We got pols who will never allow gun control! We already got plenty of AR-15s on da streets and stashed away! Look at all da mass shootings! We're allowing people to openly carry guns!

"Fuck democracy! Authorertarian power is da way to go! We got more pols changing election laws! They get dark money from billionaires! They're restricting voter drives and registration, getting rid of polling places, early voting, and mail-in ballots. Gerrymandering the hell outta urban districts, that keeps the Blacks from voting! Billionaires buyin' off judges that override the results we don't like! Even ones on the Supreme Court! And like Ratty says, don't think we don't got violent talk on the internet! It goes together! And big future plans—we're gonna round up illegal aliens and anyone that looks like 'em, right off da streets and deport 'em! We're gonna send troops into Democrap cities and say there's too much crime—that'll keep people in line! But our best work is comin' up: a lotta white Christian religious guys are planning to storm the freakin' Capitol building and get in! It's gonna be an insurrection! We gotta take back the government! It's all planned byootifully wit' lawyers! They're gonna go after the Democraps and even the chickenshit vice president! We got 'em by da balls!—if they had any—bwhaha!"

No way, I scoffed to myself. Storming the Capitol building. Insurrection. That's hyped-up bluster, that's bullshit....

"You boys are doing alright," Ayn Ratnd said with a dismissive wave of her cigarette-holding paw. "And yes, we need the Fux Fake News disinformation machine, the TheocRatic Christian nationalist lies and authoritarian conspiracy theories on social media, and the menacing muscle of the fascist racist rat boys to keep people in line. But I'm the one who's gotten into everyone's *head.* My philosophy has taken over the culture. Selfishness, greed, and cruelty are *virtues.* I've convinced millions to cherish their individual freedom over the government's idiotic collectivist plot to force people to wear masks and distance themselves. Public health, the public good, is a myth. As a result, over half a million weaklings have died. We've thinned the herd of those not fit or worthy to succeed. A bonus has been that we've shortened Black and Brown lifespans much more than whites."

She looked at her cigarette holder as if she were about to light up, then thought better of it and finished off her cup of ghislin.

"People now believe everything—success, failure—is entirely their responsibility," Ayn Ratnd continued. "Lots of anxiety and depression, that keeps them from questioning and rebelling. The corporate social media has got into the heads of kids: girls, to get them to buy into peer pressure, to feel inadequate and blame themselves for failing to look like winners; boys, to never feel manly enough, then blame and bully girls and gays. Some of the men who get the message—take complete responsibility for your failures! Yes, blame yourself! —end up dying. People call it deaths of despair—alcohol, drugs, suicide. They self-destruct. It's because these men take my philosophy to heart! I can't make it, it must be my fault! But it's fine that they die, since it shows they must have been weak in the first place. They're losers. We don't need them!

"What's even better, big corporations have adopted my views. They get the workers to adjust and monitor themselves; buy wellness products, since it's all about the individual, not any so-called system. There is no system! Happiness, success, it's all up to each person, it's all about me me me! Government, business, even schools have all adopted my worldview. Consuming things, promoting yourself, competing with others, asserting your dominance, is the way to succeed. Caring about others is a waste of time and energy, except to maximize corporate profits. The wealthy are the most deserving of all, and everyone wants to be rich themselves. Venture capitalists, Silicon Valley tech founders—they love my books! They're the rulers of the universe! Corporations need freedom! Makers, not takers! Billionaires are sexy! Death to a multiracial democracy!

"We have allies in the Supreme Court, states, Congress. Tax cuts for the rich! Deregulate corporations from government control! Privatize the post office and public schools! Health care for profit!"

Ayn Ratnd wasn't through.

"Do you realize that since the so-called *Citizens United* ruling by the Supreme Court, billionaires can provide as much money to candidates as they want—unchecked, unlimited spending! So our man, Eelong MuskRat, and other billionaires, could bail out Our Boss anytime they want! Wipe out his debts to banks and lawyers! Bankroll his permanent campaign to restore his permanent presidency!"

"We're gaining power, not just in the US but around the world," Ratty snorted.

"Rat powuh!" Pete shouted. "They try to poison us, keep us down, we're back even stronguh!"

The more I heard, the more alarmed I became. These weren't just rats lounging around and bullshitting in a fetid, subterranean lair. They were demagogues, racist power brokers whose slime leaked upwards and infected even the crevices of the everyday world above.

"Do you three sometimes venture above ground?" I asked.

"No need," Ayn Ratnd sniffed. "We're in constant touch with our allies upstairs: The Ratpublicans. The CorpoRat Executives. Right-Wing Government AutocRats. The Billionaire Dark Money Oligarch PlutocRats like Eelong MuskRat. The Rat Boy militias. And, of course, Ratpert's Fux Fake News. They do all the work for us."

"Don't forget the religious right, dear, the TheocRatic Christian Nationalists," Ratty said to Ayn. "They want to get rid of democracy and impose an authoritarian theocracy. They want strong government control over people's lives, to bring about a Christian nation and get rid of everyone else. Pete, for example, loves a powerful government that gets people in line with the right way to behave."

"Well, that's where I differ somewhat, darling," Ayn Ratnd spoke. "My philosophy is atheistic, not religious. I also want little or no government laws or regulations since they get in the way of the individual, the strongmen and corporate leaders pursuing their vision as creative capitalists. The less government the better. Almost all government spending is for nonsensical do-gooders. It ends up wasting my people's time and money."

"Yes, but you must admit, Ayn, you still like a government run by a powerful leader who uses it to give tax cuts for your guys! Destroys the mommy state regulators who keep us from making profits! Props up and subsidizes the strong at the expense of the weak!"

"True enough," Ayn replied.

I realized there was a split among the rats between right-wing, laissez-faire capitalist individualists who want the government to enable their greed (Ayn) and Christian nationalists who want to impose a theocracy (Pete), with Ratty straddling both sides.

Ratty pointed to the one thing they shared that unified them. "Look, so we both love a strong, bold, confident alpha male, a man of action and control, a hero, a savior, as head of the country! An unconventional leader unafraid to speak his mind, who ignores the norms and niceties, who can do no wrong, who takes charge in all situations! We all love an authoritarian! We despise democracy! We can agree on the one person who embodies these qualities, from both sides. We can agree on our savior, Our Boss!"

They all raised their glasses of ghislin. "To The Boss!" They toasted in unison.

I had other worries, though, at that point. I had to size up how they operated with respect to me. In personal terms they were crude and crazy. Self-centered, deluded, and mean-spirited. Yet they acted as both witnesses and mirrors to my own conditioned life. They were a hateful, forbidden part of me, burrowed within, a part I don't want to bring to light, let alone accept ... my lower self ... I'm part rat....

CHAPTER THIRTEEN

The Dogen Potion

"Hey Pete, we're running low on the spiked ghislin," Ratty slurred. "Order some more."

"I'll call the Muslim delivery service, get a girl over here," Pete replied. "Meanwhile, let's give Jake our gift." He went to a small bureau near the couch and began rummaging through a drawer.

My mobile buzzed. I took it out of my pocket and saw a text from XK. "Order the ghislin. U pay. Insist."

"Hey," I called out, "the next round of ghislin's on me. You've been gracious hosts. It's the least I can do." I kept the cellphone at hand, ready to punch in the number.

The two men put up a weak protest, but Ayn was pleased at my offer. Ratty gave me the number and told me what to order. "Tell 'em to spike it, then just tip the girl." He winked at me.

"Get a rum and coke for yourself."

Pete found my gift. He held it up with pride, a black T-shirt with the words emblazoned in flame type: *Honorary Inner Rat. Hell Inc.*

"Here ya go, Jake," Pete said, "we all agree we want you to stay down here and join us. You got the brains, you got the right stuff, you'd be a great addition to our team. We can set you up wit' whatever you want."

I put the shirt on over my own and kept calm. "Thanks all of you, I appreciate your generous offer. But I must respectfully decline, I have a life above ground. I'm trying to get back to my wife...."

There was an awkward silence. Everyone's mood changed. The three looked at each other with knowing glances and darkening expressions.

"Think it over, Jake," Ratty said in an oily, menacing voice. "Let's wait for the next round of drinks."

I read the room. It was getting ugly.

There was a knock on the door.

"That's the Muslim girl, "Ayn Ratnd told me. "They're not allowed inside. Get the booze from her and pay her with your card."

I went out in the sewer tunnel. "Shut the door behind you," the Muslim girl said. She was wearing a black niqab that covered her face except for her eyes and carrying a delivery bag.

It was Xen Kohen.

"Drink some of this now and bring the mug inside with you."

"The Dogen Potion."

She nodded. I took a swig, a kind of rosewater. "Bring them this bottle. I'll wait for you here."

"How will I be able to leave? They want me to stay, they're getting fucking nasty."

"You can, you'll see."

I re-entered Pete's rathole, closed the door, and put the bottle of spiked ghislin on the table. Pete grabbed it and started refilling the others' Solo cups. They were getting drunker, louder, and more aggressive.

"Hey Jake," Ratty yelled. "A toast! You're staying with us!" His eyes were threatening.

I stood by the door. I raised the mug of Dogen Potion and drank it down along with them.

"You're goin' nowhere, man," Pete said, and began to move toward me. The other two did the same. My back was toward the door and I kept a sense of where the handle was.

"Sorry, that's just not gonna happen. I've learned a lot from you, but my visit is over."

At that moment I entered a deep meditative awareness. It was a feeling of timelessness, not the usual sense of passing time.

I could hold all things at once: my thoughts, the rats, the entire context of our experience, all contingent relationships, past, present, and future.

I looked straight at the three of them and they froze in their tracks. They just looked back at me, puzzled, eyes glazed.

I could see some of myself, my own past, mirrored in them.

I asked myself: Do I see how I have been conditioned to indulge my rat self? Do I recognize my own racist and sexist biases? Do I have non-idiot compassion for the rats, for myself? Can I heal, nurture, forgive myself and others, for our own conditioned lives, for what had gone on in the past, and make amends?

In that moment, or non-moment, I could honor the rats' presence, not as Others, but as feeling beings. I knew they were my threatening enemies, even criminals who would have to be held to account and yet could also see them with fierce compassion. I could see things about them they couldn't, their childhoods, their personal histories. I could see them inside and out.

Ratty had a tough, mean father who'd had a troubled life, arrested for armed robbery as a youth. He did time in Sing Sing, was a bouncer who collected gambling debts, and suffered from anxiety. His uncle was a bookie and loan shark with Mafia connections. Ratty himself treated his inner circle like a Mafia family and valued loyalty above all.

Ayn's childhood was marked by trauma. A totalitarian government confiscated her father's business. Her family suffered from periods of near starvation. She built a psychic wall around herself.

Pete was a fake, hollow inside, no solid sense of himself. He never knew his real mother and grew up on the streets. His stepmother, Zardulu, used him for her own purposes and emotional neediness. Like the other two he needed authoritarian criminality and the rush of power as a fix for his emotional emptiness.

They had grown up in a sick society and swallowed its evil poison whole. Yet the society produces millions of other injured, fearful people who crave what these demagogues offer. For them the rats fill the vacuum caused in part by sell-out liberal elites who are indifferent to working people and ignore the systemic cruelties.

They turn to the rats in the absence of a well-organized democratic left that could expose and counter their lies, delusions, meanness, and criminality and fight for a decent society for all. They mistake immoral disdain for convention as higher wisdom. They indulge their lower selves by blaming others: immigrants, women, gays, people of other races or cultures. To assuage their profound fear, they find the rats' false promises for security appealing and comforting: from Ratty, authoritarian certainty; from Ayn, a philosophy that justifies selfish greed; from Pete, the visceral rush of angry power and violent domination.

Unlike the rats, my past wasn't full of misfortune and terrible suffering. In some primal sense, in some ways, though, it resonated with theirs—being conditioned and rewarded for self-centeredness, self-promotion, self-delusion, pettiness, indifference to others. I saw I could grow from it all, make some changes for myself and with others, let some things go, even forgive myself and others—maybe my enemies, the rats, as well.

Standing there, with conventional time at a standstill, I went into a profound sadness, a melancholy, a mourning. For me, for the world, for everyone and everything in it.

Fragments from *Letters to a Young Poet* by Rainer Maria Rilke:
The more still, more patient and more open we are when we are sad, so much the deeper and so much the more unswervingly does the new go into us, so much the better do we make it ours...

...Perhaps everything terrible is in its deepest being something helpless that wants help from us...

That last thought from Rilke knocked me out.

At the same time, I saw the rats were immoral and dangerous enemies. For now, I needed to get the hell away from them. More than that, I saw their pain and anger, their woundedness, their ability to appeal to and organize like-minded people. That those things were forces driving their malicious plans to harm the world if further allowed. Like these rats, those who cling to racist, capitalist America are on the short end of history and are fearful of losing their status and way of life. I sensed I would see these three again in some future form and together with others would have to fight and stop them.

My hosts stood a few feet from me, transfixed, paralyzed, unable to move. After some time, I don't know how long, I grabbed the door handle, backed out of the room into the corridor, and shut the door behind me.

Xen Kohen, in her niqab, was standing away from the door along the corridor wall. "Quick, take that T-shirt off."

I removed the Honorary Inner Rat shirt Pete had given me and gave it to Xen Kohen, who put it in her delivery bag.

"Put this one on." I glanced at the front and pulled it over my head. It had a sentence in Arabic.

"It's a quote from Rumi: *Love is the bridge between you and everything.'*" Xen Kohen then handed me a men's Muslim prayer cap. "Wear this," she said. I hesitated.

She read my thoughts. "No, you're not disrespecting Muslims in this case. It's saving you from harm. We have to hurry. Follow us." I put on the cap.

We moved through the sewer sludge at a brisk pace. Other shadowy figures dressed in similar garb were walking past us with delivery bags. They would knock on a door along the corridor and be greeted by the resident rat. I saw we were part of a network of Muslim guest workers delivering ghislin and other drinks.

Xen Kohen turned her head halfway back towards me. "The Muslims down here serve as bodhisattva types, compassionate witnesses to Allah's passion for justice, and to minister to the residents when they can. The ghislin is just a ruse, they produce and distribute it as a way to gain entrance. This is a way to offer service. They want to get to the top of Mohammed's mountain, dissolve the self, be one with all, with the divine."

I was impressed. "I guess they're willing to start at the bottom."

"Keep your head down," Xen Kohen warned. "When the rats come out of their stupor, they'll call the Hell patrol to come after us."

Sure enough, after a few minutes I caught a glimpse of three rats in military camouflage heading toward us down an alley to our right. I noticed they were all wearing the black military berets with the Pizza Rat insignia. We sped up and just managed to escape their view.

I think we are in rats' alley
Where the dead men lost their bones.
—T.S. Eliot, *The Waste Land*

We picked up our pace through the maze of corridors, turning left and right. I was getting out of breath. My legs ached. After about five more alleys we came to a small, darkened cul-de-sac.

"Here it is," Xen Kohen said. She felt around the wall and after a few tense moments found a switch that raised a rusted metal door. It opened to a small stairwell with a steep vertical iron stairway. There was just enough light from above that allowed us to see.

We heard the rat patrol approaching and getting louder. They shouted and taunted, "Oh Jay—cob, Jay—cob," the harsh voices echoing along the alley.

We ducked into the stairwell. Once inside, Xen Kohen pressed a wall switch that brought down the door, just in time.

I exhaled. The worst was behind us.

I followed Xen Kohen up the stairs. We had to hold on to the iron railing with both hands. There was just enough space around the ladder to maneuver.

"So this is one of those ladders, huh," I said, breathless as we climbed. "Nothing divine about it, or the ascent, except we're leaving alive."

"It is. We are. And hey, you did great down there."

At last, we arrived at the top. Xen Kohen pushed up a piece of translucent glass above us and shoved it off to the side. We stepped out into a basement of some sort. I squinted to adjust to the fluorescent lights. There were vegetables stacked in piles, and many boxes of packaged goods. I noticed a dozen different kinds of mustard, Zen Party Mix, and Earth's Best Organic Toddler Pineapple Orange Banana Smoothie baby food, for just a few. I removed the prayer cap from my head. Xen Kohen pulled a fleece jacket from her bag and handed it to me. I put it on over my Rumi shirt.

CHAPTER FOURTEEN

Purgatory: Still Your Eyes Are on the Ground

Heaven wheels above you, displaying to you her eternal glories, and still your eyes are on the ground. —Dante, Purgatory, Canto 14

I could not become anything; neither good nor bad; neither a scoundrel nor an honest man; neither a hero nor an insect. And now I am eking out my days in my corner, taunting myself with the bitter and entirely useless consolation that an intelligent man cannot seriously become anything, that only a fool can become something. —Fyodor Dostoevsky, Notes from Underground

Hipster XK

I had expected us to come up on Eastern Parkway somewhere. We were definitely not there, though. I looked around to orient myself.

"Where the hell are we?" I asked. When I turned back to look at Xen Kohen, they had transformed themselves again.

I was now face to face with a tall, pale white hipster guy in skinny jeans and a beige shearling jacket. In place of the niqab was an N-95 COVID mask that covered a scruffy beard. His sandy hair was slicked back in a man bun, and he was carrying a black leather shoulder bag with the initials XK. The penetrating eyes gave ol' Xen Kohen away.

I had to laugh. "You are a trip, man. So now you're my hip spiritual influencer."

XK signaled me to put on my mask, which I was surprised to find was still in one of my pockets. "We're in the basement of Hole Foods," Xen Kohen told me in his new-guy-but-still-familiar voice, "near the Gowanus Canal, at the bottom of Park Slope, you know, the eco-conscious healthy supermarket brought to you by conscious capitalism." Yupster Kohen winked. "No one will see us take this lift up to the main floor."

I had a question for my transformed Hired Power. "Who are you now?"

"We're Irish-Italian, a computer graphics designer. We grew up and still live in Park Slope, up the hill," he said.

"Ah. What parish?" That was once a common question you might ask of some folks from Brooklyn.

"St. Augustine's, on 6th Avenue and Sterling."

"Oh, that's a big, beautiful church, inside and out, a refuge," I recalled. "All brownstone, and Tiffany-stained glass windows and a golden tabernacle in the sanctuary—I snuck a peek once."

where the walls
Of Magnus Martyr hold
Inexplicable splendour of Ionian white and gold
—T.S. Eliot, *The Waste Land*

I learned a year later the tabernacle, worth an estimated $2 million, was stolen in a shocking, brazen, and insulting robbery. This was a blow to the church, which, like many in Brooklyn, was losing its congregation even before the pandemic. Of course, the question about church wealth always is: shouldn't that gold instead be put to better use to help people in need?

My emotional link to St. Augustine, though, was through Dylan's song, "I Dreamed I Saw St. Augustine." In his dream the saint searches for people who've already sold their souls. I always found comforting how he deals with our spiritual loss: *No martyr is among ye now / Whom you can call your own / So go on your way accordingly / And know you're not alone.* But then Dylan dreams he's one of those who kills the saint. He awakens alone in anger and terror, and in sorrow he prays and cries.

XK was following my thoughts. "Yes, we feel anguish and regret after we've given up, even killed, our youthful ideals, hopes, and dreams. We're going to visit a place with that theme now."

I looked at XK and waited to hear more.

"Welcome to Disturbia, Park Slope style," he smiled and crinkled his eyes.

Hole Foods

We exited the lift from the Hole Foods basement and found ourselves in one of the produce aisles.

"Mind the zombies," he said.

I looked around at the masked customers who otherwise appeared serious and focused. Hole Foods: its self-righteous motto could have been *Good for me—I'm helping the world as a conscious consumer*.

"Are we back to so-called normal here?" I asked, still trying to place myself in time. Park Slope hipster Kohen raised an eyebrow at me.

Right—normal for whom?

"Yes and no," he said. "We've returned to the present. It's mid-March, 2021. You were down there with the rats and then stood and meditated for almost three months."

"Getouttaheah. I need to move my car for alternate side parking! I need a shower and a shave, I gotta cut my nose hairs and clip my nails, I gotta take a...."

"Not a problem," said millennial XK. "You froze in time. You're not sleepy or hungry, right? We took care of your car too. Everything's cool."

I rubbed my beardless face, looked at my fingernails, and exhaled. "Hey, you could make a killing around here moving people's cars."

I thought of Sandy Denny's song *Who Knows Where the Time Goes?* And what Nina Simone said before she sang it: "Where does it go? What does it do? Most of all, is it alive? Is it a thing that we cannot touch and is it alive?"

Who does know? It was beyond me. I had just come out of a three-month Being-Time deep consciousness … an even longer time away from Maya….

I needed to check my phone. I had kept texting her, called her sister Jill's number, no one ever picked up. Nothing from Maya. What the hell. Does she not give a damn? Is she okay? I had quite a few messages from my group, though. *Mr T., what's up? Where are you? Now we're really worried!* Damn. I texted them, saying I was okay and that I had needed to go on a winter quarantine retreat upstate by myself and had turned off the phone. I apologized for not telling them and wrote I was just getting back. I thanked them and said I'd check in with them soon.

I scrolled through a news synopsis hipster Kohen had downloaded for me about what I'd missed. Right-wing thugs did in fact storm the Capitol, like Pete had predicted. Holy crap, they pulled that off, while I was down there! We were far from through with the con man and his cult, who insisted the election was stolen from him, the Big Lie, as Ratty claimed. And COVID continued to kill many Americans, mostly those in Red states who refused to get vaccinated and wear masks.

I turned back to XK and shook my head.

"So it's been a year of the pandemic. When is this damn thing over?"

"Not yet. It's funny and sad, many are nostalgic for the early days when everyone stayed home and baked banana bread and hoarded toilet paper," Xen Kohen said with a sigh. "A lot of anxiety happening though, people are gonna have a lot of work to do together. We've had you vaccinated. Twice. They're still not making it easy for people to get the shots, especially Black and Brown folks. Some still don't trust the vaccine, either. And then, as you just read, there are some Ratpublicans that have no sense of public health and many think vaccines are a hoax. There are more available now, though, and more places are starting to open."

"Thanks. Hence my sore arm."

"Hole Foods typifies Disturbia, so this leg of your recovery starts here. The corporate founder thinks the solution to all our problems is what he calls conscious capitalism."

"An oxymoron."

"Yup. Here's the deal," Xen Kohen continued, "You will see things both on the surface and at a deeper level. You are going to see how things could have been different, for you and others. Many here in Park Slope and elsewhere, white people in particular, have traded their dreams for a zombie existence, for material comforts, for the privileged perks of a racist system, and for what they think is permanent security."

I could relate.

"So, you fail to live up to the best of what you desired and expected of yourself and even others," I said. "Society says you've made it. Yet you're vaguely unhappy and don't know why. It's like being a mensch manqué."

"Haha, mensch manqué. Yes. They've been infected with mild variants of the Hell virus—greed, meanness, and delusion—now disillusion. They can't see how they've been poisoned. They live in a bubble. They get complacent, they settle. It's all about them. They think they're very decent people. They're cut off from the less fortunate and have little compassion for their pain. So the poisons are more toxic, harder to see and get rid of."

"Denial. I know it."

"What makes this toxic virus harder to cure," Xen Kohen went on, "is that it's systemic. It's in the air we breathe, it's invisible, like the COVID virus. It's not just a quality of each person. It's between people. It forms the boundaries of thought, it sets the limits of how people see their lives and of society. It's like in a computer, the toxic part is the operating system you don't see, and your thoughts are the files. It takes on a life of its own, and people breathe it in. A lot of folks refuse to, or can't get their head around, anything that's not concrete.

"People can identify personal suffering and suffering from violence and oppressive conditions. But this third kind, Rogers-Vaughn, a pastoral therapist, points out, leads to a vague, amorphous dread, a fragmented self, feelings of guilt and loneliness…. It's invisible, hard to pin down, but we need to name and address it."

I picked an organic cantaloupe from a bin, bounced it up and down in my hand, and felt its scaly surface.

Xen Kohen took out a pair of hipster glasses from his satchel.

"You'll be wearing these, XK AI Anti-Google Goggles. They look and work like your own glasses. Put yours away in your case. This is AI from the future that's used for public good, not corporate profit. They allow you to see beneath the surface to the invisible structure of things. It shows you how everything is related! It enables people to demystify the bullshit and work together to transform it. It took us years to develop this level of awareness. Then more years to distill that and turn it into this techno app that everyone can wear and see what's going on. Just touch them here when you want to use them."

Brownstoner Kohen handed me the frames. He showed me a tiny piece in the top right corner I was to pinch between thumb and index finger.

"So, these are different than the latest Facebook RayBans," I said.

"Sure, those take photos and videos, answer phone calls, and play music and podcasts. They also let you take pictures of people without them knowing it and of course they collect data on you. All part of that megalomaniac Zuckerberg's control fantasy to meld the virtual and actual world into his sicko metaverse."

"That's an invisible form of power and control right there."

Xen Kohen nodded. "And Apple is coming out with its own version of high-tech virtual reality goggles. With ours, you can see the poisonous ideology we breathe in. They're what Slavoz Žižek calls 'critique of ideology glasses.' He saw them in a sci-fi movie he liked. He says we tend to think of ideology as lenses that, when we remove them, will reveal the true world. But these lenses instead expose the poisonous crap that's invisible beneath the everyday surface."

"I would have thought you'd all have glasses that show us what a future utopia looks like instead of uncovering the present-day toxic garbage."

[The function of utopia] *lies not in helping us to imagine a better future but rather in demonstrating our utter incapacity to imagine such a future—our imprisonment in a non-utopian present without historicity or futurity—so as to reveal the ideological closure of the system in which we are somehow trapped and confined.* —Fredric Jameson, "The Politics of Utopia"

"No," Xen Kohen continued, "like Jameson, Žižek argues the opposite. His point is that we need to uncover the ideology that infects our uncritical everyday relations."

"Žižek's point is that no one is compelling people, like in a dictatorship. They actively participate, they do it to themselves. They adapt the corporatized beliefs as their own. They never feel they're good enough. No one quite feels connected to others, no one quite feels alive. This hidden ideology infects our own thinking and mental health. Even the so-called sharing economy, sharing your stuff, is commodified—Uber, Airbnb, YouTube videos...."

"Ayn Ratnd crap," I said.

I was price checking, comparing items with the Park Slope Food Coop. Everything was higher—organic strawberries, organic Haas avocadoes, organic heirloom tomatoes.

"Yup, her crap, among others. Go ahead, check them out."

I put on the XK AI Anti-Google Goggles, pinched the button, and looked around. I could see dead zombie zones of flesh on some customers. I could hear what was going on in some minds, depending on where I focused my attention. One guy eyeing the kale was thinking, "I'm worthless, feeling unproductive this week." A woman was comparing herself to women shoppers nearby. "Great haircut. Nice boots. Mine suck."

I saw mostly African American and Latino workers stocking shelves and produce bins. I saw there was no union for them, they had to keep reminding themselves to be polite, even-tempered, think of the team. "Team, my ass," one thought to herself.

As I turned my head, I saw Marva Williams, who wore a mask like the other workers and was stacking tomatoes in a nearby bin. She winked and spoke to me without talking aloud.

"Check out the cantaloupes near you." I heard her voice in my head. "And they're having a Prime sale on chicken thighs, across from aisle five." She smiled with her eyes and turned away.

I walked back to the bin of organic cantaloupes and picked up another one. This time I could see holographic images projected in my field of vision. One showed Mexican farmworkers, non-unionized, exploited, vulnerable to the COVID virus and pesticides, bent over, picking the cantaloupes in the California sun. In another, the agribusiness owner of the field was seated with a laptop checking his profits. Other screens showed the truck drivers who transported the cantaloupes to the stores and the grocery workers who unloaded and shelved them. I could see a picture of the person who would choose that cantaloupe and the family cutting it open and eating it. I saw the rinds and all the unsold ones go into composting, though the city program would be imperiled by future budget cuts.

Everything was connected. Touch the goggles and you could see the exploitative relations, the power structures, the historical events that brought about the one commodified cantaloupe.

Wearing the goggles in the Hole Foods store I could also see the hidden myths of conscious capitalism. (NB: The images were footnoted from Nicole Aschoff's book, *The New Prophets of Capital*.)

The biggest myths floating across my screens like chyrons were "1: conscious capitalism can make the world a better place and still compete in the market and make money. 2: if you personally shop at Hole Foods you're caring for the environment and supporting good working conditions. 3: investors and workers are stakeholders with equal power.

"In fact", continued the rolling caption, "Nope. A company must pick profit over decent values to survive the market, stay in the game, and compete. Money talks, so the investors rule."

I shut off the feature. "Wow."

"The more you see, the more the connections are clear," said Xen Kohen. "It's not about people in power pulling the strings. It's about how ideas that serve the system infiltrate consciousness and keep some people in power. The false ideas people literally buy into are that everything is a market from which you get what you need."

Just behind Hole Foods is the Gowanus Canal, one of America's most polluted bodies of water, its fetid, toxic sludge nicknamed black mayonnaise, a sad repository of the many forgotten—or ignored, or denied—residual wasted dreams of a broken land. After a while, as with the smells in your own house, with those of your own body, you no longer notice them.

Fragment from *You Can't Go Home Again* about the Gowanus Canal by Thomas Wolfe:

... there is in it not only the noisesome stench of a stagnant sewer, but also the smells of melted glue, burned rubber, and smoldering rags, the odors of a boneyard horse, long dead, the incense of putrefying offal, the fragrance of deceased, decaying cats, tomatoes, rotten cabbage, and prehistoric eggs. And how does he stand it? Well, one gets used to it. One can get used to anything, just as all these people do. They never think of the smell, they never speak of it, they'd probably miss it if they moved away.

Thanks to a coalition of local environmental activists, the canal was finally being dredged as part of a Superfund cleanup, only to be quickly rezoned by the city for billionaire developers who bought up both sides of the canal. Later I learned that locals were fighting to make the area a green space with affordable housing, which gives me hope.

I felt like taking a quick look. We walked around the back and saw Hole Foods had built an adjacent waterfront esplanade, a kind of Hollywood-set façade to make the canal seem wholesome. We sat for a moment in silence on one of the benches looking at the black water.

At once a large gray rat slithered alongside the bench, stopped to eye us, and quickly disappeared.

Fragment from *The Waste Land* by T.S. Eliot:
A rat crept softly through the vegetation
Dragging its slimy belly on the bank
While I was fishing in the dull canal
On a winter evening round behind the gashouse

Just before it did, I switched on the goggles. In detail the rat's cold, sneering side glance and red lips were those of Ayn Ratnd's. I felt a cold shudder from my neck down through my spine, and I turned to Xen Kohen.

"I thought we were through with those bastards."

He looked at me, pursed his lips, raised an eyebrow, and shook his head.

We began to head up the hill on 3rd Street toward Park Slope. We passed the reconstructed Old Stone House, the site of the Battle of Brooklyn during the Revolutionary War, close to the canal. An outnumbered, heroic militia of Maryland soldiers was slaughtered there in a valiant effort to hold off an army of British and auxiliary Hessian troops. Their sacrifice gave Washington and his men enough time to escape across the East River through a thick fog.

Into a rain of British fire the Marylanders charged, and Cornwallis recoiled, stunned by the unexpected rebel onslaught. Though the ground became littered with dead and dying Maryland militia, Stirling formed them up again. Again, they attacked, their numbers diminishing by the minute. Six times Stirling charged, and twice the assaults drove the British from the stone house. — John J. Gallagher, *The Battle of Brooklyn 1776*

Fragments from "The Centenarian's Story" (in *Drum-Taps*) by Walt Whitman about the Battle of Brooklyn by the Gowanus:

... Who do you think that was, marching steadily, sternly
confronting death?
It was the brigade of the youngest men, two thousand
strong...
Jauntily forward they went with quick step toward
Gowanus' waters...
... Ah, hills and slopes of Brooklyn! I perceive you
are more valuable than your owners supposed;
Ah, river! henceforth you will be illumin'd to me at
sunrise with something besides the sun.

The hills of Brooklyn, the Gowanus creek, for Whitman, forever imbued, brightened, with the lives of the young martyred men.

One of the great mysteries for me, is, though: Why do people bother to go on and fight, despite the pain and sadness, when they know they're not here for long? When we're just passing through? When we know we're going to die? What are we fighting for?

I thought of a song we learned in camp, *Passing Through*, covered by both Pete Seeger and Leonard Cohen. The transhistorical narrator asks the same question to George Washington about his men. Washington answers that even though folks know they're just passing through, they will fight and even die for what is right.... Then I remembered the Lincoln Brigade, another battalion that fought and died for a belief in a better future, in which all people could live together.... Yeah, maybe....

We found some more benches in a parkette across from the Stone House. I sat down and put on the goggles and turned to gaze at the area across from the House. After a short time, I could see scores of American soldiers in tattered blue uniforms come into focus, in horrifying hand to hand combat with the Redcoats and other soldiers shouting in German.

Like Whitman I could see the hills and water transformed. And along with the Americans' cries and screams of pain, I could hear their thoughts. The first ones had to do with sheer self-survival. *Move! Push harder! Look out!* As I zoomed in on their awareness, I heard them thinking and caring about their comrades right alongside them, and their feelings of loyalty and respect for their general. Then I could see what they were seeing in their minds—images of their sweethearts and families back home.

Next I began to hear some quieter thoughts, though still strong, maybe they were coming from the goggles, like signal beams bouncing between future and past: *for love of freedom and justice ... for our new land....* Then, like a faint voice that came from the bottom of a deep well: *to make things right ... for the love of all beings and things ... for the love in the universe....*

I was overwhelmed and exhausted by this uncanny vision and needed to shake myself out of what I'd heard and seen. I removed the goggles, stood still for a while, then turned to Xen Kohen and said, "That Stone House was also the site of the first clubhouse of the original Brooklyn Dodgers."

Taking the Dodgers out of Brooklyn was devastating, not only to me but to the entire borough. I had no idea as a kid that the Brooklyn Dodgers could ever be taken away. And it taught me a little bit about capitalism: that somebody, against the wishes of everybody in that borough, could simply move [the team] *to Los Angeles.* —Bernie Sanders, in *Bernie's Brooklyn* by Theodore Hamm

To honor all Brooklyn fans everywhere who still feel abandoned and to this day will never forgive O'Malley and dem Bums, I added, "and you shoulda stopped them from leaving for LA."

Xen Kohen just laughed. I joined him.

"When we get up the hill and head along 7th, we'll leave you at your joint, Café Regular," he said. "They've reopened just this month. We've set you up with a meeting with three other guys, it's a men's zombie recovery and peer support group. They're starting it up at the café today."

"They scored a table? That place is tiny," I said.

"We arranged it," coffee maven Kohen winked. "The one outside, it's warm enough."

"Are these guys your, uh, clients too?"

"No, we saw a post on the Food Coop bulletin board, they were recruiting other members. We left them a text and said we had a friend interested who would come around today."

"And what do you know about them?"

"Oh, we vetted them for you. They've all been vaccinated for two weeks. White boomer guys like you. They all have some familiarity with mindfulness. One's a media studies professor, another is an actual mindfulness coach and consultant to corporations, the third is a social worker like you but does some private practice and also works with local police, military, and politicians on mindfulness. They all have issues being too comfortable."

"White liberal guilt."

XK nodded. "It keeps them from doing anything about it. They've given up values they believed in for material success. They live a kind of complacent but empty life and don't know which way to go with that."

"I get that," I said. But besides being an introvert I was never big on men's groups. "We guys need to get our shit together but..."

XK jumped on my thoughts. "Yeah. A lot of men's groups tend to wallow in defensive self-pity. Or even blame women..."

"... or glorify some narrow version of masculinity," I continued. "And then they want to go drumming in the woods or some crap. I don't know the answer to how we get rid of the toxic stuff, maybe it's a start. I don't have to be so cynical, I guess..."

"This group by its very flaws can help you. They're calling themselves the Brooklyn Codgers. Hang in there."

When we neared the café AI hipster XZ said he would see me when the meeting was over and headed up the hill towards Prospect Park. What he didn't tell me was this was going to be another temporal marathon in which horizontal time stops until we stop.

CHAPTER FIFTEEN

The Brooklyn Codgers: A Men's Zombie Recovery and Support Group

Io non morii, e non rimasi vivo. I did not die, and did not remain alive. —Dante, Divine Comedy, Inferno, XXXIV, 25

I was neither / Living nor dead, and I knew nothing, / Looking into the heart of light, the silence. —T.S. Eliot, The Waste Land

All four of us arrived at Café Regular around the same moment at the outside table, each masked up. We fist bumped, sat down and shared our names, exchanged some pleasantries and small talk, then took turns going inside for our coffee. When I went in I glanced up at the mural: *L'enfer, c'est les autres.* "Hell is Other People." Let's see about these guys, I thought.

On everyone's return we removed our masks, agreed to go around and say more about who we were, why we were there, what we were stuck on, and explore stuff as much or as little as we wanted. Since we were all meditators, we also agreed we'd sit and meditate at various times if the moment called for it and left it up in the air as for how long.

I flipped on the eye switch. Under each guy's clothing I saw patches that varied in size of zombified dead flesh. I also saw some body parts that were luminous and looked downright healthy in a way I couldn't explain.

I switched it off and turned off my cellphone. I wanted to concentrate.

The first one to share was the professor, Jay A. Profwreck. He was twirling a coffee spoon in his cup, lifting and pouring the coffee back in.

Jay Profwreck

...most people will stay in limbo because their fear of hell outweighs their hope for heaven. And they're willing to keep treading water, whether it's a bad relationship or a bad government or a bad neighbor situation or you hate your boss. —John Sayles

"Hello gentlemen, glad you could come. I set this group up along with my friend here, Bob Frawst. I thought I'd never be able to share my story and felt like I was always in a kind of hell. So at least I'm trying to move to purgatory.

"I teach media studies at Columbia. I'm tenured, I have a wife, a middle school daughter in a good private school, and a brownstone here in Park Slope. We've managed the pandemic okay, we're fortunate no one's gotten ill. I teach online, my wife works from home, and my daughter's school classes are online too. Life is good." He paused.

"And that's the problem, it's too good. When I was young, I had some dreams about what I wanted to say and do and to impact the world. Over time I didn't notice how I kept compromising myself, bit by bit. I was offered a teaching job and learned to write journal articles that weren't about what I wanted to say but helped me get tenure.

Do I dare
Disturb the universe?
In a minute there is time
For decisions and revisions which a minute will reverse.
—T.S. Eliot, The Love Song of J. Alfred Prufrock

"The college administration let me buy out some teaching time if I served on bullshit committees that helped them out. I did some PR work for the university, which is all about status and competition—since I'm good at hype. Overall, it got so I was always figuring out how I could get ahead, I would study people, plan my moves to win them over, down to the last detail."

Professor Profwreck took his plastic spoon and poured and re-poured his coffee, then took a sip with the spoon.

"I had some ideas ready to challenge my field but didn't dare publish them. There were colleagues I thought were full of shit but I said nothing. I feared the thought of them dismissing my theory. I still ask myself: what if they just didn't get what I was saying?"

And would it have been worth it, after all
Would it have been worth while
—T.S. Eliot, *The Love Song of J. Alfred Prufrock*

"I don't know, 'till now I've made a kind of uneasy peace with myself. Yes, I'm a privileged white, upper-middle-class guy, we all are. There was a time I could have stood up for what's right, for what was closer to who I am—well, or was. I admit, I haven't had the courage. I'm a media consultant who can write a fancy sentence and keep it just vague enough. I discovered I could win academic debates with clever arguments and obfuscation. It got so I lost the sense of what's true from what's just bloviation. And I like comfort. So, I played it safe. I kept telling myself, there will be time, there will be time to fix things for myself. But then I find there isn't."

He sat back.

"It got me where I am today. But where am I, really? I feel like some kind of zombie. Lately I've had dreams where I'm on the bottom of the ocean, hoping to be rescued. Then I wake up and still feel like I'm drowning...." His voice trailed off.

"I've started practicing some mindfulness, to help me try to stop fooling myself, maybe even help the world rid itself of disinformation, since I'm good at detecting it. It's helped me try to see what's true, at least with me, what I really know and feel...."

Jay Profwreck was depressed. I felt for him.

After we sat and meditated for a while, he then turned to his friend, Bob Frawst.

Bob Frawst

The most regretful people on earth are those who felt the call to creative work, who felt their own creative power restive and uprising, and gave to it neither power nor time. —Mary Oliver

"Thanks Jay, hey guys ... ah, sorry, just one second, gotta record some things on the cellphone...."

He looked down at his mobile lying on the table in front of him, spent a few moments swiping and typing, then looked up sheepishly.

"Bob Frawst here, I'm a retired CEO. Until recently I've been consulting with corporations on mindfulness, to help them de-stress their employees, get them to be more positive and productive. I coach fellow execs. I bring in a nice fee on the workshops and have a good pension.

"I always thought it's good to help people take control of their lives, literally every minute of it. Mindfulness as self-regulation. For much of the time I've been trying to live it myself and teach it to others. I loved all those apps, like Fitbit, you can monitor everything you do—eating, walking, sleeping. The mindfulness app Headcase got me going for a while. I even used it lifting weights. I've been in love with positive psychology, constant self-improvement, thinking positively about everything. I mean, there's enough negativity in the world, why focus on that? And, hey, modesty aside, I've been successful. I have a couple of houses, a great pension. I shouldn't need to worry or obsess about anything, really."

His mobile beeped. Bob looked at it, nodded to himself, and thumbed in a few words.

"Sorry, that's what I mean! I'm monitoring a few things, my heart rate and also noting down what thoughts I have at random times as a mindfulness exercise.

"I'm in a funny place, though. The more I'm mindful of my thoughts, the more I watch my mind, trying to catch the moment, the *now*, the more stuck I feel. I'm conscious of being conscious. I can't get *out* of my mind. It's still about *me*. And I always feel I gotta be somewhere else, be productive; there's always something more. Like *I'm* an unfinished project, I'm never enough. I sometimes feel empty. My secret desire is to sometimes just do nothing, to get off the hamster wheel, quit the rat race. That's crazy, I'm retired! It's an old, ingrained habit—in my head! The pandemic has only made it all the worse.

"Lately, though, it's even led me to change direction with my mindfulness training with corporations. I'm telling them, look at why you're stressed! Why do you need to be so competitive? Is it all about making money? Here's what got me to question what I stand for.

"This fall I bought myself a Maserati. Love that car, incredible horsepower. In fact, it feels like I'm driving a damn horse, it's a personal relationship! I can read this car's mind, she knows me too!

"A few months ago, on the day of the winter solstice in fact, I'm taking her out for a spin to Connecticut to just try and chill. The snow's on the ground, beautiful. I decide to take some back roads. I find myself on one where I think a former corporate partner has some property, a big estate, but I think he's in Florida, lucky dog. I decide to stop in front of his land for the hell of it and get out of the car. The house is set back from the road, you can't even see it. There are woods next to it. Then it starts to snow. My mind right away goes into overdrive. Wait, I'm not even sure it's his place, I *think* it is!

"And well, if it is, I'm *thinking* he might see me! But how could he? I mean, even if it *is* his house! And I guess he wouldn't mind if I just pull over here sort of on his driveway, I mean if it is his house, and even if he's there! The point is, this is all in my mind, see."

He glanced at his cellphone on the table in front of him.

"I mean really, who cares? So then, I'm looking at my car. I can't just be present. Get this! I imagine the car is looking at me funny. I'm thinking *she* must be thinking, what the heck is this guy doing, just stopping like that, out here in the middle of nowhere in the snow! Her engine even starts to sputter! The damn car, just an organized bunch of metal, is alive, it's talking to me!

"So, then I catch myself with mindfulness. I try to just be there, just relax, clear my head. I look around. I look at the woods.

"But nope, after a nanosecond, there goes my mind again. I'm watching it, monitoring it. It jumps to a future thought: I got stuff to do back home, workshops to prepare, people I need to get back to. And I know the longer I stay the more traffic is gonna build up and it'll take me longer to get back to Brooklyn."

Bob's mobile beeped and he typed something in.

"Sorry again. We've become enslaved to these things!" He gave a self-conscious smile and continued.

"Anyway, I get back in the car, turn around, and drive back. Sure enough, I hit traffic. I try to breathe through it, take it as just something that is what it is. So much for mindfulness, huh."

Bob Frawst took a gulp of his coffee and gave us a nervous smile. The guy was anxious. The mindfulness practice he preached to the corporate types turned into a feedback loop for always watching his mind, a tool for personal productivity and success. He was beginning to doubt his own values, which even affected his corporate consulting. I felt for him too.

We sat in silent meditation for a while.

Bob Frawst then turned to the third guy.

Jess B.

When we are spiritually bypassing, we often use the goal of awakening or liberation to rationalize what I call premature transcendence: trying to rise above the raw and messy side of our humanness before we have fully faced and made peace with it. And then we tend to use absolute truth to disparage or dismiss relative human needs... —John Welwood

"Hey guys, I'm Jess B. I understand Bob's anxiety. I'm convinced the solution is to practice mindfulness so that you just *be*, you just are. That's what Bob really wants. It's what I do in my own mindfulness consulting practice. It's what I teach the police force, the military, and even the world government leaders I work with. I think it's even the solution to racism as well. You get beyond distinctions like race. You go beyond differences. We're all one. Never mind judgment, or even thinking, thinking just goes round and round. You just have to be! Then there will be great harmony. There won't be any stress or conflict! Here's some lines of a poem I know, "Tasting Mindfulness," by a guy I admire, Jon Kabat-Zinn."

Jess B. took out a folded paper from his jacket, put on his reading glasses, and read to us. I paraphrase it here.

The poem asks the reader, Can you stop so completely, can you be so completely in your body and life, that everything, past, present, future, what you know and didn't know, hold no anxiety?

"See, if Bob could have just stopped completely in front of those woods, Jess continued to read, it would be a complete moment of just being, no need to want something else or to escape or fix something.

"Being is where it's at," Jess paused his reading. "If each one of us practices mindfulness just to be, we'll solve our problems, because mindfulness of being benefits our thinking. The police will know what's the right thing to do. So will the armed forces. Government leaders will stop feeling they have to compete and stop destroying the world." He read another passage that described a timeless moment—just seeing, feeling, when life just is, and that "is-ness" takes hold of all your senses.

"No need for critical thought, no need for religion, or a set of moral values. Knowing the right thing to do, knowing what's good, come purely from mindfulness which gets you to pure being. This is a universal practice! And you don't have to take anything personally. The universe is just unfolding.

"Here's part of another poem I like about just being," Jess said. He read a few lines from "Of Mere Being" by Wallace Stevens. A bird with gold feathers sits in a palm tree at the end of one's mind. It sings a strange song, without human meaning or feeling. It's beyond the last thought. It just is.

Jess B. finished the poem and nodded to each of us with a slight bow of his head. He was well-intentioned. Yeah, there's merit in meditating and getting to the state of pure awareness, of mere being, past thoughts and judgments, past feelings of pain and taking things personally. It's nice to go *beyond the last thought*. But I was skeptical; if that's all you do, look at where you end up: *without human meaning, without human feeling....* Besides, I've never heard a bird that doesn't sing for pure joy, because it can, that's meaning right there for birds, and humans too.

We sat and meditated.

It was my turn.

The Left in Purgatory

Here is a place where time stretches on. Where food has no flavor. Where we grow neither old nor young. It's not bad, exactly. But it's not where we had hoped to be. Don't worry, American socialist, you're not in the Inferno—hey, it's not like we've ever had the power to err and commit mass crimes—you're in Purgatory! ... Yet there is something dangerous about being large enough to be a political presence in parts of the country ... but far too disorganized and powerless to carry out your political program. —Bhaskar Sunkara

"Well, guys, I share some of what you've talked about, a kind of uneasy complacency about many things ... I'll tell you about it. But we also gotta look at the injustices of the world in which we live, that we're a part of.

"I've had visions of what I wanted to do, about ways to help the world, since, I dunno, well, at least college and before. Things I *woulda* done. But I haven't had the wherewithal, the confidence, or drive, or just the damn courage, to keep at it. I sometimes felt I needed to get *asked*. I missed some chances, let some beautiful, happy things go. I took some things, some people, for granted, took advantage of them. In some ways, still do.

"In college I started wrestling with the old mind/body problem. How do you connect them? In an English class on *Ulysses* I found a passage that was like a lantern, or a flashlight, in dark woods.

Fragment from James Joyce's *Ulysses*:
In woman's womb word is made flesh but in the spirit of the maker all flesh that passes becomes the word that shall not pass away.

"I couldn't quite figure it out but kept meditating on it. Years later I found a way to make some sense of it. I learned you can't solve the mind/body problem with your ordinary rational, scientific sight. You need to see it all with your third eye. It envisions things all together, no separation.

"When I meditate sometimes with my eyes closed, I can even see the eye, in the middle of my forehead. But I developed a lazy third eye, and after a while it closed off....

"I loved that passage for another reason. All flesh, all things, when they become the word, that's when consciousness, as universal spirit, doesn't die!

I stopped and took a sip of coffee. I felt myself tearing up. In all three eyes.

"My wife has separated from me, I'm hoping it's temporary, I'm having a tough time ... I was—uh, am—pretty self-absorbed. I say I'm a feminist, but a lot of old conditioning sometimes gets the better of me. I am working on some stuff and trying to earn her back.

"I retired last year, a high school social worker, the kids were the best part. We did counseling groups with meditation. I organized them around some social action too, to try to change some of the crap we were going through in the school and the whole system. I'm still in touch with them.

"I wasn't happy working in the bureaucracy, but hung around, and like Jay, kind of settled for some job security, and let go of some visions of what I thought real education should be, and also got tired of fighting the idiots running things, who had no vision or imagination, also many had no sense of, no feeling for, what the kids' lives were like, which used to pain the hell out of me.

"In graduate school and later, a bunch of us wanted to start a school, I don't even know where they are anymore, everybody just went their different ways. We used to make fun of people for selling out, I realized later that's not fair, life in this fucked up country is more complicated than that.

"I also once wanted to start a community service agency, or at least find one already around, that could put it all together, critical thinking and education about society, personal therapy and social work, social justice, community organizing. I used to joke about looking in the *Times* want ads under R for Revolutionary. I thought I could do it myself, but didn't have enough drive or confidence, and I was always disappointed in the places that seemed like they could do that. I realized there were too many bureaucratic and social barriers to getting to that, and hell, no one's gonna fund a radical organization that challenges the system in the first place, they *want* you to keep things as they are, and of course not change anything in a radical way. That's what social workers are for—not to solve people's problems, just manage them.

"So I abandoned my dreams. I got complacent, and discouraged, and well, a bit depressed at times, and just tried to help the kids. So yeah, it's a kind of purgatory, an unresolved melancholy.

"Look, I'm working to avoid becoming a certain kind of left melancholic—you know, blame yourself and your comrades, argue over minor differences, get impatient, wallow in self-pity, obsess about your marginality, dwell on what might have been, get attached to the feeling of loss itself....

"I think we need to talk about our losses. To mourn them, feel them, deal with the melancholy. Accept our wounds, find ways to support each other and others. Then imagine the kind of future we want, and move on...."

Jay interrupted me. "Sorry, Jacob. Did you see that rat? The city can't get rid of them, it's getting worse than ever."

We all turned toward the street and looked at the fat rat casually walking along the curb. He stopped and eyed us for a long while.

While it paused, I touched the XK AI Anti-Google Goggle button. On its face in brilliant definition was Pete's vicious scowl.

The rat then darted down the hill, crossed the pavement, and disappeared behind a brownstone.

... an exterminator had told a friend of mine about rats: "A rat looks at you like you *is the problem." —Roz Chast*

I shivered and removed my glasses. I rubbed the heel of my hand between my eyes and put my head down on the table for a moment.

"Hey Jacob, are you okay?" Bob Frawst asked.

I sat up. "Thanks, Bob. He reminded me of someone I know."

The others laughed and nodded.

"He came to join our discussion about the rat race," Jess said. We laughed again.

"Or maybe he's an influencer rat," Bob said. "My daughter's always on this TikTok thing. He looked like he was posing for a video, like that Pizza Rat awhile back, and hoping it'll go viral."

I winced but joined in. "Yeah, I'm surprised he didn't take out his mobile for a selfie." They didn't know how close they were to Pete's story.

We decided to write down some topics we wanted to talk about. After some back and forth, we ended up with three: Living in a Fucked Up Society (my suggestion), Being a White Guy (Jay's), and What is Time and Why Don't I Have Enough of It (Bob). Jess was happy to just "be" with our topics.

CHAPTER SIXTEEN

Mindful Purgatory

Living in a Fucked Up Society

We're all lonely for something we don't know we're lonely for. How else to explain the curious feeling that goes around feeling like missing somebody we've never even met? —David Foster Wallace

"I feel isolated a lot of the time," Jay said. "Of course, the pandemic made things worse, but it's not all due to that, I felt that way before then."

Bob concurred. "It's a gnawing feeling, I was always taught to be competitive and that I needed to figure out and do things myself, to not rely on others. It's all about self-regulation. There's some link here as to why I don't have many guy friends, don't quite see it, though."

I activated my glasses and stayed on the app.

"Not much sense of community among us guys," I said, "so it's not surprising if we feel we gotta be out for ourselves."

"If everyone could be present, maybe they could feel more connected...." Jess wondered.

"Well," I replied, "that's an individualist solution. That doesn't account for why so many feel split off from others. We have a loneliness epidemic, especially with guys."

"It does suck to have so much inequity around us," Jay said. "Also, you feel you have to keep up with your own way of life, often at others' expense."

"Neoliberalism," I said, "the market turns us into both products and consumers. No more sense of community. Everyone out for themselves. Measurable data instead of faith and hope. Networking instead of friendship. If others win, you lose."

"Huh," Bob said, "I've been coming across that word. I've started to read about what I'm hooked on, all these cellphones, apps, social media where you're always looking for likes, where the companies monitor what you look at and buy. You know, we give them our data, like I do, we're both the masters and enslaved, there's no need for some Big Brother surveilling us, we're our own Big Brother."

"And of course being hooked on the phone and social media further alienates people, especially with kids," I added. "There's less face-to-face interactions to work out social skills, I mean, I was thinking this meeting would be a bit awkward, but it's good, I haven't done this in I don't know how long."

We sat in silence for a while.

Jay then spoke up. "Another issue that bugs me is not just the pressure to be well but you have to be happy all the time."

"Yeah," I said, "toxic positivity. You're not supposed to focus on anything negative. Bob, you said it yourself, there's too much crap in the world to focus on, so you don't. Jess, it sounds like you want to float above it. That falls into what the corporate powers want us to do, just breathe through your lousy work situations and be happy."

"And they make big bucks off it as well," Jay said. "The wellness industry, there's an oxymoron for ya."

Bob nodded, while Jess looked uncomfortable.

"Well," Jess said, "I think the point is to get to where we don't have to take things personally, which is where mindfulness meditation helps us—detach from our egos."

"There's truth to that," I replied, "but gotta say, Jess, some things you have to take personally, you have to take some things to heart."

We sat for a while.

Jay then spoke up. "The scary stuff today is the extreme right. How did we let these assholes get so much power?

"And so many are racist and antisemitic as hell," Bob added.

As hell. I thought of the rats again and shivered involuntarily. "I hope there are enough of us who oppose and will even fight these bastards," I said.

"If it comes to that, I'd do it somehow," Jay said. Bob, even Jess, nodded in agreement. "It needs more than us though."

Bob spoke up. "I'm getting a light bulb over my head."

"LED?" Jess asked.

Bob smiled. "Via a virtual surge protector."

We all turned to him.

"Look, you've got many of these right-wing working-class supporters, who, okay, maybe shouldn't have been called 'deplorables,' that wasn't helpful. Because of the changes in the world economy— not even their fault—a lot of them lost their way of life, their decent pay and jobs, their self-esteem.

"Yes," I said, "and then there's the cultural changes around the family, women, gender, all that stuff. The Democratic Party has abandoned them by failing to deal with economic inequality. Instead, they chose to keep chasing after money from their corporate donors. They focused on social issues and identity politics so they could look liberal while distracting from any desire to challenge the economic status quo. So, a lot of working people feel dismissed and dissed by us, the coastal elite libs."

"They blame us and resent us," Jay continued the point. "They think we're the establishment who did this to them, and that we look down on them. We read the *Times*, drink lattes, eat sushi, drive foreign cars...."

"Hey, I resemble that remark," Jess said. We laughed.

"They want to give us the middle finger," Jay said.

"The connection again," I continued, "is an unjust system and mindset of self-centered, competitive, corporate greed and the privatizing of everything. Many of these folks, though, don't have an understanding and analysis of it like some of us do. They take a wrong moral and emotional turn. They indulge in racism, revenge, violence, and destruction. It's dangerous for the country and for everyone. Follow the money, too. A lot of white grievance is manipulated and supported by right-wing institutes and foundations. They led the fight against affirmative action, teaching about racism, and DEI programs."

"Damn." Bob shook his head. "So then, how do we fight back, patch up this society, and reconnect?"

We sat for a while.

Being a White Guy

Equal rights for others does not mean fewer rights for you. It's not pie. —Jesse Williams

"Let's move on," Jay said. "Speaking of racism—being a white guy: easy or hard?"

"I admit I seldom have to think much about it," Jess said. "So I guess I'd say, easy."

"That's a privilege, then, isn't it," replied Jay, "not to have to think about or deal with one's privilege."

"Jeez," Bob said, "it's hard for me, I feel guilty a lot of times, thinking about all that white privilege we do have."

Jay said, "Yeah, white fragility is a bitch, having to face racism as a white guy. So it's tough being fragile, how's that for an oxymoron."

"I'm trying to find a higher way to deal with it," I added, "one that's not defensive and guilt laden. Or, on the other hand, being complacent where you avoid having to look hard at your own position."

The other three waited for me to continue.

"First, some who say 'all white people are racists,' to which our natural response, as we all know, is, 'but not *all* white people,' which they then dismiss—that's bullshit. That's a defensive response that accepts the false assertion in the first place. If you do, then there's no way to counter it.

"It's because there's a failure to distinguish between directing your anger at an individual white person without taking into account the racist system that divides people and automatically gives white guys a leg up, whether we consciously want it or not. If you're saying I'm personally racist because I'm white then why should I bother sharing how I see things, why bother having a dialogue or discussion with you or anyone who says that to reach some higher common ground? There's no point. Anything I try to say is racist. And yeah, a lot of liberal white people on the receiving end of the statement also don't make that distinction. They then naturally take it personally and feel guilty and defensive and shitty."

"The white fragility charge," Jay added. "The more you deny it and defend yourself, the more you're accused of it. It's lose-lose."

I nodded and grabbed my coffee cup. It needed a refill.

"On the systemic, societal side," I continued, "can that be done without guilt, in some kind of grown-up way? Germany has done some of that since World War II. They've acknowledged and educated around Nazism and have made some amends. In this country they're doing some of it, tearing down Confederate statues, setting up new museums and commemorations even in places like Montgomery, Alabama. Still, not much real change on the systems side. Lately, though, there's a lot of backlash from parts of the system that reinforce white people feeling threatened. We gotta keep fighting this crap!"

I stared at my empty coffee cup.

"On the personal side, like others, I say, okay, we're living in a fucked up racist system—we didn't create it, and we don't like it. Are we anti-racists? Hell yeah. And here we are, we worked hard, and the system enabled us to succeed, unlike others, who also worked hard, and we are who we are, successful white guys. So, what do we do?

"Look, Isabel Wilkerson has a good analogy. We inherited a beautiful house, but its structure is damaged, it's got stress cracks and fissures in the foundation. We say, well, I wasn't there when they built it, I have nothing to do with past sins, neither did my own ancestors. Okay, but we're here now, we inherited it, and we have to deal with it. Any further damage, it's on us.

"If we don't try to wrestle with that system, including its history, if we don't find ways to stop contributing to it, and if we don't look at how the system has conditioned our own thoughts, feelings, and actions, and allowed us to take advantage of its own injustices, and then if we don't work with others to challenge and change that, then we *are* part of the problem.

"So okay, there's a personal side to all this we're each responsible for. Can that happen on a mass scale? I doubt it but always hope so."

Jess challenged me and the others. "So, Jacob, have you been able to do that yourself? Have any of you? That's a tough way to go."

"I struggle with it," I admitted. "It's easier to not work on that. Like Jay said, we have the privilege of not having to think about our privilege. And I kick back even more when I'm feeling isolated."

The others agreed that besides trying to be kind and fair to people of color in day-to-day encounters they don't think about it much in relation to themselves and aren't doing much else.

"So, if we only do things on a personal level, that doesn't change the racist system," I said.

We sat for some time.

"Well," I spoke up again, "while we admit we're just a bunch of white guys sitting around talking, I'm gonna indulge in another rant. I have a different, even more radical take on white privilege I don't hear about.

"I think the argument of white privilege is not the most helpful way to think about this. It not only implicitly blames white people for being who they are, it buys into an either/or, you win/I lose, all or nothing, zero/sum framework. It's based on the myth there's only so much to go around, and we have to fight each other for it.

"The secret is when you let go of your artificially inflated, white privileged status, it doesn't mean you lose your identity. It doesn't mean that if people of color gain, you must ipso facto lose. That's a false, zero-sum game those in power want you to believe. They're happy to let us fight each other while they get and stay rich.

"We need to turn the notion of privileged white people on its head: It's not that white people have privilege; it's that *what we have all others should have as well.* There're enough good things to go around without us giving up stuff other than our artificially manufactured privilege.

"Heather McGhee wrote that when people replace the zero-sum myth with solidarity across race, with collective action, you get what she calls a "Solidarity Dividend"—everyone benefits in all kinds of ways."

A xen kohen: *Is compassion a zero-sum game? Is there enough in the world to go around, does it multiply when we work together? Or is it finite and measured out in Prufrock's coffee spoons?*

"First, we need to agree that what people call white privilege is, sadly, wrongly, and dysfunctionally normalized—that's the critique of racism by people of color, and they're right: white people are seen as normal, as the standard, and others are not. We get housing loans and don't get redlined, we can move into good neighborhoods, we can borrow money and accumulate savings, we have better health and health care, we don't get tailed in department stores, or stopped and even killed by police, all that stuff we take for granted. Whiteness is also the default standard of beauty, of health, of how to speak and behave. That stuff is fucked up and has to go.

"So then let's take it further and say, all those things we call privilege *should* be normal—that is, what counts as privilege should be for *everybody*.

"So every privilege, every advantage, we have had: *everyone* should have as well—all Black people, all people of color, all working-class people, everyone. *Everyone* should not just have the *opportunity* to *compete* for good things—that's neoliberal bullshit. That just keeps the competitive and individualist system as is, a pyramidal capitalist structure with a small top that only allows a few to climb over others and do well.

"Instead, every disadvantaged person should *have* the same high quality, well-resourced schools the rich have, the kind your daughter goes to, Jay. Everyone should *have* the same excellent health care, the same decent housing, a decent livelihood, the same access to the arts, et cetera. Everyone's unique beauty should be appreciated. And yeah, you want to be creative and inventive and even entrepreneurial and get rewarded for it, go for it! Just don't exploit others and climb on and over their backs and allow a system to deprive others of decent human needs and rights, which is what this zero-sum capitalist system is about."

I sat back and looked at the guys.

"Man, that's radical as fuck," Jay said. "That impugns competitive capitalism right there, all that racist and class divide-and-conquer shit."

I nodded.

Jess wrinkled his forehead. "Do you really think this country can afford to have good quality schools for all, the kind that Jay's daughter goes to, for all these kids in Brooklyn?"

"Damn," Jay said, "most of the public schools here are not very good. It's no accident there's hardly any white kids who go to them, except for the few who have the resources to get into to the few elite high schools. That's why we sent our daughter to a private school."

"The right wing wants to privatize all schools," Bob added, "they hate public education."

I turned to Bob. "You work with Wall Street guys." I looked at Jess. "And you work with the military. Do you think there's not enough money in this country for a better quality of life for everyone? The income disparity between the few billionaires and corporate execs and the rest of us is insane. To make it worse, a lot of people don't even think others *deserve* equity, that they deserve what we have! Maybe deep down some of us think that too. If so, it's because we buy into the zero-sum, you win/I lose belief. If others deserve and get what you also have you think that means you'll lose your bogus status that comes with your bogus white identity. Now there's a guilty white thought to meditate on...."

No one said anything. We sat for a few moments.

"Look, another rat," Jess pointed to the opposite sidewalk. It was in no hurry to go anywhere.

"He's jaywalking," Jess said.

I flipped the goggles on. I could see Ratty Ghouliani's long face with the hair dye stains. His eyes shifted, then he looked straight at me.

They all looked at me in turn. "Yeah, that's the other guy's twin brother," I said, trying not to show my fear, and they laughed. I had now seen all three of the rats from whom I had managed to escape. What were they doing up here?

We sat and meditated for longer.

What is Time and Why Don't I Have Enough of It

Work and life become inseparable. Capital follows you when you dream. Time ceases to be linear, becomes chaotic, broken down into punctiform divisions. As production and distribution are restructured, so are nervous systems. —Mark Fisher, *Capitalist Realism*

... the great force of history comes from the fact that we carry it within us, are unconsciously controlled by it in many ways, and history is literally present in all that we do. It could scarcely be otherwise, since it is to history that we owe our frames of reference, our identities, and our aspirations. —James Baldwin

"What is time?" Bob asked.

"Well," Jess said, "if we can stay in the now, then there's really no sense of time, just flow. The world goes round and then returns. Even the cycle of seasons, of birth, death, then re-birth ... there's no real beginning, no end."

"So, there's no real time, it's all just cyclical?" I asked. "What about history? What about trying to *make* history for the better?"

"Being in the now overrides the sense of passing time, of the good and bad in history," Jess stated. "That's what makes things better."

"Earth to Jess," Bob was a bit peeved. "Are you able to make time for yourself in everyday life? I have a hard time with it."

Jess said he could do it.

"So, you can afford to live like that. Kinda privileged there, too, huh?" Bob said. "They always tell you to stop and breathe and take time for yourself. Not everyone can afford to...."

"Right, not if it means being late for you shift or taking a mental health day if you don't even have sick leave," I added. "Reminds me of one of my favorite John Lennon songs—that line from 'Working Class Hero' about how *you're given no time instead of it all...*"

Oh yeah," Bob said, and picked up his iPhone. "Lemme find it on YouTube." He swiped and punched around and then played it for us. Lennon's singing over a lone guitar cut to the heart. The pain numbs you out, Lennon sang.

"Wow," Bob said. He scrolled ahead. "And this is what we were talking about before too. Jeez, I forgot what a great song this is." You can reach the top and join the rich, Lennon sang, but first you gotta learn to smile while you kill.

Jess wasn't convinced. "I think Lennon needed to slow down. I also work at not hurrying and teach it in my seminars," he said, "even the police and the military can benefit from that."

"Sorry to be skeptical," Jay replied. "Again, it's not that simple in this society. I read that even us privileged types have what's called Hurry-Up Time Sickness. Never enough time, always rushing towards the future."

"The future never arrives, does it," added Jay. "Just one broken moment to the next..."

"There's no flow," I said. "Moments feel like fragments, cut off from seeing, feeling the whole pattern of what you want to do in some larger sense. Well, it would be nice to have more of what Jess describes."

"The pandemic wreaked havoc on time," Bob said, to which we nodded.

"Yes," I replied, "traditional capitalist work time became more undone—at least, the pandemic got us to think there are other kinds of time."

We were fumbling around, no one had a clear grasp of the issue. I felt we were caught in some kind of liminal consciousness, between an oppressive, horizontal time, what the Greeks called *chronos*, and the possibility of another, uncertain but hopeful kind of time, *Kairos* or Dogen's time.

What I find in chronos *is not comfort but dread and nihilism, a form of time that bears down on me, on others, relentlessly.... In contrast, what I find in* kairos *is a lifeline, a sliver of the audacity to imagine something different. Hope and desire, after all, can exist only on the differential between today and an undetermined tomorrow.* —Jenny Odell

We were in purgatory all right, somewhere between holding on to ourselves, staying in our personal comfort zone and the conventional time afforded by our positions in society, and letting go of our ego, stretching ourselves towards some unknown, greater good.

I then remembered a work of art that expresses that doubt, that hesitation, that pondering, that pain and hope before an unknown, uncertain tomorrow, before one lets go of one's ego, even one's life, for a greater good....

"Hey, have you guys ever seen the casts of Rodin's statues of *The Burghers of Calais* in the Brooklyn Museum lobby? They put it out sometimes. I also got to see it in the British Museum a few years ago."

"Oh yeah," Jay recalled. "The English invaded France and took over Calais, way back when. They were gonna lay waste to the city. The local councilmen offered to sacrifice themselves so all their fellow citizens would be spared...."

"That's it," I replied. "Well, Rodin captures this moment in time in these guys' lives, between clinging to their own life and a moral drive to let it go for something beyond themselves. The agony they feel right then is embodied in their faces, their bodies, their gestures.

"And I learned that my man Rilke admired Rodin so much he came to Paris to serve as his apprentice for a while, and he didn't know a lick of French. He nailed down that moment too, when he wrote about one of the figures."

"Found it," Bob said, already scrolling his phone. He read us the English translation of Rilke's description.

He created the vague gesture of the man 'passing through life'…. As he advances he turns back, not to the town, not to the weeping people, nor to those accompanying him. He turns back to himself … his hand opens in the air and lets something go, somewhat in the way in which we set free a bird. He is taking leave of all uncertainty, of all happiness still unrealized….

"Here's what the Brooklyn Museum says," Bob continued, "sounds like they kind of riff off of Rilke."

… the body exposes the agonizing physical and psychic price of placing the collective good above personal survival. His disproportionately large hands recall the unconscious gestures that might accompany an intense internal struggle, and his feet, one planted, the other pivoting—simultaneously suggest hesitation and propulsion toward a destiny that has been accepted.

We sat in silence for a while.

"So, what happened to them?" Jess asked.

"According to the story at the last minute the English Queen convinced the King to spare the Burghers and everyone in the town." Bob read.

"Whew. Like Abe and Isaac," Jay said.

"Well," I said, "there's no clear evidence or account things happened this way. It's more a French patriotic story."

The others looked surprised.

"But it's a still a good one, and it inspired great art and writing, and moral insight."

We took a break and went in two at a time to refill our coffees.

When everyone returned, I confessed I wasn't through obsessing about time. "Time is history," I said.

"Okay, Buddhists say we are the crossroads of an infinity of causes and effects, co-arising at once. If you let go of the illusion of trying to grasp a solid, existing self, which is part of that eternal web, if you become conscious of who 'you' really are in this sense, if you see your being as at one with eternal wisdom and love, you lose the fear of death.

"But we ourselves are also *history*. We—and, by extension, the material universe—evolve through history, which is time. History is *time. We,* material beings, *are time.*"

I started telling them about Dogen's time, then deferred to Jess to expand on what he had begun to tell them earlier. His problem was he was out of love with historical time. At best a sense of eternal time was his strong suit.

Jess then asked that we sit and meditate for a longer time, how long I didn't know or realize.

I had a hard time settling in. Old doubts and feelings of despair were revisiting my head. Why bother trying to make things better? Why bother helping others? Why not just stay comfortable? Does that mean even letting go of working to get Maya back, not seeing that as worthwhile? Maybe all this really is just emptiness, nothing....

In the middle of our sit my mobile buzzed. What? I thought I had turned the thing off during our meeting. I saw the text was from my counseling group.

CHAPTER SEVENTEEN

Sic Transit

We're still figuring out the tricks time pulled over the past few years, how it stretched and contracted, sped up and slowed and there was, for a while there, time to contemplate it. —Melissa Kirsch

*H*elp Mr. T was the first line of the text, which gave me a chill. I turned to the men and apologized; I said I had to answer this one and walked a few feet away up the street.

We been trying to reach u. We're in deep shit at the school, Mr. T, plz come now if u can, boardwalk same place

I thought you were all online at home! I texted back.

School opened in March. We're back.

March? This *is* March.

When I looked around the leaves were on the trees. It was a warm spring day, verging on summer. I checked my phone and saw it was June 4. Had we been sitting there for over two months? How did the phone work now when I had turned it off? I checked my messages. Nothing from Maya, all this time. Jesus. I touched my face. I didn't need a shave.

The pandemic kept fucking with my, with everyone's, sense of time. I gave up trying to sort it out.

See you soon, I texted back.

Right after that, I got another ping from XK. *It's OK, head out. See you there.*

See you there? What the fuck. The dude had played with my head, and with time, *my time*, all over again. XK had turned on the phone too, of course.

I returned to the guys and said I was sorry to leave like this but had a kind of emergency; my counseling group has never asked me for immediate help before. I told the guys I had to take the subway out to Coney Island, not far from the school, and meet the kids under a gazebo on the boardwalk, where we'd often gather after classes.

They were concerned, wished me the best, and offered to help in any way if they could. I thanked them and said I was grateful for that and for feeling I could call on them if I needed. I said I found meeting and sharing with them surprisingly meaningful and enjoyable, and I hoped we could do this again soon.

The guys seemed unfazed at the passing of time, but Jay looked puzzled and worried when I said that. "Of course, Jacob, see you next week as usual."

"Each week I feel we're making progress," Bob enthused, "meditating all these weeks, checking on what we're stuck on, helping each other!"

"We're a bunch of recovering complacent white neoliberal assholes," Jess added, to my further surprise, and we all laughed.

I couldn't begin to explain to them, let alone to myself, what I was going through, what I'd been doing, where I'd been, all this time, all these weeks. I apologized. "Hey, yes, of course. This text from the kids has just put me in a frazzled state."

"Go Brooklyn Codgers!" Bob said.

I smiled and tried to look as if I wasn't going out of my mind, which I was, then took my leave.

I headed over to the 7th Avenue station to take the B train, which runs express to Brighton Beach, then would switch to the Q to Coney Island.

B Train Crossing the Terminal Moraine on a Ladder of Gradual Ascent to the Outwash Plain, Passing the Site of a Stairway to Nowhere

As I rode the uncrowded B train car, my mind was swirling. Where the hell had I been these two months? Did I go home each day and then return to the Codgers meeting at the café once a week? I had no recollection.

And what was XK doing with my head? When he, I mean she, damn, I mean we … shows up in whatever form, I'm gonna give, well, *them* a piece of my mind. What was left of it.

And what changes had the kids been going through and why were they so upset now? I sat with my anxiety as best I could.

Along the way I noticed the train trip itself moved up a kind of three-step ladder. It took me not to Heaven but to another level of Purgatory, to another part of Brooklyn on the other side of the terminal moraine, the outwash plain.

You catch the B train at the 7th Avenue Park Slope station. Straightaway it crosses the terminal moraine by traveling underground beneath Prospect Park. As a second step it then emerges through a cut in the earth, in the open air but below street level. After passing a few more stations the B train ascends to the third level, toward the ocean, on an elevated track.

The B skips the Neck Road Station and as we went past, I tried to catch a glimpse of the stairway to nowhere I once read about, known to some older local residents. But it had been demolished as part of a so-called station revitalization project.

The Post-Traum-atix

… adolescents are lightning rods for the zeitgeist. They live at the fault lines of a culture, exposing our weak spots, showing the available array of solutions and insolubilities. They are holding up a mirror for us to see ourselves more clearly … we all have these questions about how precarious life has to be in this country, how

to live with the hopelessness about the future that is merging…. Adolescence, then, is not only an attempt at a cure. It is the chance we have for finding one, not only for them, but for all of us. — Jamieson Webster

We need, in every community, a group of angelic troublemakers. — Bayard Rustin

As with all kids, the social isolation caused by the pandemic has taken its toll on my group. They missed being in school and hanging out with friends, along with other students from whom they could learn about themselves and others. Everything was virtual—on Zoom, Instagram, through texting—piss-poor substitutes for in-person connections. Some lost family members to COVID and are still grieving. Pandemic angst is always in the back of their minds. Given the need for masks, it's also literally on and in everyone's face.

Each feels the pain of growing up today in an uncaring society that squeezes and blames each of us, obscures the social sources of the pain and stress, and blocks people from connecting. Young women get depressed from the increasing harshness of peer and sexist pressure about their bodies and looks, the bullying, intimidation, and slut-shaming from social media and from the unchecked misogyny among many boys and men. They're anxious about the threat to their right to control their bodies. The boys feel a different kind of pressure. They are struggling to find their way through changing roles and expectations. Transgendered young people face their own challenges that include the threat to their right to be who they are.

All my kids are aware of the gun violence both in Brooklyn and in mass shootings around the country that include those in schools.

They are in their last year of high school and set to graduate the end of June. They've all planned to go to Brooklyn College next fall and stay together in Brooklyn.

Each is stressed about their future. Will climate change make the Earth uninhabitable? Will they be able to earn a living and succeed in anything? They feel the pressure from their family and school to be perfect, and from everywhere about whether, when, and with whom to have sex, relationships, and perhaps a family. For some even their sexual identity is in constant question.

Then there's the background stress from the right wing, threatening their very existence. Each one of my kids is a target for some damned hateful, ignorant, xenophobic, misogynistic, homophobic, transphobic, racist, antisemitic, anti-Latinx, anti-Asian, anti-Muslim/Palestinian, conspiratorial asshole....

I hadn't been with the six of them in a while, so took mental notes to refresh my memory.

Each is Brooklyn to the core.

Cami is Afro-Dominican. Some African American kids who meet her tell her she's Black like them, but she says no, I'm Dominican. It's something she wrestles with: can I be both? Derrick gently questions her about it at times. When the pandemic first hit, she lost her mami, who had asthma, to COVID, and she grieves every day. She lives with her father and an older, lighter-skinned brother who identifies as white. He is a right-wing business major at Brooklyn College, and they often quarrel about politics. Cami is damn smart, not just an excellent student. She speaks her mind and is insightful and attuned to other people.

Dina is Palestinian and wears a hijab. She's Cami's BFF and just as bright. The two tag team and can argue anyone to the ground on something they think is unjust. They sometimes finish each other's sentences, in a good way, not like I try to do with Maya. Dina is even-tempered and has a calming influence on Cami. The two will challenge teachers if they think something they said is unfair. That's earned them the dislike of some of the more conservative ones—like Dotty Beckerman, their history teacher—who are threatened by any challenge to their arbitrary authority. They both follow social media and keep up with all the fake rumors in school circulating on Instagram and texts. Dina's parents keep trying to set her up with family friends' sons, but she is not interested and tells them she finds them too macho and traditional and threatened by her.

May May is Chinese American, slight with delicate features, transitioning to a woman. She has felt she was a girl—gender dysphoric—since she was young. She had gone through a lot of comprehensive assessments with medical and mental health professionals and her immigrant parents. We were glad they accepted the transition, unusual for Asian parents, and it was agreed she qualified emotionally and physically. I had worked with some school administrators and the other counselors to try to build a supportive school environment. We knew that discrimination, stigma, and a hostile social milieu contribute to troublesome outcomes like suicidal thoughts and actions for transitioning teens. The good news was the administration and most teachers accepted her. She and her family have also experienced some hateful incidents since the right blamed the Chinese for COVID. May May seems to have a healthy sense of herself and has been taking judo classes to feel like she can handle herself better. Her role model is Ryka Aoki, an Asian American trans woman and science fiction author with a black belt in judo.

Derrick is African American. He is the oldest sibling, and his single-parent mom relies on him to watch over his younger brother and sister. After joining our group he's become less alienated from and angry about school and toward his father, who left the family. He recently managed to leave a gang, some members of which he was close with, but most are now angry at him and think he's a traitor. He started following and working with a Brooklyn community group called the Violence Interrupters who work in local organizations and neighborhoods to ward off and resolve potential conflicts that start out as rumors. Derrick caught fire learning about the Black Panthers in an American history class.

Billy is gay and from an Irish/Italian Catholic working-class background. When he decided to come out to his parents his conservative father became angry and told him he was disappointed in him. The father has begun to get involved in the high school PTA and at meetings pushes for more punitive and restrictive school policies. Their relationship is strained, and his mother tries to mediate but has limited success. Billy is president of the Gay-Straight Alliance at the school. All the kids in the group are members. He is a visual artist who is learning digital art and is a voracious reader of comics and graphic novels.

Arielle comes from a liberal, secular Jewish family and is an all-around activist. She's an ardent feminist and has a close network of like-minded women friends who, along with Cami and Dina, confront and educate boys around bullying, shaming, and harassment. She is a skilled organizer and works with Dina and other Muslims for Palestinian rights and against antisemitism, and she's co-chair with Billy of the Gay-Straight Alliance. Arielle is also a leader in the school around climate change and has organized students to join environmental groups and go to demos. She's got the socialworker gene, fierce compassion for all, and a sense of humor.

I had to stop myself from worrying about them and figured I would wait and see what was up. Not easy. I focused on the ride and breathed.

I changed for the local Q, took it three stops and got off at the Coney Island–Stillwell Avenue station, where I removed my mask. I walked down a few blocks and looked at the famous amusement park, which opened in mid-spring. The beach itself opened Memorial Day weekend.

As a resort and beach, Coney Island has seen its day, but each summer still draws thousands of New Yorkers. How many world-class cities have a boardwalk that stretches along a great sandy beach with swimmable ocean water? Some greedy pols and businessmen now want to build a casino there. They bait the locals with the promise of a few jobs while creating another way to suck dry working people's pockets. In its heyday Coney Island was the summer respite of millions of working-class New Yorkers who sought relief and escape from their insufferably oppressive apartments and heat-absorbing streets.

I flipped on the XK AI Anti-Google Goggles and could see what it once looked like, endless crowds in the amusement park, on the boardwalk, and on the beach, as far as the eye could see, families lying inches away from each other's blankets.

I climbed up onto the Boardwalk, turned right, and headed towards the gazebo where my group and I would meet after school on warm afternoons like today. Beneath it are short benches and four small chessboard tables with benches on each side. I saw the kids, who had managed to grab a table and were sitting on top and on the benches. I felt I was ready for anything.

I was wrong.

CHAPTER EIGHTEEN

The Post-Traum-atix on the Beach: Wednesday

What shall we ever do? —The Waste Land, T.S. Eliot

The kids, of course, were checking their phones and taking selfies. A few gathered around one phone, laughing. When they spotted me, they put them down, got up and shouted, and broke out in big smiles. We ignored the COVID rule and shared hugs.

When we sat down on the benches, I noticed a seagull with a black mark on its head that looked like a yarmulke, hanging around the table. The kids were feeding it some crumbs from a Nathans' hot dog bun. It even landed on their shoulders, oddly friendly, persistent but not aggressive. Some were taking selfies with the bird. It was so distracting I had to focus back on the kids.

"Oh man, Mr. T., we missed you so bad," Dina said, as she fed the bird out of her hand.

"Where you been? You been okay?" Cami asked. "We were afraid we'd never hear from you."

The bird jumped from the table to Cami's shoulder. Derrick took a photo with his cellphone.

"Long story gang, I'm really sorry for being out of touch. I missed you all too, but I'm okay and here now. Let's skip our go-'round check-in and tell me what's up."

I switched on the XK AI Anti-Google Goggles as a way to concentrate, I figured.

Nope.

Instead, the group froze and faded into a gauzy background, like a damn movie or a Saturday Night Live skit.

The Jewbird

"Hey Yankel! Got a nosh? We'd love a bagel with a schmear. A nice piece herring mebbe?" The familiar voice was coming from the bird. XK was now a seagull with chutzpah and a Bernie Sanders accent.

I was not amused. "What are you doing? Oh, I get it, you pulled another Malamud trope. The Jewbird. Very clever, you've come to lay some guilty *tsuris* on me and remind me I can't escape my tribal demands. Just remember the guy in the story finished off the bird."

I was pissed but good. "And don't tell me you're a cousin of that pseudo-spiritual schmuck, Jonathan Livingston Seagull, either. Feh."

XK, the Coney Island wise guy, ignored all this and went right on. "So *nu,* you gonna introduce us to your kids awready?"

"Listen, stop *schnorring* off them and enough with the *kibitzing*. They're in some kind of trouble, as I'm sure you know. Now *I* need to know so I can try and help."

"Of course!" But instead of answering, XK the *meshugeneh* seagull started flapping its wings and made ready to take off. Then it stopped and waddled closer to me on the table.

"Sohh, boychik … first tell us what ya loined from the Codgers group."

What a noodge. Still *hakn mir a tshaynik*. Rattling me like a tea kettle on the stove. I sighed and collected myself. "Well, we admitted it's easy to live in limbo and comfort, and after gaining conventional success in our lives, to let things we value just slide.

"The Anti-Google Goggles have come in handy. I've seen even more crap and tried to help the others see it too. We've committed to helping each other and others in Brooklyn not doing as well as us. What else are we good for?"

The bagel-loving *momzer* puffed up its chest with what looked like pride. "Dot's good!"

"We got work to do … I guess," I continued. "But I don't know … sometimes it doesn't feel worth it, it feels like it could all come to nothing…." My voice trailed off.

And would it have been worth it, after all
Would it have been worth while.

XK, the smartass bird, code-switched and in a serious, still familiar voice gave me a part dharma, part coach-at-half-time pep talk.

"Look, you doubted yourself, you lost faith, it happens. That regret you all shared in the Codgers group—okay, you mourn your losses. If you can't let them go, you learn to live with them. Yeah, a lot of life is a bust. But you can go on! You've also tapped into the larger timelessness of love and wisdom. You have it within you. It's also outside us, it's all around us. You literally went through Hell! Look at how these kids pulled you right out of your doubt and despair! And think of Maya!"

I stopped and took this in. I tried to connect it all with my loss of Maya but it wasn't yet clear. Maybe nothingness, emptiness, in the broodhist, not the nihilistic sense, is liberating. If you can let go of your damn ego, accept the imperfection of the world. Maybe then you can even do the right thing and love without getting attached to any outcome.

"Okay," I said to my bird. "Now please tell me how I—how we—can help these kids, will ya? I still need to know what's going on with them."

XK reverted to his schtick, Groucho's boid with the magic woid from the fifties' TV show *You Bet Your Life*. "Hokay, boychik, *the kids'll* tell you. And we'll be around, we gonna help 'em, you'll see!"

The wise guy seagull made to leave again, then stopped and turned its head. "Don't you wanna finally know the answer to Dylan's xen kohen, whether birds are free from the skyway, hah?"

I looked out at the ocean. Some families were setting blankets down near the shore. A ship that looked like a freighter was perched on the distant pencil line of the horizon. Like a gluttonous seagull I went for the bait. "Okay, I give up. Are they?"

XK, the *tumler* Jewbird, gave what my grandma would call a *geschrei,* a screech, next to my left ear. I tried to block the noise with my hand, scrunched my face, and turned my head.

"Hah, do you know they have a Gull Scream competition in Belgium; they choose the winner who can make a sound just like us! The organizer said he wants to make seagulls sexy again!"

"Mazel tov. That's about as sexy as nails on a blackboard. I'm still waiting for my answer."

"Well, that's for us to know and for you to...."

I was disappointed and interrupted. "Yeah yeah, very mature. We used to say that in junior high school. Go study your haftorah, your Bar Mitzvah's coming up soon."

"Not to worry about the kinder!" XK shouted at me like Jerry Stiller. "You gonna help them but good! See you around!" and flew off into the sky in a flash of rainbow light.

I blinked and found myself back with the group under the gazebo. Our eyes were all drawn to what was now on the table, two shoe boxes enclosed in some kind of teal iridescent wrapping.

"What. The. Fff..." Derrick said. "Where'd those come from?"

"Someone musta left them," Billy wondered. "But damn, how come we didn't see them before?"

"I know, the seagull dropped them off for us," Arielle said, and everyone laughed at the absurd joke.

"And it just took off, we didn't even see him go," May May said. "I was starting to get used to him."

Arielle was right. And I knew what was in them. What a freakin' trickster. I scooped up the boxes and held them next to me. "Well gang, I, uh, was hiding them and brought these as gifts for everyone. Don't ask for the details now, I'll tell you about them and give them to you soon, I promise. Just tell me what's going on."

Low School

But now is the time to think like poets, to envision and make visible a new society, a peaceful, cooperative, loving world without poverty and oppression, limited only by our imaginations. —Robin D.G. Kelley, *Freedom Dreams*

"The school has gone wack, Mr. T.," Derrick began. He looked over at Cami and Dina.

"The teachers, plus Mr. Martinette and his APs have turned into *pendejos*," Cami said.

Dina continued and took turns with Cami. "They act like mean bullies towards everyone who doesn't go along with them...."

"...like us, of course."

"We don't know who they are anymore!" Dina shook her head.

"... It's like something or somebody took over their brains!"

"They've created these really stupid rules—like no talking in the halls...."

"They got rid of the student council!"

"They got a bunch of gangsta wannabes to patrol the halls...."

"... and they're allowed to push us around, physically, since we don't go along with the program!"

"They let the guys bring knives, even guns into the school, it's freakin' scary!"

"The guys are forming militias and...."

"... are running the school, practically!"

"Then in class they're throwing total *basura* at us," Cami said. "There's no teaching, just lies about—everything!" She turned to May May, who continued.

"Like, immigrants are fucking up this country. Trans and queer folks are harming and perverting little kids. We can't say anything bad about America! It's just ... bullshit! They're piling the work on us too—more tests, more useless homework, and telling us we need to be more productive."

"If we question anything, they give us an F and kick us out of the school," Billy jumped in.

"The librarians are working with some parents to get rid of a bunch of books," Arielle said. "The administration won't even let us read some. Unbelievable! Like Nazi Germany!"

"Yeah, even the counselors are acting wack," Derrick added. "We can't figure them out. They still like us, but they want us to 'develop ourselves' as, like, *brands,* so we can succeed. They now say competition is the way to go."

"Plus, they now tell the girls to not have sex and that abortions and being gay are immoral and sinful!" May May said.

"Get this, Mr. T.," Cami said. "You know a lot of us girls get down on ourselves from all the social media, TikTok and stuff—we get sucked into comparing ourselves to others, we take it all to heart. You and the other counselors used to help us with that, to think about those messages from those—waddayou call 'em—clickbait sites that just want to make money, and to resist that shit, to understand where it's coming from, fight the bullying and peer pressure, and help each other...."

Dina jumped in, "They're saying we need to get over feeling down, that we even *should* blame ourselves for not looking good and not working on ourselves, and we should stop blaming social media—technology is business that's good for the country or something like that!"

"And the counselors also stopped those mindful moments before school and in our counseling groups when we could meditate for a minute," Derrick said. "They want us to pray instead!"

Arielle said, "The school is now the opposite of doing the peace and contemplation stuff you brought in..."

"...We're trying to practice that ourselves at least," May May added. "Mr. Martinette and his APs hold these weird assemblies," May May continued. "They are saying we should do prayers, not meditation. They want us to follow their Christian values! We're not even Christian! They closed down the service clubs where we help others, like the Gay-Straight Alliance. It's insane!"

"The school is filthy, too," Arielle said. "There's trash everywhere. They stopped picking up the food from the cafeteria 'cause of budget cuts. There are now tons of rats down there! We're seeing rats everywhere! They run wild! In the halls and classrooms too!"

Everyone nodded at the word *rats*. Some shuddered, as did I.

"It's like the school *likes* the rats," Derrick said, "it's like they're letting the rats run the school!"

Letting the rats run the school. I sat there overwhelmed. It all came together. My three rats from hell, Pete, Ratty, and Ayn, who said they never came above ground since they never had to, decided to operate in Brooklyn. I saw them here. Worse, they're in my group's school. *They're here to get back at me.* They've found the way to run the school all right, found a way to infect the administrators, teachers, counselors, and students.

Somehow the rats managed to elevate the worst tendencies already present in high school—the pressure to conform, to compete, promote yourself, and win; the tendency to bully weaker people and resist solidarity with others; the robbing of time that allows you to pay attention, reflect, and think critically; rewarding instant gratification and distractions that benefit those in power…. The rats are not just demagogic wannabes. In this fractioned, hypervigilant society they're also dangerous anti-contemplatives.

In the counseling group last year, we had been working on the idea that sometimes doing nothing—meditation, contemplation— can be a deliberate, radical act that resists capitalist time. We talked about how if you're strategic about it you can make meditation even more than a way to listen and become self-aware. You can see it as a conscious political, rebellious, freeing action in personal, historical, and cosmic ways. When you let go of attachment to your ego you begin to see how we're all interconnected.

"So what are we gonna do, Mr. T.?" Arielle asked. Everyone looked at me with glum, worried faces.

We sat for a while and passed around furtive glances.

I looked down at the two boxes at my side, then along the boardwalk, then out at the ocean. A mild breeze was blowing off the water toward us. I turned and looked at each one of them before I spoke.

"Listen, I met some ... bad people ... they were ... like rats," I began, "I don't know how to explain this exactly, but their thinking, their beliefs, their actions, were just like what you're seeing. I think somehow, they've infested the school."

But how did the rats do it? How did they manage to turn it into a rat lab for their own agenda? I didn't know yet.

The group was silent and just looked at me.

"We're gonna fight back," I said. "We have to prepare ourselves and use all our skills. Like never before."

After a while Billy, the graphic novel maven, spoke up in an excited voice. "Hey, we could be like these comic superheroes I've been reading about. There's a digital web series online about these three superheroes who have to rescue the New Brooklyn, which takes place in the future—the Brooklynite, The Purple Heart, and Red Hook.

"I'm checking out one of them, Red Hook, he has a team of superheroes. It's kinda like us! In the story, the whole borough of Brooklyn becomes New Brooklyn, its heart is broken, it splits off from America, which is, like, cold and greedy and inhumane, and Red Hook, the hero, stands for art and personal expression and altruism. He forms a group of, like, different but united superheroes to take back Brooklyn against a bunch of bad guys, just like we could, and...."

"Woah, slow down Billy," I interrupted. "So, you're saying there's a role model group of superheroes who save Brooklyn?" I had to credit these guys who came up with this idea straightaway, otherwise who knows, they might think I stole it from them.

"Yeah, this guy Dean Haspiel came up with Red Hook, a superhero," Billy replied. "It's cool, he does things like using a subway station as a leak in time, like a cosmic portal, and there's an angel in there. Red Hook makes peace with his inner demons. He embraces his heartache, he and his team of superheroes vow to save Brooklyn...."

Jeez, I thought, cosmic Brooklyn minds think alike. I'm just hearing about this now.

"... I showed it to May May," Billy continued, looking over at her. "You were reading it, right?"

May May nodded. "We could pick up on that story by fighting the bad guys in our school. Red Hook says only altruism, love, can save the world—but hey, so do we, so do a lot of people. I mean, we share a lot of the values in that comic, but we're also different, and we have to find our own way to be Brooklyn superheroes," she said.

"We don't have superpowers though," Derrick said. "Wish we had."

That was my cue.

"Look, gang, you already do! First, you've been practicing contemplation. You know how to slow down time, slow down your mind, to really see and listen and accept what's happening, with yourselves, with others, and as a way to resist a lot of the crap thrown at you. Second, you've been becoming aware of how things work to keep people down, the hidden myths and power structures that govern how people think, what they believe. And third, you have a just vision of what we need to do, how things could be, how they *should* be, for ourselves, for everyone."

I stood up, paced around a bit, and looked at each of them. I thought of the rats and scowled and raised my voice.

"Well, fuck it! We're gonna build up our superpowers, fight these rat-brained bastards, and take back the goddamn school!"

The kids looked startled and stared at me. I had always been careful not to curse in front of them.

"Wow, Mr. T., we never heard you talk like that before," Arielle said.

After a moment Dina and Cami broke the tension and high-five'd each other and started laughing.

"Awright!" both said.

The others relaxed and smiled too.

"You all have, what," I asked, "just a couple of weeks left before you graduate?"

"Yeah, and finals," May May answered.

They all looked at each other.

Dina finally said, "Mr. T., a lot of us have been cutting school, not just 'cause we're seniors, but we can't stand what's going on there."

Derrick sucked his teeth. "Damn, you know, we been cuttin' since we been back, last year and the year before too, even before this shit went down."

I knew that what educators call absenteeism is a chronic problem in many schools. Schools tend to see it as a problem within the kids and don't bother to see how they fail to meet and help them where they're at. The pandemic made it worse as some kids got used to not coming in when the schools reopened.

Last year we talked about hanging in there as a conscious choice. Do it for your highest self, I implored, not because authorities are making you conform, but neither do you want to act out in a way that doesn't solve anything and just messes you up.

"Well," Arielle admitted, "we gotta get through this crazy year or they won't let us graduate."

She looked at the others, who nodded.

"You're right. And you will," I said. "It means, though, you gotta go back to the school until the school year's over."

We sat for a few moments, until I broke the silence.

"Okay, here's what we're gonna do. We're gonna train over the next few days and work on our superpowers. Then we'll be ready to kick ass. Everybody good with that?"

Derrick looked at the others and spoke for the group. "Yo, Mr.T., we all have different projects and things we're doing after school. Like May May is taking judo classes, Billy is doing his artwork, I been goin' to workshops for, you know, working with the Violence Interrupters. But hey, we're down with this shit, and we'll meet every week for as much as we can," he said, his eyes blazing.

The others nodded in assent.

"Good enough," I said. But I worried whether we could get enough training in given the little time we had left.

I turned to the two boxes. The first one I opened, as I suspected, had six large teal vials with child-proof type safety locks, each with one of the kid's names on it. The Dogen Potion. The note inside was for me and gave instructions on how to open them.

The second one had six different customized stylish frames of XK AI Anti-Google Goggles in locked, transparent cases, also with each kid's name embossed on the top, and a similar note.

"Hang on to these two things 'till we meet next time," I told them as I handed out the vials and cases of glasses. "I'll explain how we'll use them to boost our superpowers."

"Wow, these frames are exactly what I love." Each kid said almost the same thing as they showed them to each other. "How did you know this is my style?"

I smiled and shook my head, as much at XK as anything else about the whole crazy scene.

At the same time, doubts flew around my mind like pesky birds. Can we really pull off defeating the rats and overtake the rat-infested school? I shut my eyes and breathed. After a few moments I managed to watch the doubts fly away as passing thoughts, like seagulls soaring out to sea. *Hell yeah, we have to.*

One doubt lingered longer. Was I going to be one more stereotypical Hollywood and comic book-style white male superhero—not exactly in his youthful prime, either—who leads a colorful, diverse league of young sidekicks with special talents? Was I going to play the counterpart of the Magical Negro, the powerful, benevolent White Guy who helps rescue the poor, marginalized, oppressed minorities? The cool teacher, counselor, white shadow coach, the wise, wizened Yoda?

As best I could I was determined to not let that happen. If somebody wanted to see me that way, too damn bad. This wasn't about me, or even about my getting back at the rats. I was gonna work to divest my ego. Yeah, I'm just a white male geezer, some will say, and am not up on everything these kids are into, the latest songs from Beyoncé, Taylor Swift, Bad Bunny, and Megan Thee Stallion. But I'm open to learning and paying respectful attention to where they're at. And I was gonna share things I had the benefit of knowing to try to help the group and the school reach a higher plane. And fine, I'm helping myself too. I vowed to be part of an authentic league, a fellowship in which we all worked together.

If you have come here to help me, you are wasting your time. But if you have come because your liberation is bound up with mine, then let us work together. —Lilla Watson, indigenous Australian, who says she did not first say it

I returned to the second box to close it. At the bottom I almost overlooked an envelope addressed to me. I recognized Maya's handwriting. My heart began to beat out of my chest.

Dear Jacob,
I miss you as much as you miss me. I'm doing Okay. I know it's crazy but I've been following you these last months and am proud of you. I love you and will see you soon—I know you have more to do, so get back to work!
Love, Maya

I felt great joy and relief and started tearing up. A moment later I wondered, what the fuck? That crazy character XK had arranged this. How does XK communicate with her? Why are they keeping this all secretive and leaving me out?

"Mr. T., you okay?" Cami asked.

I nodded and wiped the tears with my hand. Arielle handed me a tissue she pulled from her purse. I thanked her and mopped the rest of my face, blew my nose, and tried to muffle any blubbering I felt was coming on.

"A nice surprise love note from my wife," I managed, "we've been away for each other awhile..." my voice trailed off.

The young women uttered a couple of sympathetic "awws," the two guys sucked their teeth, and all looked concerned.

Whoah, besides feeling embarrassed, so much for my pledge to avoid What About Me-ism. I just broke a basic rule of Socialwork 101: "The client is not there to help *you* deal with your issues. You can disclose and share something appropriately personal if you think it helps them move on."

Well, sometimes things just happen. Maybe they even benefited from seeing me curse and cry despite myself. They—and we together—were now a league of Brooklyn fighters against evil. But they were also young people with varying degrees of vulnerability, and they looked up to me.

I collected myself. "Thanks for your empathy, gang, I really appreciate it. My wife said we'll see each other soon." Not quite, but I hoped.

I then said, "Look, we all want to imagine a great future together and make things better for ourselves and everyone. But hey, we're also here to listen to, and care for, and accept and support each other. That's what we're about too, no matter what happens."

They nodded in silent assent.

Derrick spoke up. "Okay. But calling ourselves superheroes is, like, you know, kinda old..."

"Passé," Arielle broke in.

"... I mean," Derrick went on, "I love Black Panther and Afrofuturism and all but...."

"Yeah, I like the Marvel ones," May May added.

"Nah, DC. Wonder Woman rules," Dina argued.

Cami said, "Yeah, we can be superheroes but that's already a cliché, like all the comics and movies...."

"... and all the sequels," Dina added.

"Time to change our name," said Cami.

We sat in thought.

"How about the BK Dream Team," Billy proposed.

"Yeah!" Arielle shouted. "Any great coach would dream about putting us together as a team. Right, Mr. T.?"

"Of course."

"We fight great together against evil and dumbass stuff," said Dina.

"And we dream good, too, about what everyone needs and should have," said May May.

Derrick had the last word and the last laugh, though. "Well, we ain't no Afrofuture comic book types. But we still superheroes, y'all."

The group and I agreed to meet over the next week. I said I'd see them tomorrow and took the train back to Park Slope and walked home, up the terminal moraine.

CHAPTER NINETEEN

Rat Fighters

We will dance around the poles of awareness and unawareness, attachment and indifference, hope and grief, responsibility and guilt, exploring how these show up in our body, heart, and mind—individually and with others. We will explore how modern life takes our attention, narrowing our salience landscape and diverting our focus from actions that are in support of the greatest depth of consciousness, for the greatest span of sentient beings. — Gail Hochachka, Steffen Munzner

This separation between past, present, and future is only an illusion, if a stubborn one. —Einstein in a letter to the family of his friend, Michele Besso, who had just died

On Thursday, shortly after school, I met the group at our spot on the boardwalk on Coney Island. We sat in a circle around the chess table.

"How are you all?" I asked. "How was your day at school?"

I was met with silence and averted eyes.

"That bad, huh?" I said after a few moments.

"Yeah Mr. T.," Cami then spoke up. "*Mucha jodienda.*"

"Like we said yesterday," Derrick said and sucked his teeth.

I decided to let it go for now. "Okay, we'll move ahead."

We sat and meditated. As often happens afterwards, the group was more open to sharing and listening. I asked how they were feeling and if anything had gone on for them over the weekend.

"I'm tired and scared," Arielle began, "I feel it in my stomach and my chest. A lot of times the last few days." She turned to Derrick.

"I don't know," Derrick said, "I'm kinda numb. Like a blank screen saver." He paused and looked down. We waited to see if he had more to say.

"Well, my homies, I mean some of the dudes still in my old gang, I ran into them on the street Saturday. Same shit. They said I was a pussy for leaving and hanging out with you all, and for stayin' in school. One of them, though, said he heard on the street there was a lot of fighting going down at our school and said they should go over there and bust some heads. We almost got into a fight ourselves. Then they all got distracted. Oh yeah, we saw a big-ass rat, just stopped and stared at us. Our 'hood is full of them. I was able to walk away."

The group was silent and took it in.

"Wow, that's cold," May May then said.

"Hell yeah," added Arielle. "We're really glad you chose to hang out with us."

The others nodded. May May went up to Derrick and gave him a fist bump that led to a hug from her and Arielle, sitting beside him.

Derrick looked down. "Thanks, y'all," he told them, and after a while he glanced up at everyone.

After another long silence, Dina spoke.

"I have waves of stuff in my body—feeling helpless, then anger, then hope, then helpless again," she said.

We waited. She shook her head and hugged herself. "That's it for now," then turned and looked at May May.

"Same," May May said, sighing. "Just trying to deal with my stuff, I guess, going through all these changes. I got plenty on my plate." She then looked at Billy.

"Scared and feelin' down," Billy said.

I nodded. "Anything up at home?"

He looked at me and the others. "Yeah. My dad..." he started to choke up, then managed to go on.

"You know, he's been mad at me since I came out. He won't even look at me, forget about even saying anything. He comes home with *The Post* and turns on Fux Fake News and sits there all night. He even has an old buddy that works there, calls him Jimbo. My mom, she, she just tries to keep him from going off. Brings him his dinner with a few beers in the TV room. Yesterday he's in there, watching the Mets game in between the Fux liars. I had to go in and cross in front of the TV and get some of my art stuff from the closet. Then he goes off on me."

Billy started tearing up. Arielle, a regular socialworker, always keeps tissues handy and passed him one.

After a moment Billy mimicked his dad's angry, ugly face. "'Get outta my way,' he snarled at me, 'go play with your dolls!' Then he tells me he's going to the PTA meeting at the high school this week—it's tonight, in fact. My mom told me he'd found out on his social media site they were cracking down on the libs and other pussies in the school and started going last month. He never showed any interest in my schoolwork or artwork or anything before. 'I'm gonna run for office!' he says. 'We're gonna kick some ass, that means all a youse perverts, illegal aliens, A-rabs, all your trans whatever pals! I'm gonna get Jimbo to help me!' I ran out as fast as I could."

The others stood up, as did Billy, and they gave him a collective, swaying hug.

"Thanks, guys," he said, and sat down. After a few moments he turned and nodded to Cami.

"Well, I'm more pissed than anything," Cami scowled. *So much for mindfulness calming you down*, I smiled to myself. Sometimes we need righteous anger, too. "I wanna get going on how we're gonna get these *pendejos* who are messing up our school."

"I hear ya, we will," I said. She seemed more angry than usual, though, and I said that to her. I sensed something else was going on. "How're your dad and brother also doing?" They were all still coping with the death of her mami.

Cami raised her brows in a sorrowful way. "Papi's still so sad, I help him out as much as I can. As for Roberto, or Rob as he now likes to call himself, he can go to *el carajo*. He's become this asshole *blanquito* who even admires that idiot you-know-who. He hangs around with these white guys in the business school and—sorry, May May—some other Asian business majors, they all just want to work on Wall Street and make a ton of money. They don't give a damn about anyone but themselves. Like, they think the homeless and immigrants deserve what they get, it's their fault and their problem. We're always arguing about stuff like that."

Cami was agitated enough to stand up.

"The other day, though, I, I couldn't believe it, I caught him in my room, reading my journal I had left open! For like a second I had to run out to help papi with some clothes and didn't get a chance to lock my door."

Some of us gasped, me included.

"I was so, angry! I screamed *get the fuck out of here*! He just looked at me with dead eyes and left the room. I couldn't calm down. What's even worse, I had written down what we've been talking about here and how we want to take back the school. He must have seen some of that! I'm mad at myself too!" Cami started to tear up.

"Girl, you can't blame yourself," Dina moved next to Cami and hugged her. Arielle gave her a tissue.

Cami blew her nose, then said, "Yeah, maybe not totally. He came back and he ... Dina what's that word? Like this." She made a face.

Dina recognized it. "Smirked."

"Yeah, he smirked," Cami went on. "He said he already knew what was going on at our school through his socials and was glad the school was cracking down on us *radicals and troublemakers. Coño pendejo!*"

"We're going through a lot of pain," I said, and didn't have to suggest another group hug—they already formed one.

After a while Cami returned to full strength. "I'm ready. Let's move on!"

I had been thinking about a strategy that could use the group members' various strong points and skills to combat the very three poisons embodied and promoted by the three rats in the school: delusion, lies, and disinformation (Ratty), greed, selfishness, competitiveness, clinging to ego (Ayn), and meanness, bullying, and controlling and harming others (Pete).

"Here's what we'll do," I said once we'd sat again. "You'll work in pairs. You'll practice and engage in your superpowers. Your higher self-awareness is gonna help you. We're gonna be strategic as hell."

They looked at each other, then sat up straight and leaned forward.

"Dina and Cami, you're the Bullshit Busters. You're gonna oversee confronting the right-wing lies, authoritarian thinking, and conspiracy crap they're spreading in the school like you already do. Now, though, you'll power up—speak truth to power, ramp up ways to bring in more critical thinking, question the ways people look at things."

I looked off at the ocean for a moment.

"Arielle and Billy, you're the Community Connectors. You're skilled organizers. You're gonna fight the selfishness, the myths they want you to believe that competing and winning and branding is the only way to be, that greed is good and that giving a damn for others is for suckers. The way you challenge their mean-spirited, antidemocratic, racist, BS is to organize our allies and show a better way for everyone, through care, empathy, and fierce compassion.

"Derrick and May May, you're the Defensive Disarmers. You're gonna use your fierce compassionate warrior minds and disciplined, defensive, nonviolent fighting skills and strengths. You're gonna work to disarm the bullies and authoritarian fools who think they can force people to think and be like them. You'll work with those who are open to change and peaceful ways to help themselves and others.

"Each of us, though, is gonna use all our powers at some point, everything we've been practicing and thinking about. How we've become aware of our feelings and our relationships; how we see their connections to what's happening in the school, in our community, and society. How everything is connected."

I looked at each one. They were all on high alert. "What do you think?" I was making this shit up and hoped they'd go for it.

Everyone said they were good with their assignment and were eager to get going. I told them we'd go over and discuss their assignments tomorrow. They all agreed we would reconvene then, and they would bring their superpower boosters that we'd unlock and learn how to use.

I continued to obsess about how we'd manage to find both the means and the time to prep for the battle to come.

The Cosmic Disembodied Dogen Retreat Center

I'm so far ahead of my time, I'm 'bout to start another life. —Jay-Z, "Hovi Baby"

That Thursday night I had a lucid dream. I was walking on a bright green, moss-grown path through a lush thicket of trees that led up a gentle slope. Ahead was a three-story wood-frame building, covered with shimmering, multicolored mosaic tiles. At first sight it was a kind of zendo. I looked again and it appeared to be a synagogue, then a mosque, then a church, the way a house of worship designed for one group changed hands in different epochs, like in Spain or the Lower East Side. A sign in front said *The Cosmic Disembodied Dogen Retreat Center: Welcome Brooklyn Dream Team.* Smaller signs pointed to the left for *The Bullshit Busters*, right for *The Community Connectors,* upstairs for *The Defensive Disarmers.*

When I awoke on Friday, I knew what we had to do.

The afternoon was humid with a white sky over boardwalk and ocean. The group was anxious and eager to get started, even after we meditated.

"Okay, we're going to a place that doesn't exist," I told them, just to shake them up. They looked at me like I had just grown a second head. Some made that dismissive *pfihh* sound when you hear bullshit.

I smiled like some kind of idiot. "Everyone please get out those little bottles and take a tiny swig."

They made sourpuss faces, and some sucked their teeth but did as I asked. After each had downed the Dogen Potion, Derrick smacked his lips. May May smiled and said "Ahh." Dina and Cami gave each other a look of pleasant surprise. "Not half bad," Billy declared. "A presumptive blend of Chardonnay and Dr. Pepper," Arielle said as she raised her pinky.

"Okay, now take the eyeglasses out of the cases and put them on," I said and instructed them on the unlocking process. "Ooh." The gals started posing in pairs, made duck lips, touched heads, and took selfies with each other.

It took a few minutes for the Dogen Potion to kick in. "Now touch the button on the side of the frame. Take five slow, deep breaths." They each did. "Now allow yourselves to be ... transported."

I shut my eyes, touched the frame button, and visualized the Cosmic Disembodied Dogen Retreat Center for the Brooklyn Dream Team, somewhere in cosmic time and space. Wherever the fuck that was.

In a few more moments we all found ourselves on the moss-grown path leading to the Retreat Center. Everyone looked around at the woods and each other.

"Holy shit!" was pretty much the collective response.

"This way," I said and led them up the slope. The group was stunned into silence. When they saw the signs, I told each pair to follow them to their assignment.

I was able to attend all three workshops/morale-boosting sessions at once. Don't ask me how.

The Bullshit Busters

The Bullshit Busters session was run by some cosmic Black Americans who spoke truth to power. They rejected lies and deceit and wanted to help create a society based on righteous honesty and awareness. Paul Robeson, the singer, actor, and civil rights activist; Brooklyn feminist and progressive politician Shirley Chisholm; and political intellectual, anti-racist, and author James Baldwin. They were accompanied by musicians who had sung the truth: leftist activist Woody Guthrie, conscious rapper Tupac Shakur, and martyred anti-fascist singer and songwriter Victor Jara from Chile, tortured and murdered by the US-backed military coup arranged by Henry Kissinger, who was invited by Woody and Tupac. Everyone sat around a circle, introduced themselves, and took turns speaking to the kids.

Dina and Cami, like the others in their sessions, could hardly contain their excitement and kept putting their hands over their mouths and looked at each other. They furiously took notes on their cellphones and snapped plenty of pictures.

"Here's the main theme, yo," Tupac began. "Don't believe everything you hear. *Real eyes, realize, real lies.*"

In his deep voice, Robeson told them, "Find common ground where possible. They stick to what they believe out of fear. Listen to what they *aren't* saying, between the lines. They delude themselves as well. Show them a better way to meet their real needs."

"Be fearless. Don't let anything go unchallenged," Chisholm added. "And do the research. Take on the book banning. Call out the rumors and BS being passed around in school, on social media, and from Fux Fake News."

Jara said, "*Use su entendimiento de cómo piensan o la visión del mundo de sus opositores. Hechos nada más no convencen a nadie; esta gente necesita ver el mundo de otra perspectiva.*"

Cami translated for Dina: "Use your understanding of people's mental frameworks or worldview of your opponents. Facts alone don't convince people; they need to see the world differently."

Robeson nodded and said, "Challenge their authoritarian worldview. You're also Bully Busters. They love revenge and think bullying is the way to get back at those they feel have wronged them. That's deluded, distorted, and immoral thinking and always comes back to bite them."

Baldwin paused and looked at both Dina and Cami before he spoke. "Another distorted belief that needs to be challenged is the zero-sum myth—that if Black people gain, it must be at the expense of white people. People's rights don't diminish the rights of others."

Guthrie smiled and strummed his guitar. "Speak as if you have an imaginary smart audience who's listening—point out to 'them' what your opponents are saying."

Tupac told them to speak the truth everywhere. "Ask them, who do you think gains from the lies and delusions? *They have money for war but can't feed the poor*."

"You can't reach everyone, though," Baldwin stressed. "You're not going to win over all the cultists and trolls, so don't waste time by just being rational or playing nice, or lose your cool and slip into moral outrage."

Chisholm smiled and winked at Cami and Dina. "Flummox them. Use humor to point out how they're being defensive. Don't hesitate to mock them when they fight dirty. Kill them with sarcasm and repeat!"

The Community Connectors

The Community Connectors session for Arielle and Billy was run by fearless cosmic American organizers: Harriet Tubman, leader of the Underground Railroad; Chicano rights activist Cesar Chavez, co-founder of the United Farm Workers union; Elizabeth Gurley Flynn, IWW labor organizer of the 1912 Lawrence textile strike; Jane Jacobs, anti–Vietnam War protester and community activist who led successful fights against Robert Moses' urban highway projects; Harvey Milk, political activist leader for the San Francisco gay community; and Bayard Rustin, leader in movements for civil rights, socialism, nonviolence, and gay rights and who organized the 1963 March on Washington.

"You'll need to use all your organizing and social skills," Tubman began. "Find the kids who are allies and form solidarity and support groups, like you've done with the women and the Gay-Straight Alliance and the Climate Change Fighters in your school."

"Keep expanding them into bigger networks," Gurley Flynn added. "Encourage them to speak with their friends and keep building the movement."

Jacobs said, "It's a strength to organize a variety of regular people and stand up to authoritarians."

Rustin told them, "Notice what the other side gets out of what they do. If it's no longer profitable for them, it will weaken them."

Chavez smiled at Arielle and Billy. "*Si se puede!*"

"Wow," Arielle whispered to Billy. "He and Dolores Huerta came up with that!" The two shivered with excitement.

Chavez continued. "Every moment is a chance to organize. Everyone could be an activist. Every minute gives us a chance to change the world."

"You're gonna do this not just by calling out these myths but by showing a better way to be, by your smart, compassionate actions," Milk said to Arielle and Billy. "Teach and practice what you've learned about caring and generosity, and empathy and wise compassion."

"Yes, mutual aid is very important. You want to nurture and support your group spiritually, in the name of freedom," Tubman told them.

"You have to have collective action to make changes," Rustin affirmed. "Find ways to stay unified, find common ground."

Milk said, "Stay aware of how you can turn anger and frustration into positive action."

Jacobs added, "Refuse to let them marginalize you. Don't be intimidated by those in power. You have your own strengths."

"We'll leave you with the song about our martyred union organizer, Joe Hill," Gurley Flynn smiled and said, "And joining us in the song is ... Joe Hill!"

... And standing there as big as life
and smiling with his eyes,
says Joe, "What they can never kill
went on to organize,
went on to organize

The Defensive Disarmers

The Defensive Disarmers meeting included an international group of moral leaders, defenders, resisters, and warriors who fought and, except for one, were martyred in the service of universal righteousness: Martin Luther King Jr., assassinated nonviolent civil rights and anti-war leader; Pedro Albizu Campos, Puerto Rican national hero and revolutionary, leader of an island-wide strike, imprisoned, harassed, and murdered by the FBI and US government; Marek Edelman, Bundist leader who fought in the Warsaw Ghetto Uprising and survived, working in memory of his martyred comrades and the six million Jews; Minerva Mirabal, who led the revolutionary resistance movement in the Dominican Republic against dictator Trujillo, who murdered her and her two sisters; Fred Hampton, Black Panther and founder of the Rainbow Coalition, a multicultural alliance of street gangs that worked to end infighting and work for social change, before being murdered by the Chicago Police; and Mahatma Gandhi, who disarmed the British colonialists and liberated India with nonviolence and was assassinated by a religious fanatic.

May May and Derrick were stunned and tried to stop shaking as they listened to their teachers and took notes.

Mirabal spoke first. "May May, you will mobilize your judo class. You have all been learning how to turn an enemy's own physical and mental energy against them. With your skills practice centering your energy and your focus on this task, you must work to disarm them."

King said, "Derrick, you will lead some of the other young men in your Violence Interrupters and peace makers workshops. Bring them into school to help them see the misunderstandings and resolve conflicts."

"You both know how to mentally and physically disarm bullies," Gandhi followed up. "You're going to use as many nonviolent practices as you can to stop them."

Campos told them, "You'll encircle them with fearlessness and demonstrate to them you're not intimidated. You'll show them and tell them that that's real strength. At bottom, bullies are cowards who shrink back when you challenge them."

"See through the enemy," Hampton said. "See what makes them act that way. Most are scared inside."

Edelman spoke. "If at some time, only when you must, you resort to defensive fighting, use your meditative skills when you do. You're going to try to be nonviolent, like Martin and Mahatma say, but sometimes you can't—some enemies are too far gone."

"You know what I've said: 'Be the change you wish to see in the world,' Gandhi said to them.

"You two can do it!"

May May and Derrick looked at each other and shook their heads.

"No one said it's easy to love your enemy," added King. "It takes a spiritual practice. I'm happy to see you and your friends are doing that. Channel your aggression and anger toward making the world better."

Mirabal told them, "You are not just resisting to help liberate your school, you're fighting for your communities, and for all people."

"I want to second that," Edelman added. "Yours is a struggle that is both for your own people and for the sake of human history."

Campos chimed in, "You have the right to fight to be yourselves, to be free of others controlling and enslaving you."

"When you must fight, hold the vision you have of a decent and just society and world in your mind's eye," Hampton said.

Mirabal spoke last. "We'll leave you with a stanza from the poem, "Still I Rise," by our cosmic sister Maya Angelou. Here she is!"

You may shoot me with your words,
You may cut me with your eyes,
You may kill me with your hatefulness,
But still, like air, I'll rise.

Afterwards

Afterwards we reconvened and I walked with the six of them a short way down the verdant path. No one said a word. We were all exhilarated and exhausted.

"You all have some idea what you're gonna do tomorrow in school?" I asked.

They nodded.

"Wow, they were so inspiring!" May May said. "Plus we learned some incredible stuff we're gonna use, from these..." her voice trailed off.

"Cosmic superheroes," Arielle said.

"Shit was dope!" Derrick shouted.

Dina brought up the difficult and the unspoken. "Uh, yeah, Mr. T., but these, like, cosmic superheroes, they're all, like, dead, right? And how did we get here? I hope you can get us back."

Here we go. Too much to explain in a short time.

"First, not to worry, we're going back the same way..."

"Ah," Billy figured. "These glasses had something to do with it, right?"

"... and that stuff we drank," Cami concluded.

"Yes. Listen, I'm gonna give you the short of it for now since we gotta get back and fight the rat ... the rat-brained people right away. The potion, the glasses, I, I, was lucky to get them from someone I met with their own superpowers, and then get them to you...."

I was starting to sweat. I could feel their eyes locked on me and took a breath.

"These boosters, they're hacks, shortcuts, to get us to realize that … time, history, we're all part of it … those great leaders you got to be with just now, yeah, they died, but what's real is that the past is always here, it's always with us, and so is the future. We touch both, we touch everyone…. *You* all embody your past ancestors, *you* all embody our future…." *Along with mine, after I'm gone.*

I was afraid I was losing it, almost doubting it all, and had to pause for another breath.

"And these people, especially, they let go of their egos in the service of a greater good! Some were martyrs, they gave up their lives for others. They melded their selves into the eternal love of the universe! So, like, by doing that, in that way, they *didn't* die! So, you, just now, you got to see something true, those people are always here, it's just a different kind of here … it's a different kind of now … and you could hang out with them because of your own superpowers of meditation and insights into history and justice for everyone…." I stopped, exhausted.

"We know, Mr. T.," Arielle stepped in and saved me. "Tell him, gang."

"For real," Derrick said, "when we meditate, we can slow down and expand time."

Dina said, "We practice centering ourselves…."

"and being patient…" added Cami, "although I can't always, it's a pain in the ass," she laughed.

"I'm starting to realize what I call *self* is not something to own, like how they want us to own everything…" Billy said.

"We want to send out smart compassion for all, starting with ourselves, expand it out to everyone," said May May.

"Even *pendejos*," Cami added.

"Sometimes I can see the hidden threads, we're all connected with everything," Billy said, "with everyone that is, was, and will be."

"We can see a great future, where people know themselves, where they work things out and get along!" Arielle said.

"I love watching my mind," May May added, "how it tries to catch me with its own nonsense, but I get on top of it and let it go, I go to a higher place. I don't have to follow it."

"Yeah, we get to know our mind and how we feel," Derrick said. "Plus, we're not fooled by the bullshit out there that keeps us down and from being our best selves."

"We know about the hidden sources of power, of how and why people are so fearful and hateful..." Dina said.

We gotta use our superpowers to fight all this shit," Derrick said, "there's too much dumbass racist ignorance...."

"And mean, greedy people..." said Billy.

"And *pendejos,*" Cami chimed in.

"Even *pendejos* need our help!" Arielle shouted to laughter.

"... and our love," Dina said.

"Thanks gang, you got it, you always have," I said, relieved as hell.

"And we have each other," May May said.

We joined hands in a circle and breathed. "On Monday, take another swig from that bottle, and use the glasses the way we went over them," I said. "They'll boost the superpowers we've been practicing all this time we've been together. Plus, the ones you learned today."

After a few moments I told them to pinch the side of their glasses and visualize returning to their homes. It was dusk but still light out. I wished them lots of luck and love and a good weekend and said we'd meet Monday after school at our usual place on the boardwalk. After pinching my own goggles, I found myself in my apartment, and I promptly fell asleep on the couch with my clothes on.

CHAPTER TWENTY

Late Stage Purgatory: O'er Thyself I Crown and Mitre Thee

Behold the sun there shining on thy brow;
behold the tender grass, the flowers and shrubs,
which here the soil yields of itself alone.
Until in happiness those lovely eyes
appear, which, weeping, made me come to thee,
thou mayst be seated, or among them walk.
From me expect no further word or sign.
Free, right and sound is thine own will, and wrong
were not to act according to its hest;
hence o'er thyself I crown and mitre thee.
—Virgil to Dante, Purgatorio XXVII, trans. Courtney Langdon

Surrealism is the exaltation of freedom, revolt, imagination and love...[It] is above all a revolutionary movement. Its basic aim is to lessen and eventually to completely resolve the contradiction between everyday life and our wildest dreams. By definition subversive, surrealist thought and action are intended not only to discredit and destroy the forces of repression, but also to emancipate desire and supply it with new poetic weapons. —The Chicago Surrealist Group, 1976, in Freedom Dreams, Robin D.G. Kelley

I spent part of a restless weekend trying to clean and vacuum the apartment, filled with hope Maya would return soon. For the time being, I decided to let go of trying to figure out how my rats got to infest the school and what we had to do to stop them.

No visit or text from Xen Kohen, either. Ah, who needs them, I tried to convince myself, I've got the tools for now, I can help the gang do this on my own. On the other hand, of course, I still owed XK, in more ways than one, and had just found out my Hired Power was a crucial link to Maya—how, I didn't know. Well, XK wasn't Virgil, he could still show up in some form or another.

That Friday night I dreamed Maya and I were in the kitchen—she, as always, the creative and talented cook, assembling a curried vegetable mélange, me in my usual role of unskilled sous chef. The radio was playing some kind of low-key classical piece on WQXR, like one of Bach's cello suites. Suddenly it switched to Linda Ronstadt's cover of the Stones' "Tumbling Dice." *Rank outsiders. Partners in crime.* We dropped the utensils and started dancing and laughing like crazed teens.

I woke with a vague feeling Maya had something to do with summoning Xen Kohen, to help me recover. Now XK was gone, as was she.

Early Saturday morning, feeling sleep deprived, hallucinogenic, I rode the subway to Manhattan and sat by the river in Battery Park. I walked up and across to Chinatown for some chow fun, further up to Washington Square, and beyond to Central Park. There I sat on a bench and closed my eyes....

Manhattan, Island of Dreams Dyspeptic and Divine

How often have I had this longing for an infinite walk—of going unimpeded, until the movement of my body as I walk fell into the flight of streets under my feet—until I in my body and the world in its skin of earth were blended into a single act of knowing. —Alfred Kazin

Fragment from the Great American Novel, *Raintree County*, *by Ross Lockridge Jr.:*
He then dimly understood that every moment of his life, like every journey of his body, returned at last to the same mysterious place that had nothing to do with space. And he wondered at the miracle by which he had been spun out of the substance of his mother's flesh in some prehistoric era that had nothing to do with time. Somehow he had sprung without a pollution into the world of names. And the names made all the difference and rescued him from the feeling of being lost in a void of earth and night.

Before the pandemic I would wander about Manhattan, island of dreams dyspeptic and divine. I was all over the place. I tried to hold on to the way things are supposed to be. To stay grounded, as the saying goes. I could not. The ground has disappeared everywhere. Everything has become unmoored. Everyday life is spinning out of control. The lack of community. The lack of ease with oneself. The way people self-monitor as personal brands. The way people divide themselves....

You might have found me on a pier in the lower Hudson on a blue flame October afternoon. The foghorn bleats, the choppers buzz, the tugs slice through the gilded foil of the river. Manhattan feels like the still point of the turning world.

Without warning the pier breaks off from its base. It starts to float away and swirl in a slow eddy. Nobody notices. I want to enjoy it but am getting vertigo. Somebody offers me a Xanax with an IPA chaser. I start to relax. The pier is now airborne and floats over Manhattan. Some office workers wave. The sun turns from day-glow orange to lethal pink...

I might have shown up in the courtyard of the Frick Museum on a hot and humid summer day. The air quality is deemed unacceptable. I do not accept this air, and no wonder. The air is comprised of visible particulates of leftover crap from a forgotten era: iPods, fax machines, floppy discs, walkmen, phonebooks, squeegees, and Whip Inflation Now buttons.

All this is suspended in a gelatinous mass in front of my face like a bad Calder stabile. The heat causes the fountain in the museum courtyard to boil over. The air is so saturated there is no place for the water to go. The Vermeers start to sweat and melt into Dali-esque globs. The acid in the air eats the polish off the antique chairs. The entire museum has become a soft sculpture by Claes Oldenburg. I step outside. On a bus an ad for a health club says All Butts Are Off. Another says HEADCASE Mindfulness Studio: Have a Nice Day....

You might have seen me in the cellar of a restaurant down in Chinatown at 1 a.m. on a weekend, staring at a plate of undulating noodles. The room is a fluorescent biosphere. We are close to the earth's core. Any closer and we are in China.

The waiters know something but won't tell. The chopsticks are trying to tap out a message. The tea leaves do synchronized swim patterns in the glass. I order the house special, blastula with sautéed tao-fu in spicy sauce. To go. I ask them to hold the MSG.

Soon green smoke starts to pour out of the kitchen from a wok in heat. It envelops the room and the patrons, who are from New Jersey, yell, "What the fuck is that?!" But I know. The waiters know too, and nod at me. They place my food in a plastic I Love NY bag. I climb the stairs with my order while the others are writhing on the floor. They try to get up but can't. Their cellphones explode in their hands. One crawls to an ancient payphone behind the counter. Of course it spits back his quarter. Outside their cars are being towed away....

Now I wanted to be a contemplative urban flâneur, open to any experience, losing myself in the sights and sounds and crowds, freely reflecting on my dilemmas.

Instead, since the pandemic lockdown, I have more often felt forced to expend my energy dodging all sorts of traffic, crowded pavements, larger vehicles, anarchic drivers, cyclists, e-bikes...

Today, my inner flâneur has been replaced by a neurotic curmudgeon.... There are few more effective ways to think through a philosophical or personal problem than by taking a long walk...But this is possible only as long as the flâneur's peaceable, rhythmic perambulation remains relatively uninterrupted…. A city that no longer accommodates wandering no longer accommodate wondering, too, and a flâneur without freedom falls into a sort of zombified routine. —Shaan Sachdev, "Baudelaire Would Be Run Over in New York City Today"

At best I was a social critic. With the AI XK goggles I could see beneath the surface of the everyday injustices and sadness of the city. I saw the life history of some disheveled homeless men. I saw stores forced to close during the pandemic, having fought a losing battle against high rents and no business.

And I was reduced in part to neurotic broodhist, obsessing over Maya, the group, the rats, unable at times to get out of my head and lose myself.

I felt the need to ride the subway to mystic Nicholas Roerich's Museum, housed in an elegant brownstone on the Upper West Side, and disappear into some of his Buddhist paintings of the Himalayas.

Rat Dream

That night I had a disturbing lucid dream. The three rats were sitting around plotting how to get back at me, but I couldn't make out the details.

Ayn: Get to his wife. Kidnap and hold her ransom.

Pete: We can't find huh. My boys have tried, threatened huh co-workers at the hospital, they don't know nuttin about where she is.

Ratty: My cyberhackers can't locate her either. They say she's behind some new kind of firewall they can't breech.

Ayn: We'll get to the school where his counseling group is. Change its consciousness, how it operates. Enlist the school bully boys. Flood everyone with disinformation.

I barely slept. On Sunday morning I rose at dawn and decided to walk through Brooklyn to try to process what I'd dreamt and clear my head.

I walked over to Prospect Park, then south to the border of Green-Wood Cemetery, through a bit of Sunset Park. It was a fine spring day with low humidity that yielded a clear sky.

Fragment from *Brooklyn, the Wide, Low Borough of Light* by Pete Hamill:
... in Brooklyn, the visitor, whether native son or total stranger, can experience a very special sense of beauty.... Brooklyn is still the wide, low borough of light, bouncing off the harbor and the ocean (out by Coney Island), a place of big skies, a place where you can see weather, not simply defend against it.... The light is immanent, muted, a promise.

Among artist Jacob Lawrence's many works, I love *Fulton and Nostrand,* a painting from the mid-1950s of a lively street scene in Bed-Stuy when he lived and worked nearby. It always felt like some kind of warm community scene I wanted to join.

Life itself—being alive—has a rhythm. It derives from all its gathered moments of resistance and flow. The dynamic is fueled in part by the tension between inner life and company.... Lawrence painted this rhythm.... Lawrence yields only so much to the prevailing taste for abstraction. He loved people. He loved street life. He loved narrative, psychology and secrets. All of which he squeezed into this picture. —Sebastian Smee, "Inside Out," on the painting Fulton and Nostrand

It took me a few subway lines to get there. The spot now resembled little of what was in the painting, so with the flip of the XK AI Anti-Google Goggles I stood on a corner and entered the time and space Lawrence had rendered.

By the way, these futurist goggles are superior to the commercialized so-called Immersive Experience virtual reality ones in which people pay to "be" inside a Van Gogh painting like *Starry Night.* With these XK goggles you are transported inside the painting to the past or even some future and witness the scene as if you were there, because you are.

Just walking around in my twenty-first-century pandemic clothes I must have stood out like a white cannellini bean that fell into a pot of *frijoles negros.* On a corner I spotted Marva Williams carrying a shopping bag and went up to her with a big smile.

"Wow, this is great to see you!" I said. She looked askance at me, then around at the all-Black neighborhood from which white people had fled. This was in the fifties, remember, although since then white millennials have been moving in, buying and fixing up Bed-Stuy brownstones.

"Jacob, watchoo doin' here?"

"Well," I sputtered, "I always liked Jacob Lawrence, and his vision of community, I don't get to feel it much...."

"Don't tell me you're looking for the magical Negro to save your ass," Marva Williams said, and laughed.

No, I'm here 'cause I need, I don't know, all the connection, support, and inspiration I can get. Hey, I mean, like I always admired leaders like Harriet Tubman, Rosa Parks, Michelle Obama, they're great..." As I was saying this, we both noticed a group of young girls on the sidewalk jumping double Dutch. "See, even those girls right there, their skill, their teamwork, it's inspiring, I don't know how they do it!"

"Yeah, I used to be good at Double Dutch myself. And I can tell you, in a few years some of us Black women are gonna deliver some justice to this racist system. Meanwhile, ol' XK told me you're helping your kids, fightin' the rats. Way to go. Stick with it. There might be a time I can help."

"Hey, just hearing from an XK alum who's doing well is support enough for me, thanks."

I wondered how she met up with XK.

"Look, I'm a descendant of Harriet Tubman. I've always been angry, always looking for both the inner and the outer underground railroad. One night XK came to me in a dream."

Marva paused.

"At first I did a lot of arguing with XK. It's like in the Old Testament where some of those guys talk back to God. You know, Abe, Moses. More, though, like your guy Jacob with that angel. Sometimes I didn't know if we were wrestling, hugging, dancing, or maybe even getting it on." She laughed.

Is that what I've been doing? I took a deep breath and looked around at the bustling street.

"After a while XK helped me find a way I can keep my feelings and still work toward real freedom that I, that we all need to do."

Marva winked but then said, "Keep an eye out for some saboteurs close to your kids. Mind everything."

I gave her a puzzled look but before I could ask her what she meant, Marva turned on her heels and quickly walked away. I called out to thank her again as she disappeared into the crowd.

I returned home and tried to nap but could only manage a restless, dreamless, semi-sleep. I woke up groggy, then crossed Eastern Parkway and caught the last few open hours of the Brooklyn Botanic Garden.

The Garden is a sanctuary for Maya and me, as it is for many, especially in the warmer seasons, but really anytime, it is a place as near to heaven in Brooklyn as anyone could find. Maybe it is damn heaven. Or at least on the border. Recall, it's on the terminal moraine.

One of my favorite sections is the Shakespeare Garden. It's scattered with quotes from the bard's plays that reference herbs, staked on mini signposts next to the herb plants themselves. I stopped in front of some thyme adjacent to a sign with a line from Oberon, the mischievous and unfaithful fairy king, spoken to his servant Puck, in a *Midsummer Night's Dream*, a dreamlike, playful play:

I know a bank where the wild thyme blows,
Where oxlips and the nodding violet grows,
Quite overcanopied with luscious woodbine,
With sweet muskroses, and with eglantine (Act 2, Scene 1)

I sat on a favorite bench of ours and pondered the dream about the three rats. I could see what they did but still didn't know how they did it. I also knew I had to look out for what Marva Williams said about saboteurs.

I reread Maya's note, which I carried everywhere. Brooding on it, I feared I would share the same fate as poor Malvolio, whom Maria, observing him shadow boxing from behind a boxwood bush, predicts for him in *Twelfth Night*. The quote was posted on a staked sign adjacent to one such bush:

He has been yonder i' the sun practising behavior to his own shadow this half hour. Observe him, for the love of mockery, for I know this letter will make a contemplative idiot of him. (Act 2, Scene 5)

To try to get another angle on things, I walked a few feet across the path to the Japanese Tea Garden and sat on one of the covered benches inside the viewing platform next to the pond. No one else was there, which was unusual.

The weeping cherry trees on the other side of the pond were past their peak but still beautiful. I gazed out at the red wooden Torii Gate farther out in the pond itself. A Torii, I looked up, represents entrance to a sacred space, the boundary between the secular world and holy ground. It signals the presence of a Shinto shrine nearby, and Maya and I sometimes visited the one hidden on the hill on the other side of the pond.

The time has to be right; one has to be, by chance or intention, upon the border of two worlds. And sometimes these two borders may shift or interpenetrate and one sees the miraculous. —Loren Eiseley

The pond itself is stocked with koi, some golden orange, others white speckled black, that often gather just below the platform. They likely have been spoiled by people who have thrown bits of food at them in the past and so are always hoping for more.

I looked up koi with my goggles. They are intelligent and spiritually significant. In Japanese culture koi stand for luck, new beginnings, and resilience, persistence, and strength of purpose in the face of adversity. They also symbolize love and friendship, and more people worldwide see them as standing for peace. The word *koi* in Japanese is also a homophone for a word that means affection or love. Maybe they'll help me out in some way, I hoped.

Seeing the koi in the pond reminded me of the fish in two of my favorite poems. In each one the poet's longing for connection with another and with nature transforms the fish into a human form of love and desire. I was feeling the same deep need.

One fish with whom my inner teen—a hopeless romantic still pining after unobtainable objects of desire—will always be in love is the little silver trout in Yeats' "Song of Wandering Aengus." The narrator went fishing, out to the hazel wood, he tells us, *because a fire was in my head* and caught a trout in a stream. The fish transforms into *a glimmering girl/ with apple blossoms in her hair* who calls him by his name and runs away. The narrator, now an old man, refuses to give up pursuing and realizing his dream—*till time and times are done*!

My second fish is Richard Brautigan's "Your Catfish Friend" (1968), a poem I've loved since the seventies.

Just so you know *I* know what *you* already know: the word *catfish* is now a verb used among Gen Z online daters to refer to the act of creating a false identity in order to lure someone into a romantic relationship, which has sometimes even led to dangerous and lethal outcomes.

Some well-intentioned words get corrupted—for example, right-wing assholes have managed to convert "woke" and "social justice warrior" into snide put-downs. For years, Madison Avenue hucksters have appropriated "spiritual," "radical," "cosmic," "zen," "mindful," and "revolutionary" to sell us a variety of crap. Not here. I'm holding on to the original meaning of my catfish.

So, in Brautigan's poem, the narrator imagines he lives as a catfish at the bottom of a pond, and if you, lonely, troubled reader, were to come by, admire the pond, and say "I wish somebody loved me," *I'd* love you, the catfish says, and you'd then no longer feel lonely but would be at peace....

I could have used a good cry. Instead, I fell into a semi-conscious state between missing Maya—despite her note, she still wasn't returning my texts or calls—and meditating and brooding about all the sadness and pain in the world and what to do about the rats.

My reverie was short-lived.

"Ah, Jacob san." I jumped and opened my eyes. I knew the voice but didn't know where it was coming from. I turned in all directions to look around. No one else was there on the platform.

"Down here."

No.

I bent down along the side of the platform and saw one gold koi that had broken off from the others. Its head bobbed to the surface and its mouth was open.

"Where the hell you been?" I was more exhausted than angry and didn't feel like arguing or getting into anything stressful.

"Here and there, Jacob san," XK, the Japanese Garden pond koi said, with his head well above the water. "I thought you could use a break and carry on without me."

I sighed. "Yes and no. I still need to figure out how to help the group gear up to fight the rats in short order. And now I know you know where Maya is, and she's working with you somehow. Thanks." I was just too wiped out to be sarcastic or even press the issue.

"Well, I guess it's fitting you're a koi," I continued, "you're a spiritual being who's supposed to give me peace, love, and hope through perseverance."

It began to rain very lightly. I leaned back under the roof of the platform out of the rain with Xen Koi still in sight but silent.

"So, how 'bout it? I was hoping for some kind of helpful reply."

Instead, I was treated to a haiku, by the poet Shiki—XKoi recited it in Japanese. Great. I kept the goggles on for a translation.

Yudachi ni Utaruru koi no atama kana.

Summer rain --
It drums on the heads
Of the koi

I bent down over the railing, back into the rain. "Is that it? Nothing else? Aw, c'mon man," I said to XKoi. But the fish had already disappeared beneath the pond.

Drums on the head. The haiku had become a xen kohen. I stayed leaning out over the pond and let the rain drum on my head and face and had my good cry after all. Like the Everly Brothers sang, when your heart is broken you can sometimes hide your tears and do your *Crying in the Rain...*

It took me a few days to absorb the effects of the haiku XKoi had recited.

CHAPTER TWENTY-ONE

The Battle of Brooklyn

The Battle of Brooklyn Day One: Monday

It is a serious thing
just to be alive
on this fresh morning
in this broken world.
—"Invitation" by Mary Oliver

I was anxious about how the group would do and decided to get to the boardwalk early. It was another beautiful mild June day. Instead of switching to the Q, I got off the B train at Brighton Beach and found one of the Russian restaurants with outdoor tables on the boardwalk. I had a bowl of borscht and a plate of piroshki and people watched. After lunch I walked down the boardwalk toward Coney Island to try to score one of the tables beneath our gazebo, which I managed to do. I sat and tried to meditate while waiting for the kids.

When they all arrived, everyone looked serious and wanted to skip meditating and the usual schmoozing and checking in. We got right down to it.

"Who wants to go first?" I asked.

"We will, the Bullshit Busters," Cami said, and looked at Dina, who nodded.

"So, we took them on in every class. We argued back, especially in Ms. Beckerman's...."

"We didn't let the teachers get away with anything...." Dina continued.

"We wore our cool glasses," Cami said, "they helped us see right through the bullshit, for real!"

"We countered every lie with facts. We asked, who's the source of these beliefs? How did you come to believe that? Who's making money off them? We interrupted them all the time...."

"We kept laughing out loud!"

"Enslaved people learned skills during slavery that helped them once they were free," Cami imitated Ms. Beckerman's serious tone. "She says slavery was actually good."

"Oh man..." Derrick groaned.

"We used sarcasm..." Dina said.

"Yeah," added, Cami, "like, ooh, so the former slaves learned how to polish white people's shoes and their *nalgas*!"

Yeah," said Dina, we know facts alone don't convince people. They need to see the world differently...."

"So you have to just stick to your own vision and frame...."

"We see it like this, we said—we think people are generous, not selfish. We want a democratic school, for us, not one run by, by...."

"... authoritarian *pendejos*..." Cami added.

"... or people that say selfishness is good, like Beckerman does."

"So we stood up in the middle of Beckerman's class and interrupted it...."

"We said: as a little kid you believed your parents when they told you go to sleep or the boogeyman would come. If I came around and told you then 'that's no fact, it's made up,' you wouldn't have believed me. Now you look back, you can see it was superstitious stuff they tell kids...."

"... You got older, you changed your way of thinking, you questioned what grown-ups told you. Now you can think for yourself. So hey, think for yourselves!"

"Of course, they kept kicking us out of class and sent us to Mr. Martinette...."

"He usually loves to boss everyone around. But he didn't know what to do with us and would send us back...."

"We were there in Beckerman's class, the last period," May May said. "Dina and Cami were awesome!"

"Her class ended early, though," Cami told us. "A huge rat snuck in through the door and ran all around the classroom. Everybody jumped up from their desks. She dismissed us and we all ran out screaming!"

Shit.

"Our turn," Arielle said, "the Community Connectors," and turned to Billy.

"We texted our groups in the morning and told them we'd hold a meeting of all of us at lunch in the cafeteria," he began.

"The Gay-Straight Alliance, the Women's Group, the Climate Change Fighters, Black Lives Matter, Jews and Muslims for Palestine and Against Antisemitism, the Radical Mindfulness group ... that's us," Arielle added.

"We made a huge circle around the entire cafeteria. Me and Arielle had a megaphone and held a kind of teach-in and demo...."

"Our groups were all really disciplined and focused, it was great!" Arielle shouted.

"Some of us held hands," Billy continued, "others were like the Black Panther Party, just stood there with their arms folded, staring at the other kids."

"It was mad cool," Derrick said.

"Some hecklers—guys—yelled stuff and tried to drown us out," Arielle reported.

"Yeah," Billy said, "but we kept going and shut them down."

"Me and Billy took turns speaking. We said, 'Hey! You're worried about stuff, you're angry, the way to go is to join together and resist the powers that get you to feel that way! They tell you the only way is to look out for number one and fight each other! Not true! The way is to be together, to hang out together, to help each other! This is what we do, this is where we each get our strength! Join us, don't fall for this selfish crap!'"

"Look at what Martinette is trying to get us to do!" Billy continued. "He's become a religious nut! He's trying to make us behave according to his screwed-up beliefs! He's dividing us against each other! But we're fighting back, we're helping each other. We have more in common than differences. We want you to join us so we have more power to fight this BS!"

Arielle turned to me. "We were just getting going. Guess what happened then, Mr. T.?"

"I think I know."

"A couple of rats came outta nowhere!" Arielle answered her own question. "I mean, well, it's the cafeteria, the food is next door in the kitchen. They created a scene, running around under the tables, jumping at the kids' legs. The students poured out of there. The rats broke up the rally!"

"At least we got to say some stuff we wanted to say," Billy said. "We were in a calm, meditative state the whole time."

I gave a hopeful nod to mask any sense of weary resignation, which I was fighting.

"Okay, how about the Defensive Disarmers, May May and Derrick?"

The two looked at each other. May May nodded at Derrick, who began.

"We caught the text rumor in the morning there was gonna be a beef after school," Derrick said. "The Bully Boyz, the school fools picked by Mr. Martinette and his APs, were gonna go after some of us that weren't going along with the program."

"So, we also texted our posse early," May May picked up, "the girls from school who are in my judo class, and Derrick's Violence Interrupters...."

"We told them to meet up after school, on the school grounds, not on the street," Derrick added.

"Sure enough, those guys show up. We know a lot of them, they're in our classes! But we're there first. We're solid," May May said. "Right away, we make a huge circle all around them."

Derrick said, "Yeah, that messes with their head, they get confused, it like busts them up. They turn to their leader to see what to do."

"Then they start dissing Derrick and his guys," May May said. "'You just a bunch of pussies, y'all can't fight,' stuff like that."

"Yeah," Derrick continued, "so we just stand there, arms folded, like at lunch, like the Black Panthers. 'Nah,' we tell them. 'We could fight, but it ain't worth it. We choose peace. Y'all just tryin' to trip. But if we refuse to be bullied where's that leave you? We can talk stuff out if you want. We know how. We're here when you ready. Y'all should know, power's not the same as strength. There's strength in not fighting. And we plenty strong.'"

May May said, "They don't know what to say, and just stand around and curse. Then they look at me and my judo group. They say, 'Okay what about you girls, we hear you actually like to fight, you all practice for one.' The leader says, 'We don't like to fight no girls usually but hey, let's have one of you go up against one of us.'"

"The girls then look at each other, like they thinking who's gonna be the one," Derrick told us. "I said yo, fair fight only, no one jumps in even when you losin'. They all laugh at that and then the leader said aight."

"I jumped right into the center," May May said. "I was ready! They start laughing more and say, hey, you ain't no girl!"

"I'm getting pissed off," said Derrick. "'She's a girl who was a guy,'" I told them, "And if you think she's a guy then you should feel even better if you win. If you lose you can say well it was no girl, it was a guy that beat you.'"

"So, I'm waiting to see what they do," May May said.

"They look at each other," Derrick reported. "'Aight,'" the leader said. "Then they chose one of the bigger, taller dudes, who went into the center."

The rest of us were listening wide-eyed.

Derrick switched to present tense like he's calling a sports event. "So the two of them start circling around each other…. They take their time … May May—remember, she's *small*, yo!—takes her crouching position…. They staring each other down…. Everybody's shouting at them…. The guys are saying 'c'mon! Just take her!' … He's feelin' his homies' eyes watchin' him…. Then the dude makes the first move…. He lunges at her with his right arm…."

May May picked up the play-by-play. "I grab his arm and shift his weight, so he loses his balance … I use his own force against him, like we're trained to do. He starts to stumble to my right…."

"Yeah, then she moves her foot around and kicks him behind his right knee, not even hard, just real quick! … He goes down!" Derrick is getting worked up. "He gets up real slow. His homies are yelling at him…. Get up! Go get her! They can't believe what they seein'!"

"I get back in position," May May said.

"She was ready to kick butt! I mean, you know, keep him down…."

"And then…" May May continued.

"And then, guess what, Mr. T.," Derrick said.

"Uh huh. How many this time?"

"Damn, like maybe three or so."

"The rats are like, menacing us," May May said. "They come out from under the school! They're all around but they are closer to us than to the guys. We can't go on so we all start to walk away fast, the guys too. It breaks up the fight."

"She woulda had him too!" Derrick said.

"I don't doubt it," I said. I took a few breaths. "What a day. I'm proud of all of you, you did great."

Everyone high-fived each other. "Let's get some pizza," Dina said. "Mr. T.?"

Pizza. I had to stop myself from wincing. "Thanks gang, I'm gonna go home. You all did the work, I'm beat. Go figure."

"We'll meet you back here tomorrow," Billy said.

I nodded. "See you then!"

The Brooklyn Dream Team had scored some points and played the rats to a draw. There was more to come.

The Battle of Brooklyn Day Two: Tuesday

The next afternoon the group met me under the gazebo with somber, grim faces. It was a cloudy, humid day that matched their mood. I braced myself for some troubling news.

"Some bad things today, Mr. T.," Derrick said.

It's worse now," May May continued. "The school Bully Boys got bigger and nastier. We heard that Martinette recruited and paid off these right-wing white guys from, I don't know, Long Island or Staten Island."

"Yeah, bad dudes," added Derrick. "How they're allowed inside the school, we can't figure."

"They all come in wearing these military-style black berets with this insignia, or patch," Billy told us, "It's a mean looking face of a rat baring his teeth in front of a bitten-off pizza slice…."

Sure enough, I recognized that logo from my visit with Pete.

"That's the logo of the Staten Island Pizza Rats baseball team," Arielle announced. "My aunt and uncle moved there from Brooklyn. I remember when we visited them a few months ago, my cousin had a baseball cap with that ratface on it, in his room, he told me what it was."

Arielle confirmed what I long suspected—the rats were the ones infesting the school.

"They even handed out those pizza rat berets to all the guys in the school. Now they're all wearing one," Dina said.

"Haha, we all grabbed some too and wear 'em inside out!" Billy said.

"It's now one big rat patrol," May May told us. "Today they were patrolling the halls along with the school bullies. They tried to intimidate and push us around, and blocked us from moving through the hallways…."

Dina spoke. "Then they've like, managed to ramp up their lies and rumors, I don't know how…."

"… Somebody took over the PA system and the administration spews garbage all through the day," Cami told us. "And overnight they posted fake news, and nasty lies about people on all the hallway bulletin boards. Online they've hacked the school website, filled it with lies, bullying a bunch of us...."

"... and I don't know how, they found a way to jam our social media sites," Dina went on.

"When you try to text somebody in school you get trolled, or you just get bullshit announcements from Fux Fake News and some Christian religious program...."

Arielle spoke up. "They've also outlawed our social support groups! At lunch the Bully Boyz and their new recruits blocked the classrooms where we usually meet and herded us out of the school with police sticks!"

Billy said, "Today in every class we heard this garbage about competition from the teachers. They passed out pamphlets from corporations on getting ahead and how to brand yourself. They said they're from the school district, but they look fake. The teachers said they're starting new groups that encourage this stuff and setting up rewards in the school for the most achieving student who can pass a bunch of stupid tests."

"Beckerman loves this Ayn somebody or other," Arielle said, "she's always talking about the virtues of selfishness and how it's the best and only way to get what you want and have a winning life. Everything we're against!"

May May added, "It's like we told you last week, Mr. T., it feels like these outside forces have taken over the school, and since yesterday things have gotten worse."

It was clear my three rats had somehow been able to further spread their poisons in the school—bullying, disinformation, and selfishness. They'd recruited and brought in outside thugs, increased media manipulation, and stepped up indoctrinating the students with their greed-is-good propaganda. They had to be getting outside help, maybe from their larger network.

I worked to hide any hint of worry. "Look, you guys are making a difference," I said. "They've doubled down now that they see you starting to fight back in an organized and strategic way."

"We're gonna keep fighting, Mr. T.," Arielle said.

"Yeah, we're gonna figure out how they get away with their crap and work around it, the lies, the bullying, the propaganda..." Cami said.

"Thanks everyone. Okay, get some rest, we'll meet up here tomorrow and make some adjustments."

The Battle of Brooklyn Day Three: Wednesday

Things went from bad to worse. The group was even more down than the day before. I learned more about the saboteurs Marva Williams had mentioned, the ones who ramped up the authoritarian attacks. The rats had bought off Billy's right-wing dad, Derrick's former gang, and Cami's brother.

Billy reported first. "I found out my dad did go to the PTA meeting the other night. He got himself elected as an officer. He's already getting parents and teachers to ban books about gays, oppose teaching history classes he says unfairly present all white people as bad guys, and blames immigrants for crime and taking jobs from citizens. He bragged he's the one that got the school to use the PA system, billboards, and school website. He must have asked Jimbo, his pal from Fux Fake News, to help him. He's also the one who must have had something to do with jamming the sites we use and trolling our texts with bullshit."

"Yeah, Mr. T.," Derrick said, "and I learned my ex-gang homies came to the school and joined the other fools goin' around messing with us. They make those school bullies and Staten Island types look like kindygarten kids. You know, they want to get back at me. You wouldn't think they want anything to do with rednecks but they into power too, where they can find it. We saw them walking around the school, they were looking for me and the rest of us. They gonna teach the other bullies some shit if they can."

Everyone turned and looked at Cami. Her eyes flashed with anger. "It turns out my brother's been working with Ms. Beckerman and others on this selfishness thing. He's showing them how to get kids to buy into more, like, corporate thinking about beating the other guy and to believe greed is good and losers deserve to lose. He told me he and his pals from the business school at Brooklyn College are part of a larger group, they made up those papers the teachers then pass out to all the students, and they're getting big bucks to do it."

We sat in silence for a moment.

Arielle spoke up. "Well, at least we're applying the stuff we learned from those, uh, cosmic superheroes," she confirmed.

"And that drink we got," May May added, "it helps us meditate and keeps us focused...."

"... and the goggles boost our smarts," Dina said, "you know, we can see where the teachers and our classmates are being brainwashed, and why they're stressed out by everything."

The others nodded.

I stepped in. "I get it though, we're feeling stuck, especially now since they've come down harder on us."

Their silence confirmed it. From the looks of discomfort of the first three, I sensed something else and took a direct approach.

"Billy, Derrick, and Cami—how are you feeling, now that you know your own folks are on the other side and that you have to oppose them?"

Billy lowered his head. "I do feel ... kinda bad, I guess sorta guilty, I mean he's still my dad...."

Derrick offered support. "Yeah, gotta be tough, a racist dad helping mess up the school. But he still family."

We waited and then turned to Cami, who was close to tears. "I'm mad at my bro, but also...."

"... hurt?" Dina helped out.

"Sad, too, right?" Arielle added. "Still family, like Billy." She handed Cami a tissue.

We waited for Derrick.

Derrick sucked his teeth. "They *were* my homies, but later for them. I left them already."

May May said, "We know, Derrick, we're really proud of you...."

"Still, it's gotta be a little hard," Billy offered mutual support. "You all had a kind of loyalty to each other … you were a kind of family too, like with me and Cami. Now it's worse, they wanna go after you, and us, your new family."

Derrick looked away toward the ocean and nodded. The beach was jammed with families on blankets and under umbrellas with kids on the sand shouting and running every which way.

Amid the chaotic, noisy scene we were at a low point. To fight the rats and rat consciousness the group, with the help of the Dogen Potion, had mastered mindfulness practices and insights into the nature of the self and time. Through our weekly sessions they had gained awareness and knowledge into the hidden social structures of power and greed, boosted by the XK AI Anti-Google Goggles. They'd applied the wisdom and fighting skills they'd learned from meeting the timeless cosmic superpowers. Now I felt they needed one more strategy to get them over the hump.

CHAPTER TWENTY-TWO

The Barbie Maneuver

I turned around to face the boardwalk. A mother and two children, a girl and boy, whom I took to be Latinos, strolled by. The older boy was swatting and yelling at his little sister, who was pushing a stroller with a Barbie doll. The pesky brother was trying to grab the Barbie, but the girl was managing to keep it away from him. I studied the family for a moment then turned to the group.

"Everyone, please take out your little bottles and take a swig. We're getting outta here."

"Where we going now, Mr. T.?" May May asked.

"We've met with people from the past, now we're going to the future. The near future."

Without a word, the group did as I asked.

Like our last trip it took a few minutes for the Dogen Potion to kick in. I gave the same instructions. "Now touch the button on the side of your goggles. Take five deep breaths. Allow yourselves to be … transported."

As before, I shut my eyes, touched the frame button, and visualized a bright, pink fantasy land that didn't exist yet, somewhere in cosmic time and space. Wherever the fuck that was.

Barbie Land

We stood and looked around. Our goggles had turned into sunglasses to shield us from the glaring pink of everything, the pink beach, the pink streets, the wild pink buildings.

"Yo, this place is wack," Derrick said.

"Where are we, Mr. T.?" May May asked.

"We're in Barbie Land. It's a set for a movie that hasn't come out yet. You'll see it in the theaters or on cable in a few years, in 2023."

"Wow, the architecture here is incredible, Mr. T.," marveled Billy the graphic artist.

"I used to have a Barbie!" Arielle said.

"Not me," scoffed Cami, "they were for white girls. An older white girl in my building gave me her old one. I trashed the Barbie up, pulled out her hair and an arm, marked her face up with lipstick and crayons and stuff...."

"Nah, they make all kinds of Barbies, even Black ones, my cousin has one," Derrick said.

"They've got Hijarbie too, said Dina, "she wears a hijab, my little sister saw it and wanted it."

"They'll have a transgender one soon," I said, and looked at May May, who laughed. "But look, we're here to meet the cast, they'll be in character. It's a great story about how Barbie with the help of others becomes a real woman in the best sense. Spoiler alert: it's got a great feminist speech, and the women find a way to stand up for themselves and win back Barbie Land from the sexist Kens who took it over—we're gonna learn from the characters how they did it."

We spotted a circle of directors' chairs nearby on the beach and headed over to them.

As we were finding our seats, we saw four women walking toward us—Barbie Margot, Weird Barbie, Gloria, the mom who works at Mattel, and her teen daughter, Sasha.

"Hey guys," Weird Barbie said.

The four women joined us in the circle and smiled at everyone.

"Hey, Cami," Gloria addressed Cami, who was slack-jawed. "I can relate to what you did to that Barbie doll. As a kid I did the same thing, I wanted to make her original and different."

"That's who I am," Weird Barbie continued. "We all have a right to be ourselves."

"So here's what we did," Sasha told them. "The Kens muscled their way into Barbie Land and took it over. We got them to think they had power over us, we went along with them, played dumb, appealed to their egos...."

"But first we had to get Barbie here to get over feeling bad about going against her buddy Ken," Gloria said.

"I didn't want to hurt him," said Barbie. "I was afraid he wouldn't like me...."

Gloria said, "I had to remind her, he took your house. He brainwashed your friends. He wants to control the government."

"She and the others helped me change my mind," Barbie Margot told them. "So, I know what Billy, Cami, and Derrick are going through about having to fight people they still have feelings for. But also, I don't feel that strongly about Ken, that's just the way it is.

"So, then we turned the Kens against each other, we got them to fight among themselves," she continued. "We turned their egos inside out. They started to question whether they even have enough power over themselves, let alone us."

"What Barbie said..." Weird Barbie spoke, "You stoke their egos and jealousies, they turn on each other. While they were fighting, we got to take back Barbie Land. You guys can do the same and take back your school and help Brooklyn too!"

Everyone looked at each other.

"Sounds like a plan," Dina said.

"So, we turn their own selfishness, lies, competition, bigotry, against them," May May realized.

"We beat them at their own game," Cami said.

"Yeah, they implode on their own BS," Arielle saw the strategy.

"I'm down with that," said Derrick. "As long as I don't have to live in no pink bubble."

"Okay gang, stay true to yourselves, don't take any crap," Weird Barbie told them. "Someday maybe Mattel will make dolls out of the Brooklyn Dream Team...."

"Or a graphic comic book ... in all colors." Billy added.

"Yeah! Or a Superheroes movie!" Dina shouted.

I had to laugh, then said, "Uh gang, hate to break it to ya, none of that's gonna happen, if ever, until we at least stop the bad guys. We have to get back and finish the job."

The cast posed for group selfies, gave out autographs, and wished us all the best. "We'll see you, well, you'll see us, in a couple of years," Gloria told them. As they were saying their goodbyes Ken Ryan walked over. "Hey, I figured out things about myself and all guys too! All the things I thought were me aren't really ME. I can exist without being in relation to Barbie, or my house, or my mink … I can just be … myself!" He smiled and walked away.

The Battle of Brooklyn Day Four: The Ratocracy

The next day, Thursday, the group followed part one of the Barbie strategy—let them think they have power over you.

At our afternoon meeting, Dina summed up what the group and their allies did in school.

"We all acted like we had given up and let Martinette think he had won. When he told us to behave, to keep quiet, stand on line, and other stuff we did everything exactly as he said and kept saying, 'Yes, Mr. Martinette, of course, whatever you say!' He said, 'Well, well, this is a pleasant surprise.' We acted like we couldn't do anything and were helpless. We asked him, 'Oh, please tell us what to do, how can we be more religious and do the right thing?' We kept praising the staff and all the bullies. We asked them how we could become like them—tougher, more competitive, even lie, to get ahead of other students and become winners."

May May added, "The staff and the bullies were surprised and then happy we had given up and stopped fighting back!"

The previous night the three kids with ties to those who helped take over the school also worked on their connections.

Billy told us, "I apologized to my dad about my, uh, childish rebelliousness, as I put it, and asked him to tell me what he really cares about. He shut down at first but then after a few beers, he came around. He told me how he and his pal Jimbo from Fux

Fake News were being hired by some powerful people. They want them to expand their social media jamming and spread their bullshit and what he calls 'proper Christian morality' online in our school and beyond. What the hell?!"

Cami shared how she approached her brother. "It wasn't easy but I, like, apologized for arguing with him. I told him I had come around to agreeing with some of what he believes. After a while he opened up. I couldn't believe it at first, and then what he told me was even more unbelievable. He said he and other business school students had been approached by people who offered them what he called dark money. They want them to spread individualism in schools—they call it that!— and work with teachers like Ms. Beckerman. They want more charter schools run by Wall Street too."

Derrick told us he reached out to some of his former gang members and had a truce meeting at midnight on a corner in East New York. "They told me they were part of a network of gangs who get secret funds from rich powerful white dudes. They want the gangs to scare people enough to keep them from fighting them. These dudes want to take down the government and start their own. My boys told me this group was even gonna show off their power soon in Brooklyn. Damn. Then they invited me to rejoin them. I said yo, I had to think about it."

The group reported back to me how they'd won over the power brokers, authoritarians, and personal connections. The kids did such a convincing con job that their adversaries became comfortable enough to relax, open up, and confide in them. As a result, the group was able to learn disturbing things, which they reported with much excitement and anxiety.

"You won't believe this Mr. T.," Arielle began, breathless, "The jerks running our school are part of a larger conspiracy network that works in Brooklyn!"

"Yeah, they call themselves the *Ratocracy*!" Dina shouted. "They have ties all around the city, even in other states, with these, partners.... They call them Ratpublicans! CorpoRat Executives! Right-Wing Government AutocRats! Billionaire Dark

Money Oligarch PlutocRats! There's this other billionaire, Eelong MuskRat! Some big group of right-wing religious nuts, the TheocRats! Oh yeah, and Ratpert Murdoch's Fux Fake News! And this Saturday they're, they're...."

"... they're gonna have a huge event Saturday in three places in Brooklyn." Cami stepped in. "It's all, like, coordinated, they're finishing up the plans tomorrow."

"And not only are Billy's dad, Cami's brother, and Derrick's ex-gang members gonna take part in it, Mr. Martinette and Ms. Beckerman too, they play a big role!" May May reported.

We fell silent. You could hear us breathing.

Okay," I said, "tomorrow, two things. Now that you've won them over and they think they have power over you, you're gonna take what they stand for—lies, competition, violence—to their logical extreme. That leads to consequences. It creates conflict and chaos between them so they fight each other. That'll open up a space for us to help change the school. And second...."

"... We gotta find out what the Ratocracy conspiracy is up to with those demos and where they're gonna be," Arielle broke in, "and then...."

"... we're gonna plan how to disrupt the hell out of them," Billy added.

"... yeah, and then do it," Derrick said.

Everyone nodded.

The Battle of Brooklyn Day Five: Friday

The next day, the group carried out the second part of the Barbie plan inside the school— turning the values of lying, selfishness, and meanness upside down to create chaotic divisiveness and weaken the authoritarian structure.

"Here's what we did," Cami and Dina, the Bullshit Busters, reported after school.

"We started rumors on texts and in the halls that Beckerman was gonna take over the school, like a conspiracy, and make everyone a Ratndista," Dina said.

"A coup!" Cami broke in.

"... and that Martinette, the religious fanatic, was then gonna stop her from teaching that stuff and ban all the books about selfishness."

Cami continued. "Yeah, we created the Big Lie! It spread all over school. The two got really pissed at each other and started getting people to join their side."

"Teachers, students, everyone, one side fighting the other. They trashed each other over the PA all day. People were arguing and yelling at each other, there were nasty fights in the halls...." Dina quipped.

"... They disrupted the classrooms; the teachers couldn't do lessons."

"We created some chaos!" Dina said. She and Cami looked at each other.

"You weaponized disinformation, fake news," I said, "It was a tough lesson for you to give, for a greater educational good."

The two nodded. Dina said, "Some of the teachers and students did stop. They started to look like they weren't so sure any more about what they believed. We talked to them and said we're glad you're thinking about this. We started these lies! You see how lies are bad! Let's figure out a better way for us to have a decent school...."

We turned to Arielle and Billy, the Community Connectors, whose job that day was to disconnect people to bring home their point.

"We flipped our script," Billy began. "In the cafeteria we told everyone we changed our minds and no longer believe everyone has to care about each other, or have things in common, or believe in democracy."

"We told them that being selfish and obeying the bosses without question is really the way to go," Arielle said. "Then we set up a quick contest right there and got some of the guys who'd heckled us to divide into two teams. We based it on a phony competition show like *The Apprentice.*

"We said, okay," Billy continued, "which team can show they're more selfish and tougher than the other? We made up a couple of scenes where they had to role play mean, nasty business types who boss everyone around and act like assholes."

"Then we got the other students who were watching to take sides. We handed out bullshit posters for them to hold up with slogans like Greed is Good and Fuck Your Feelings and gave out fake free school passes and dessert vouchers to whichever side scored a point against the other team," Arielle said.

Billy concluded, "A lot of trash talk went on and fights almost broke out."

"But we set up a timer and then blew a whistle, like a TV game show, to stop it before it got out of hand," Arielle said. "Afterwards some kids even looked kinda ashamed and uncomfortable, so we started talking to them right away, letting them know this was a deliberate experiment and what we still think are good ways to come together and treat each other with respect."

The Defensive Disarmers, Derrick and May May, told us they went around telling everyone in the school they decided to renounce peace, nonviolent self-defense, and conflict resolution.

Derrick said, "We told everyone we now believe it's good to get back at others, to bully weaklings, and fight anyone you think is out to get you."

"So we invited Martinette's school bullies, the outside pizza rat gang from Staten Island, and even Derrick's ex-homies," May May continued, "to come by after school for a workshop on how to further intimidate and fight anyone you think deserves an ass-kicking."

"We then topped it off by starting a no-rules fist fight contest between the three groups and invited anyone else around to cheer on one of the teams," Derrick told us. "It was starting to get nasty."

"But we had a friend call in to the 60th Precinct to let them know there'd be a fight after school, so just as they were getting going, the cops did come to break it up," May May said.

Derrick added, "Later we found some who looked, like, sad and we went up to them and told them 'Hey, this was a set up and we hope you might think twice about a better way to work things out.'"

"This was a tough way to go," I told everyone. "You took delusion, selfishness, and meanness and flipped them on their heads as if they were virtues. You exaggerated them, parodied them, and carried them to their logical, absurd extremes. But we know they don't work; they just make people unhappy and things worse. The conflicts you created helped people see that. And it's gonna weaken the rat-infested authoritarian structure and toxic thinking that's gripped the school!"

The group told me they did see more school members start to feel the painful consequences of lying, selfishness, and bullying, while those in power became distracted by the infighting.

"Well, this gives us a chance to jump in and make some real changes in the school," Arielle said. Everyone agreed.

The group's efforts served as a warm-up for the bigger battle to come.

CHAPTER TWENTY-THREE

The Final Battle of Brooklyn

After everyone had reported back on their strategies, the group told me what they had managed to uncover from their new confidants about the RatocRat events scheduled for the next day, Saturday.

"They have huge plans, Mr. T.," Dina said. "First, they're gonna stage a press conference on the steps of Borough Hall. They'll tell a lot of lies and then announce their agenda for taking over Brooklyn."

"Then they're gonna hold a convention-type rally inside the Barclays Center. They'll have speeches and rituals and stuff," Arielle told us. We found out that Martinette and Beckerman are gonna be on a panel as speakers, can you believe that?!"

"After that, to top it off, the Pizza Rat Boyz are gonna have a militant outdoor demonstration," May May reported. "They're gonna assemble on the meadow in Prospect Park. Then they'll march to Grand Army Plaza, rush up the Library steps, and storm the Library. Once inside they plan to trash and burn as many books as they can."

Our Plans

"We'll need to mobilize our crews," I told the group. "Your school clubs, the judo class, the Violence Interrupters, the students you recruited who've come around to our side and resist the school authoritarians. I'm gonna get some colleagues to help as well."

I texted my fellow Brooklyn Codgers, Jay, Bob, and Jess. "Hey guys, this is a great chance to use your skills, fight evil, and do some good!" I found a way to leave a message for Marva Williams at Hole

Foods. I explained to everyone what was going on and what I needed from them. They all quickly got back to me and were happy to help.

We left the boardwalk and walked down to Nathans' to discuss plans for the next day over dinner. Derrick and Dina ran ahead to grab a table. When we arrived the rest of the gang picked up hot dogs, hamburgers, French fries, and other over-fried substances while I got a fish sandwich and clam chowder and paid for everyone. The kids texted their families to say they'd be home late, and then messaged everyone they knew to get ready for tomorrow.

I told them about my meditating Codgers friends who would join us —Jay the media maven, Bob the Wall Street influencer, and Jess the military and police trainer. Each one held insights into how these institutions turn malignant and how to fight their toxic effects. I said a new friend, Marva, was coming with her large network from Bed-Stuy.

After a few hours we parted, feeling ready as we could be.

The RatocRats Fake News Press Conference at Borough Hall: Saturday

The group and the public learned through tweets that the RatocRat press conference would be held at 10 a.m. the next day on the steps of Borough Hall in downtown Brooklyn. We arrived early, gathered our forces, and assembled close to the steps. Our motley crew had procured Pizza Rat caps from the bullies in school. We all wore them, even Dina over her hijab, to try to blend in.

Members of the local press were setting up their cameras and equipment. Some curious onlookers began assembling. Several men arrived wearing the Pizza Rat baseball hats and the words ALTERNATIVE FACTS MATTER on their T-shirts. I spotted Marva, who had come with a large group of her women colleagues. We exchanged nods and smiles. A number of police were standing around in a cluster and looked like they were on high alert.

Ten o'clock came and went. There was no sign of anyone who looked ready to speak to the restless crowd.

At 11 a.m., word spread that the presenters had gotten the address wrong. Somebody in their campaign network assigned to get the city permit apparently misheard the name on a garbled cellphone call not as *Borough Hall* but *Borrow Hall*, a shabby pawn shop with a jokey pun of a name on a side street a short block away. The press conference would have to be held there.

We joined the crowd and made our way around the corner, laughing and shaking our heads at their incompetence, and arrived in front of the pawn shop. The press scooped up their equipment and hustled to get to the front where some flustered men on the sidewalk were hurriedly setting up a lectern, mic, and speakers. One of them was the principal, Rush Martinette.

The group and I worked our way to the front. Billy pointed out his dad and a guy we figured was his pal Jimbo from Fux Fake News. The plastic-lettered sign with some missing letters behind them announced *Borrow Hall Pawn. Borrow from Us. Sneakers Tattoo ewelry O tical. We buy used phones We take all payment*

A bald-headed white man in a blue suit and red tie came up behind the lectern and tapped the mic. He looked familiar.

A nanosecond later I recognized him as the senior lawyer partner of Hell Inc. For the occasion he wore shoes over his hooves and had cut off his slithering snake locks from behind his head.

I touched the side of my XK AI Anti-Google Goggles. Underneath the shell of the lawyer, visible to me alone, was Ratty Ghouliani.

He gave a quick look in my direction as he scanned the crowd but I didn't think he'd clocked me. I had darkened my glasses, pulled my Pizza Rat beret over my eyes, and ducked behind a taller crowd member.

"Uh, welcome everyone, we apologize for the misunderstanding about the location," lawyer Ratty announced. He patted his chest and inserted his hand inside his jacket. I realized he was searching for his reading glasses.

"In the confusion I seem to have misplaced my reading glasses," he addressed the crowd that was growing rowdy and turned to the others in his entourage. "Does someone have a spare pair?"

In a flash I pulled out a plain second pair of the XK AI Anti-Google Goggles I was carrying in my own jacket pocket that could pass for reading lenses. Having familiarized myself with its functions, in a few quick steps I programmed it based on Ghouliani's life and lies and put it on a timer. It would kick in in about ten minutes. I handed them to Arielle, who was standing next to me, and told her to go up and offer them to him with a smile. She held them high over her head as she made her way through the front of the crowd to the podium.

"Thank you, pretty miss," Ratty, posing as the Hell Inc. lawyer said as he took them, "You're a bit young for reading glasses, aren't you?"

"They were a favorite pair of my dad's, who just passed away," said quick-thinking Arielle. "I keep them in his memory. He was a loyal Ratpublican who would be honored if you could use them here," she smiled.

Meanwhile the other Dream Team members were passing out one-page handouts on how to counter conspiracy theories; the flyers were made by my fellow Codger, the expert on challenging false narratives and disinformation, Jay Profwreck. "Look," he'd told us, "People don't give up conspiracy beliefs quickly. You have to spend time with them, find out why they believe them, raise critical and contradictory questions. This is the best we can do for now!"

Just before Ratty was about to begin his speech, Jay shouted out to the crowd through a bullhorn he was carrying, "Get ready for a conspiracy theory! You're smarter than these lies! Think for yourselves!"

Ratty hesitated and looked flustered. He had never before been confronted in public for lying. I saw Fux Fake News Jimbo's face turn red in anger as he pulled out his cellphone, probably reporting to his bosses.

Sure enough, Ratty began with the lie, "We're here to continue to protest the stolen elections! We know that our party leaders lost only through a network of cheating...."

At once Marva's Bed-Stuy crew drowned out the lawyer as they kept chanting, "How do you know? Show us the beef!" They were joined in the chorus by Cami and Dina's fellow student Bullshit Busters.

Ratty tried to continue over their voices. "Well, we have proof! We have seized voting machines; we have videotapes of election workers stealing votes...."

"Rats will not replace us! Rats will not replace us!" The counter demonstrators were laughing and enjoying themselves. "Rats are the cheaters! Rats gonna lose! Loser! Loser! All fake news!"

"You're being duped," Ratty tried to argue. "And the people in power want the immigrants to take over our city and take your houses, your jobs, they're part of a huge crime wave...."

"Hey, hey, take a look! Fux Fake News says *you* be the crook!"

Ratty the Hell Inc. lawyer was getting more aggravated. As he looked down at his speech, the XKgoggles kicked in. They acted like a kind of truth serum.

Our counter-protestors were chanting non-stop.

"Who's your daddy? You're afraid! For all *your* lies you won't get paid!"

He stopped and looked over the crowd. We waited almost a minute for him to go on.

"You know, you're right!" he then shouted into the mic. "I hope the Boss pays me! He never pays anyone! He owes me for this bullshit!"

The crowd became silent. The paparazzi began flashing their cameras with fury and moved their mics closer to the podium.

Ratty started rambling. "I don't really believe any of this crap! It's a phony conspiracy theory! No wonder they call it the Big Lie! But truth is, lying works! It's very effective! Lying is okay in the service of a greater good! People need conspiracy theories! They can't think for themselves! They're angry, they feel confused, they're sad...!"

Two of the men near the podium came up to him from both sides and gently tried to escort him away. He wrestled free of them and continued.

"Do you know I had a lousy childhood? My father was a mobster. I had to lie to him to survive! My mother couldn't help me! I went into law enforcement to get back at people! I...."

A third, larger man came up to help. The three struggled and managed to pull Ratty off the stage.

He kept shouting without the mic as they dragged him to the side. "I used to be a good guy! Remember 9/11, hah? You loved me then! Yeah, we lied to you about how toxic the dust was, okay, some of you died.... Just like COVID, they lied, you died! We all gotta die...." As he was being dragged away, Arielle just managed to run up to him and lift the glasses off his face.

The crowd didn't know what to make of it. Not only did the guy go off the deep end and suddenly cop to the Big Lie, he was also effing deluded. Who the hell did he think he was, the so-called America's Mayor?

The press conference quickly ended in chaos. The crowd dispersed. As I walked away, I glanced behind me at the stage where Martinette, Billy's dad, Jimbo, and the other organizers were yelling at each other. The Ratocracy had failed to lay out their plans to take over Brooklyn. Fux Fake News and the other media were left to spin the mess.

The RatocRats Convention at The Barclays Center

"We gotta get up to the Barclays Center," I told the group, "The rally is starting soon." We ducked down the stairs at the nearby Borough Hall Station, took the number 4 train two stops to Atlantic Avenue–Barclays Center, and walked underground to the arena.

The event was free, open to the public. Security guards checked everyone's bags.

Some of us who had been there—Derrick and I to a couple of Brooklyn Nets games, May May to a New York Liberty game, Cami and Dina, who had scraped and saved to see Beyoncé and Jay-Z a few years ago—found the Barclays Center foreign and unrecognizable. This convention was more treacherous than the press conference. The kids were feeling nervous and kept their Pizza Rat berets slung low over their face. They all wore their XK goggles and could see what was motivating much of the crowd—resentment, grievances, feeling disrespected, the need to get back at the libs, slavish worship of The Boss, who would save them.... My Codgers colleagues accompanied us as well as Marva's crew.

A huge overhead screen played continuous scenes from the January 6 Capitol Riot. Colorful pennants hung from the rafters: WELCOME TO THE RATOCRACY INSURRECTION! God, Guns, and Rats! They'll Never Replace Us! Greed is Good! Take Over the Deep State! Stop the Steal! Free the Patriots of January 6! Revenge is Best Served with Guns! Smash Obamacare!

Many of the attendees milling about wore RATPOWER T-shirts. Vendors sold Woke Tears water bottles, rat bobble heads, and stuffed toy rats wearing pizza rat berets and mini T-shirts with the various slogans. They offered hoodies, hammocks, pins, and trinkets that said *Make America Christian* as well as videos of the January 6 insurrection.

After a short time walking around, I could see the two philosophical and political sides of the Ratocracy Ayn and Ratty had discussed down in Hell Inc.

"Try not to look," Cami whispered to us, "there's Roberto." Cami pointed with her mouth in the direction of her brother who, with other Brooklyn College business majors, was staffing a table of Ayn Ratnd books, neoliberal pamphlets, and paraphernalia.

On the other side were the TheocRats, white racist so-called Christian Nationalists.

"There's my old man." Billy said and quickly turned away.

So far, the tension between the two wings was held in place by the RatocRats' common faith in their strongman demagogue Boss who shared qualities both endorsed. To the Ratnd ideologues, The Boss signified the selfish, immoral, malignant narcissistic alpha male of action they admire, a strong leader who bails out corporations and frees the capitalist class from foolish do-good government policies, regulations, and taxes. The white Christian

Nationalists regarded him with cult-like adulation as their messianic savior, a Pete-style tough guy and government TheocRat who delivers on their racist and fascist policies and protects them from godless liberals and people from shithole countries.

At the convention, that uneasy truce was now in jeopardy. The split was about to be exposed. The keynote panelists scheduled to speak soon were Ms. Dotty Beckerman and Mr. Rush Martinette, local high school educators initially chosen by the RatocRat underling bosses as model representatives of RatocRatic values in Brooklyn. Thanks to the recent work of the Brooklyn Dream Team, though, they were now enemies, forced to front as friendly colleagues.

Before the panel began, convenors were invited to come up to one of two mics placed at the front of the two aisles to ask questions and suggest topics to the panelists. Most people who queued up addressed the familiar anxious themes. How are you teaching our children to win and compete? What are you doing to stop the immigrants and non-Christians from replacing us? After each speaker, the audience cheered and applauded to varying degrees to show which ones they favored.

On the dais, the moderator, an elder woman with kabuki makeup and bright red lipstick who looked strangely like Ayn Ratnd, took notes on each. She was flanked by Beckerman and Martinette, both of whom looked miserable. Sure enough, with a flip of my glasses I recognized the moderator to be no less than Ayn herself, visiting from Hell Inc.

Fellow Codger and corporate mindfulness influencer Bob Frawst, master of the here-and-now app Headcase, which he used to promote competition and self-evaluation, awaited his turn in the queue next to where we sat. When he reached the mic he looked over at us, winked, then addressed the panel and the entire convention. He got everyone's attention off the bat.

"To all RatocRats: We are at war! A culture war! A political war for the soul of America! We have many grievances! We feel hurt! We feel under siege! From the immigrants! From the leftist elitists! From the fake media! So, why deny it, let's embrace our warrior side! We love the super bully who can out-bully the bullies that have bullied us! The reality is we have two different, competing ways to bring about our Ratocracy. So, I say to our two speakers: let us honor our fearless Boss! You know he won't be around forever! Let us honor and immortalize him by having it out with each other in his style, the bullying warrior debate style we all love: Interrupt! Hurl insults! Call the other nasty hurtful nicknames! Be selfish! Lie like crazy! Call a lie the truth! Call the truth a lie! There's no longer a difference!"

Bob paused and the crowd clapped, whooped, and whistled. He held up his hand to ask for silence and continued.

"Let's be mindful of the here and now folks! I ask everyone in the audience to take out your cellphones and download the Headcase app."

People did so.

"Now click on the program that monitors your judgments. When a panelist says something you love, click that. Something you hate and makes you mad, click that one. Keep it on your lap, it will check your heart rate and blood pressure. Use it to vote for your side. The more competition, the better for us all! Let's take this all the way!"

After the cheering calmed down, the pale-faced woman moderator was so impressed with the overwhelming popularity of Bob's suggestion for a RatocRat civil war between competing bullies she decided to implement it. "So be it!" she exclaimed to further applause and shouts.

Dotty Beckerman and Rush Martinette pursed their lips and looked down at the table.

The Ayn Ratnd moderator nodded to Dotty Beckerman, the Ratnd proponent, to start.

"Success and failure are purely personal; it's a matter of individual strength. There is no God who hands out rewards. You are your own moral compass...." she began. Before she could continue, though, the Christian Nationalist crowd drowned her out with a chorus of boos and catcalls. They fiddled with their Headcase app.

Martinette the TheocRat saw the opening and jumped in. "That's blasphemy. We are under the gun of a vast godless deep state conspiracy and powerful replacement forces. We need a strong, moral, Christian government...."

The Ratnd supporters in turn yelled and screamed. Everyone both seated and standing were checking their cellphones and monitoring and tallying up their own and everyone's responses.

"That's a lie, tiny fingers Martinette!" Dotty screamed. The crowd decibel level shot up to the rafters. "Powerful individual self-centered acts are superior to any TheocRatic laws...."

Martinette interrupted her. "Listen, horseface, if you think the transgenders, criminal Mexicans, Muslims, and other immoral types have any brains to think for themselves...."

"Religion is conformity, it's for morons, moron!"

"Hey, dotty Dotty, we stand for God, the traditional family, and law and order! We demand the government ban books and protest demonstrations! Restrict gun regulation! Ban sex education, abortion, gay marriage, and the transgenders! We oppose immigrants, unions, affirmative action, Marxist universities, and radical wokeness!"

"We don't need your stupid theocracy," the Ratndista yelled, "We don't need a controlling government! Just one that de-regulates and supports corporations! Plus, we have dark money! And we have self-made billionaires like Eelong MuskRat to give Our Boss as much money as he wants!"

"Oh yeah, well guess what, it's not all about the money! MuskRat himself also hates immigrants! He now says he wants our kind of moral Christian government as well!"

Both looked like they were ready to come to blows.

The so-called debate quickly deteriorated into a vicious shouting match with each one yelling over the other.

The convenors in the audience were now so incensed they ignored the panel, put down their cellphones, and turned on each other. Fist fights broke out, then spread into a floor fight, all against all.

I signaled our group to move quickly toward the exit. Marva and her crew speed-walked alongside us, as did my three fellow Codgers, Jay, Jess, and Bob—and the latter, as the instigator, pulled his Pizza Rat hat low over his face and ducked down to avoid being seen. He had succeeded in bringing the RatocRats' festering civil war to its logical end point. The convention had degenerated into chaos.

The RatocRats Rally at the Grand Army Plaza Central Library

We headed back down the subway, took the number 2 train to Grand Army Plaza, and walked up through the plaza to the Grand Army Library. We knew the Pizza Rat Boyz and their allies had already assembled in Prospect Park and would be marching to the plaza, where they planned to hold a rally and storm the library.

I have always imagined that paradise will be a kind of library. — Jorge Luis Borges

To turn Borges' quote on its head, you could also say a library is a kind of paradise.

We arrived before they did and were ready to confront them. We were joined by Derrick's crew of Violence Interrupters, May May's fellow judo students, the large contingent of Marva's network from Bed-Stuy that had been with us throughout the day, and many high school students recruited by Arielle and Billy.

We had just managed to position ourselves in front of the library doors when Cami pointed excitedly toward a large approaching group. We spotted many women, some wearing hijabs, and men in keffiyehs walking up through Grand Army Plaza from the subway station.

We turned and looked at Dina. "I invited some of my cousins," she shrugged, then laughed.

Dina had outdone everyone. She had called people to schlep all the way from Bay Ridge to come and stand together with us against the Ratocracy. Everyone cheered and made space for them to join us. We had now become a large mass of resisters that spilled over the sides of the stairs and was spread out across the width of the building.

Two of the mindful Codgers—Jay, the dismantler of dissembling, Bob, the corrupter of corporate competition—had already helped us fight the Ratocracy that day. Now it was Jess's turn. He would apply some of the mindfulness skills he taught to the police and military to help us combat the militant arm of the authoritarian movement.

Jess stood facing us from a few steps below, looked at our group from one end to the other, then spoke with a bullhorn.

"You have it within you to overcome your own inner fears and rage, as well as those of the people you are about to confront! With your own powers—mindful breathing, staying calm and present, being at peace, being attuned to the absolute love of the universe, you will overcome those who, out of despair, blind themselves to our common humanity. Meet them with fierce compassion! Stand and stay together!

"And, oh yes," he winked, "that drink the Dream Team has been passing out to many of you, it'll give us an extra boost to do what we must at this time." XK had left me instructions on how to increase the Dogen Potion, something like how a sourdough culture can multiply. The kids handed it out in paper cups up and down the lines.

"Here they come!" Derrick shouted and pointed toward the park entrance. Everyone turned their heads to look at the marching Rat Boyz.

"Then I suggest you drink those now," Jess finished.

We watched them moving toward us, a shouting, chanting, angry mob in colorful rat-themed shirts and baseball caps carrying banners with the usual Ratocracy slogans.

I flipped on my glasses to better see the ragged assortment of young, mostly white men. Some carried baseball bats. Among them were Martinette's high school bullies, the Staten Island

Pizza Rat group he imported into the school, and even Derrick's former gang members, in it for the power and money.

Leading the charge was a large, older bearded man, I guessed in his fifties, who wore a rat hoodie with protruding ears and a long tail. I took a closer look. Underneath the costume no one else could see was Pete himself. He was carrying a flag that pictured a rat, a gun, and the name of OUR BOSS in flame letters.

Pete brought the mob into the plaza below the library steps. He ran up a short series of stairs just above his followers but still below where we stood. He glared at us and did a double take when he saw all the Black women and hijabi Arab women. He then turned around and with a bullhorn addressed his crowd.

"We are fed up being called losers! They try to keep us down! They poison us! We're being replaced by illegal immigrants, Muslims, Mexicans, Blacks, and Jews! Our families are being destroyed by feminists, gays, and the transgenders! This building has disgusting books based on lies! Do we want to let these people harm our children and destroy their future?

"Nohhh!" The mob roared back.

"We are gonna march into this liberry! We are gonna destroy all books that teach people dangerous, filthy ideas!"

As I stood there with my comrades, I thought of some iconic photos of peaceful protestors who confronted those ready to do violence: the young woman at a 1967 anti-Vietnam war demo who walked up to a National Guard soldier with a pointed bayonet rifle and offered him a chrysanthemum. The Chinese man who stopped the tank in Tiananmen Square. The woman in Santiago, Chile, who faced a soldier in 2016 at a demo marking the anniversary of the military takeover from Allende.

I envisioned us all doing a Haka, the brilliant, fierce, choreographed, Maori war ritual that's intimidating as hell.

I also feared that our peaceful stance would be met with a violent reaction that's happened too often. The African American marchers led by John Lewis, beaten crossing the Edmund Pettus Bridge in Selma in 1965. The Peekskill riots of 1949 at which

Paul Robeson concertgoers were attacked and beaten by right-wing thugs. The 1937 Memorial Day massacre in Chicago in which the Chicago police shot and killed ten unarmed union demonstrators striking against Republic Steel. You might not know that one, but if you see the haunting newsreel footage, suppressed for years, you won't forget it.

Some victories, though, too.

The 1912 Bread and Roses Lawrence textile strike. The Battle of Cable Street, London, 1936. The Warsaw Ghetto Uprising, 1943. The Greenwich Village Stonewall riots, 1969.

Our entire group of resisters, six rows deep, forty across, locked arms and held fast in front of the library doors.

Pete's Rat Boyz mob began to move up the stairs. They yelled and screamed and raised their baseball bats.

We stared directly at them and held our ground.

Pete was about to give the command to charge when he spotted me and stopped.

"Hey, Jake! We miss you man! Come back with us!"

"Not today, Pete, not ever. Sorry."

My group of kids next to me were stupefied. They looked at me. "Do you *know* this guy?!" May May asked with anguish.

"Yeah, kids, we're old friends," Pete yelled. "You don't know this guy like I do. You might not wanna hang around wit' him if you did."

"What's he talking about Mr. T.?!" Billy cried. The group was anxiously waiting for my reply.

I was feeling calm. I smiled at them, shook my head, and waved my hands in a dismissive gesture. The group relaxed a bit.

"Not to worry, kids, we go back a ways. Ol' Pete took a wrong turn a long time ago."

Pete scowled. "Hey man, we got your wife now, you know! Whaddya gonna do about that, hah?"

Now I couldn't hide my fear and rage. Blood was pounding in my head and heart. "You hurt her and you're a dead rat, you hear me?!"

Pete laughed. "Come and get her!"

"He's bluffing, Jacob!" From a few yards down the line, Marva shouted at me. "Don't believe any of that crap! He not only eats trash, he talks it too!" I turned to look at her. She was glaring furiously at Pete.

She must have been right. Pete spat, gave me one more filthy stare, and turned back to his mob. I had to laugh at myself. Marva helped save my white ass after all.

"Let's get 'em, boyz!"

The Rat Boyz bared their teeth and began to lurch toward us. They were going to push and shove their way past us and break into the building. I was still stoked from the earlier adrenaline rush.

Just as they moved, we began chanting and yelling in a spontaneous yet organized way I had never heard or seen.

It began with the scores of Bay Ridge Muslim women Dina had recruited. They ululated at the top of their lungs. Then everyone began doing it.

When they'd stopped, others started shouting loud chants, one after another, that everyone picked up. *Ban Hate, Not Books! Black Lives Matter! No Pasarán! Feed the People, Starve the Rats!* Then the ululating resumed louder than before.

The Rat Boyz hadn't heard anything like that, either. They just stopped, frozen, and stared at us. They sensed something about us, our singular will, our aura of conviction and confidence. Like the rats in Hell after I took the Dogen Potion, all they could do was look at us with puzzled, glazed eyes

We seized the moment of their paralysis and charged toward them, yelling as loud as we could. The Rat Boyz were overwhelmed and were literally and figuratively taken aback. With an enormous surge of power, as if one being, with one singular move, we pushed them down the stairs and kept pushing them. Some stumbled backwards and fell.

After they picked themselves off the plaza they scattered. Some ran, some just walked away, turned around, and gave us the finger.

We cheered, blew kisses, and shouted back at them: *Feed the People! Starve the Rats!* We checked to see if anyone was injured. Then, still cheering, everyone hugged each other.

Heaven/Paradiso/Nirvana/The Future/The Top Of The Ladder

And now, as at the stroke of burning rays,
what lies beneath the snow is wholly bared
of what were previously its cold and color;
thee, thus remaining in thine intellect,
will I inform with such a living light,
that it will quiver when thou seest it.
—Beatrice, Canto II, Paradiso (trans. Courtney Langdon)

CHAPTER TWENTY-FOUR

Maya

Guide us, keep us, till the end of time. —Terrence Malick, The Tree of Life (2011)

Old Growth

Maya and I spent a glorious week in bed. Wouldn't you? Ah. Kind of like John and Yoko's weeklong bed-in for world peace. In this case, our peace. And no invited paparazzi.

While we were apart, Maya had stayed with her divorced sister Jill in her small house near Woodstock. From there Maya worked online as an OB/GYN nurse manager. She told me of heartbreaking and harrowing stories about overworked, exhausted nurses and scores of patient deaths that often led to her feeling helpless and despondent. Now she was back with me in Brooklyn.

It had been over a year since we were together. We had hours of pillow talk.

I apologized like crazy and said I was a changed man. She forgave me and said she knew.

"I was monitoring your progress!"

"Okay, I knew you were in on this. Tell me everything."

"Promise not to interrupt."

"Well, except when I have a question." I had a million.

"Huh." Maya gave me a look. I gulped and nodded okay.

She fluffed up her pillow and settled in.

"All right. So you know Jill's place is in the woods. The woods are beautiful all year 'round. There are many tall, stately trees, quite old. Jill described the forest as old growth...."

"Old growth! That's great! That's like us, Old Growth! It should be the name of a boomer folk rock or bluegrass band...."

"Jacob!"

"Sorry. Please go on."

Maya paused for a few moments, then continued. "Every day in the early morning I would take a walk in the woods. I would get into a kind of meditative reverie, an eerie frame of mind. Everything felt unreal. I would then come back for breakfast. Jill and I would have...."

"Hippy granola with organic blueberries and organic unsweetened almond milk?" I always got a kick out of Jill. She'd been sewing her own clothes, making her own granola, and baking her own bread long before the pandemic. She was a doula, honorable work. She and Maya used to work together with pregnant women before she divorced and moved upstate. "Breathe and Push" was her and Maya's advice to pregnant women—and to me. It turns out even doulas during the pandemic, like Maya as an OB/GYN nurse administrator, could often be as effective and helpful online as in person.

"Hey!"

I was getting out of hand with excitement. "Okay, I'll shut up, promise."

Maya gave me another look of warning before she resumed.

"One morning I stopped in front of this huge, beautiful tree. There was something amazing about it, I couldn't put my finger on it...."

Maya went on. "You're not gonna believe this..."

"Are you kidding? Nothing surprises me. The tree spoke to you."

"The tree spoke to m...." We said it at the same time.

Trees are sanctuaries. Whoever knows how to speak to them, whoever knows how to listen to them, can learn the truth.... A tree says: A kernel is hidden in me, a spark, a thought, I am life from eternal life. —Hermann Hesse

We both just stared at each other, open-mouthed.

"Xen Kohen," I said at last.

"What? Yes! That's what the tree called itself! He? She? We? I couldn't get that, it just said you needed help. I said I know! Then this Xen Kohen tree says to me, 'That's why I'm here. *You,* Maya, need to summon *me* to help him.'"

"Jeezus, that's like Beatrice, she summoned Virgil to rescue Dante from his lower self and move up the Divine Ladder!"

"Yes. Whatever, that's your area. So, I'm thinking, I can't believe I'm talking to a tree! But I was so, I don't know, in a kind of dreamlike state I still can't describe, and of course I'm worried about you. So I said, okay, I'll be back."

I bit my tongue and took a deep breath. Maya didn't know that in some cosmic sense she herself summoned ol' Xen Kohen. I wasn't going to interrupt her again, though.

"So then the tree—uh, Xen Kohen—says come back tomorrow."

"Did you tell Jill?"

Maya sighed. "I started to tell her I had this unusual, kind of spiritual experience in the woods. I would have had a hard time explaining it and worried she'd think I was getting really stressed out, or worse. So, I was relieved when she shrugged it off and said, 'Of course. Many people around here do, I have them. These woods are sacred. And trees are also powerful women that give birth, like the women we help.' Then she went and found and read me this great poem."

... every time i think about us women I think about the trees
I think about
the subversive trees laden in blood
but not bleeding
the rebellious trees encrusted but not cracking
the abused trees wounded
but still standing
I think about the proud trees

the trees with beehive tits buzzing
the transparent trees
the trees with quinine breath hovering
the trees swaying & rubbing their stretched marked bellies
in the rain
the crossroad trees coming from the tree womb
of tree seeds
Trees....
—Jayne Cortez, excerpt from "Sacred Trees"

"So, I was glad she didn't ask me for details, and I let it go."

"So, the next day you...."

"So, the next day I ... do you wanna hear this or not?"

I nodded and shut my eyes. And my mouth.

"So, the next day I returned to the tree, to this Xen Kohen, who says, 'I just need you to tell me you want me to help Jacob. There are other people too but you're the most important. I won't tell him you're doing this, though, and you have to stay silent. You can't contact him and can't return his texts and calls.' So, I agree. I was still mad at you so the silent part was not hard."

"Ah, so you're the anonymous contributor to my GoFundMe."

"Xen Kohen told you that? Who knew? I didn't even...."

"That also explains why you wouldn't answer my texts."

Maya nodded. "And told Jill not to answer your calls. Anyway, it gets weirder. The next day I notice some sort of eyeglasses in a teal blue box on the ground in front of the tree. Xen Kohen says, put these on whenever you want to see how Jacob is doing. I put them on right away, and every day. It was incredible. Over the months I could see you talk to these awful, rat-like people who showed you those videos of your life, and I saw how you handled them and then escaped! I saw you with your men's group, then your counseling kids, your visits with the dead heroes and to Barbie Land, and how you all defeated the RatocRats in the high school and later in Brooklyn and at the Grand Army Library. It was great!" She gave me a big hug.

I told her the early stuff about my dream, the Camperdown Elm, the ad in the Brooklyn Cosmic Inquirer, the earbuds, meeting the mercurial Xen Kohen in the sub-subway station, the Joy Harjo poem, and the Divine Ladder.

"Did you also see me talk to a Black baby in Prospect Park? A Latina subway conductor, a Muslim woman, a Park Slope hipster, a *meshugeneh* seagull, a mystical koi?"

"Yeah! Who were they, why were you talking to them, and how did you even *manage* to speak with those…?" Maya had a sudden insight. 'You mean, they were all…?"

"Yes. Those were all Xen Kohen, who's from the future."

"Wow. And my tree."

A Miracle

A few days later we walked through Prospect Park and found the Camperdown Elm—My Raintree. My Bodhi tree. My Tree of Life. My Tree that Grows in Brooklyn: Another Tree of Heaven. And—sibling of Maya's and Jill's sister Sacred Tree of Old Growth.

Trees are ladders between Earth and Heaven….

"Here's where everything started," I told Maya.

"Let's renew our vows of love, in front of this tree," she said, which we did.

"And now," I added, "as part of our ritual let's recite our cosmic mantra based on John Prine's song, 'In Spite of Ourselves.'" You know, in spite of ourselves, we're okay. We accept ourselves. We forgive ourselves. We can love ourselves. In spite of ourselves! Damn. We skipped the raunchy duet verses, though. You can hear the whole shebang on YouTube.

Maya took out her mobile. Wi-Fi has long been spotty in the park, but this time we were in luck. She found Louis Armstrong singing "What a Wonderful World" (green trees, red roses, for me and you!) and we slow danced to it in front of the tree.

I was happy no one was around to even think about doing that phony slow-applause thing onlookers do at the end of some rom-coms. I wasn't gonna completely give up my persona as a grumpy kvetch.

What is a miracle? When do you experience one? When you are alone and then you get close to someone you love, the world changes. A miracle, once found only in superstitious myths and pre-scientific religions, or thought to exist only in some spectacular way, appears. But they occur every day. Being next to Maya, holding her, hearing her words, felt like a miracle.

All of a sudden, the world becomes a beautiful place, a heaven.

CHAPTER TWENTY-FIVE

The Ratocracy is Gone, Some Rats Are Still with Us

Imagine we jettison the idea of production and consumption being the sole purpose of economic life and substitute care and freedom...In a world built around care and solidarity, much of this vast and absurd office space would indeed be blown up, but others could be turned into free city universities, social centers and hotels for those in need of shelter. We could call them 'Museums of Care' — precisely because they are spaces that do not celebrate production...but rather provide the space and means for the creation of social relationships and the imagining of entirely new forms of social relations. —Nika Dubrovsky and David Graeber

When you realize you are mortal you also realize the tremendousness of the future. You fall in love with a Time you will never perceive. — Etel Adnan

After the final battle of Brooklyn and my reunion with Maya everyone was ecstatic. All over Brooklyn people, danced in the streets. It was like what Amanda Gorman says in her prophetic poem, "The Hill We Climb"—all of us will emerge bruised yet beautiful: *for there is always light/if only we're brave enough to see it. If only we're brave enough to be it.*

Here's some of what happened.

The School and the BK Dream Team

... if schools cannot enter the students' collective imagination, other forms of knowledge are destined to fill the vacuum. —Stanley Aronowitz

You learn to accept the world on its terms without giving up the belief that you can change the world. That's a successful adulthood—the maturation of your thought process and very soul to the point where you understand the limits of life, without giving up on its possibilities. —Bruce Springsteen

The success of the BK Dream Team—Cami, Dina, Arielle, Derrick, May May, and Billy—opened a space in which they and other students and educators could take back the high school from the Ratocracy. RatocRats like Beckerman and Martinette lost their positions, their authority, and credibility and soon become part of an isolated and irrelevant minority. The Dream Team planned and led small democratic meetings among students and staff. With mutual support, restorative justice, conflict resolution and group problem-solving, and in mindful counseling and study groups they created spaces to help school community members heal and reflect on what they had gone through and rebuild and reorganize the school. Although they knew that trauma is part of one's history, one way to heal from trauma is to find and live with joy.

The Team acknowledged and addressed several RatocRatic emotional issues and grievances—their sense of loss of status, fear, and confusion over changing gender roles, and their mistaken belief that if others gain, they stand to lose. They helped those mired in RatocRatic feelings and beliefs, such as wanting to bully those they feel were to blame for their conditions and thinking autocrats would solve their problems, to transition to more evolved ways of thinking and being. The Team and others drew the line, however, at tolerating some people's overt biases and harmful actions, all while working to understand their underlying emotional experiences and life conditions.

As contemplative and radical surrealist visionaries, the BK Dream Team encouraged limitless imagination and everyone to act as if they already lived in a liberated world. Students and teachers began to imagine and build a decent school based on critical social analysis and thinking, and personal and communal creativity. They set up contemplative arts projects with video, writing, graphic arts, and music to create lucid dream environments that included and respected everyone.

As the Dream Team knew, living as if we are already free is not a simple matter of will. It requires awareness of unavoidable contradictions and conflicts, of how everyone to varying degrees is still conditioned by the past. It means mindful awareness—developing a compassionate relationship with one's thoughts, learning to forgive and let go of old values and patterns, and helping each other develop and practice new ones. The Team took special care to identify and work on patterns that have sometimes plagued progressive practices: self-righteousness, judgmentalism, rigidity of language, us-versus-them thinking, and overattachment to one's absolute viewpoint.

The group would be graduating soon, and so they were each collaborating with students and educators who could carry on their work after they left the school.

The Brooklyn Botanic Garden Timeless Cosmic Future Visions and Food and Music Festival

If we want a new society, we have no choice but to supersede the dominant reality—imagine a different relationship not only to the economy but also to time, to work, to the natural world, to each other. —George Clinton

Heaven and earth, the Celtic saying goes, are only three feet apart, but in thin places that distance is even shorter…. It's not that we lose all sense of time but, rather, that our relationship with time is altered, softened. In thin places, time is not something we feel

compelled to parse or hoard. There's plenty of it to go around. —
Eric Weiner

The group and I met in the Brooklyn Botanic Garden to celebrate and figure out what's next.

"We've reached heaven, gang," I said, "here in Brooklyn. We can see it and live it. Now we want to find a great way to bring it to everyone."

The Team looked at each other and then at me. Derrick spoke. "We already came up with a way to do that, Mr. T."

"We call it the Brooklyn Botanic Garden Timeless Cosmic Future Visions and Food and Music Festival," Billy said.

"It's fantastic! Wait'll you hear this!" Arielle shouted. "It shows everyone what's possible!"

"We hold it right here in the Garden," May May explained. "We have these great venues that are celebrations, with people from the past and from everywhere! Everyone can come and stay as long as they want...."

They explained the whole festival idea and each venue. I was blown away. I added some of my own thoughts, plus I lobbied for two new venues at the end.

The Brooklyn Botanic Garden is a thin place in which heaven and Earth air kiss and where there is an infinite amount of quality time. It's the crown jewel of the Terminal Moraine.

The festival, the Dream Team told me, is one big joyful celebration to be held on a timeless, endless, gorgeous, perfect late spring day. It's a bit like combining parts of the Brooklyn Book Fair (with its panels of extraordinary authors), Celebrate Brooklyn (with its lineup of great musicians), and the Prospect Park/Willamsburg Smorgasburgs (with their fantastic food venues from creative chefs). It uses all the spaces in the Garden. The trees and plants don't give a damn about the time of spring at which they're supposed to bloom, and all show off their blossoms at once: Wordsworth's daffodils, Issa's cherry blossoms, Buson's peonies, Whitman's lilacs, Rilke's roses, Blake's (and

Ginsburg's) sunflowers, and Mary Oliver's holy trees. Azaleas, tulips, wisteria, dahlias, and other flowers and bushes also run wild.

Upon entering, everyone receives a T-shirt with the line from the song "Woodstock" by Joni Mitchell: *We Have Got to Get Ourselves Back to the Garden,* and a pair of XK AI Anti-Google Goggles. There is always room for everyone. People can visit any or all venues from the past and the future. They have all the time they like. They want for nothing. The gang extended their insight that one of the best ways to overcome trauma is through joy.

These are some of the venues the group told me about that everyone could visit:

"First, we want to let people know the story of how we all defeated the Ratocracy," Dina said, "so we created a multimedia show. And we have a Q&A session."

1. The BK Dream Team Sound and Light Show and Discussion

The Team put together a dramatic presentation with storytelling, poetry, video, graphics, dance, music, and songs on how they and their friends defeated the Ratocracy in their high school.

"We also offer individual sessions," Cami said:

Derrick on *Violence Interruption and Peacemaking*

May May on *Being Trans and Judo*

Arielle and Dina on *Creating Great Jewish-Palestinian relations*

Billy on *Graphic Comics and Imagining a New Future*

Cami, Dina, May May, and Arielle on *How to Fight Together to Find Yourselves, specifically for young women*

Derrick and Cami on *Organizing Young People from the African Diaspora and the Caribbean as Guardians of Justice*

Billy and May May on *LGBTQ+ Life, Family, and Love*

"Then, we've invited all those great superheroes we met who encouraged us to share their wisdom with everyone else," Billy said.

2. The Consultants from the Cosmic Disembodied Dogen Retreat Center on How to Speak Truth to Power, Connect, and Kick Butt with Love

All are there: Shirley Chisholm, James Baldwin, Paul Robeson, Woody Guthrie, Victor Jara, Tupac, Harriet Tubman, Cesar Chavez, Elizabeth Gurley Flynn, Jane Jacobs, Harvey Milk, Bayard Rustin, Martin Luther King Jr., Pedro Albizu, Joe Hill, Maya Angelou, Marek Edelman, Minerva Mirabal, Fred Hampton, and Mahatma Gandhi.

They speak, dialogue, answer questions, and have everyone sing "I Dreamed I Saw Joe Hill Last Night." To top it off, they lead everyone around the Garden in a conga line.

"Your guys, the Brooklyn Codgers, are also happy to give workshops and share with everyone what they know," Arielle said.

3. The Brooklyn Codgers Workshops and Discussions for Park Slopers and Other Zombies Who are Stuck in Emotional Purgatory

Jay Profwreck: How to Mindfully Fight Disinformation and Self-Delusion
Bob Frawst: How to Mindfully Decondition from Competition and Productivity Addictions
Jess B.: How to Mindfully Let Go of Reactive Militarism and Be at Peace

"Mr. T., you told us you were at a sacred American Indian site and didn't just want to do virtue signaling, so we got these leaders from Native American groups to talk about how people can help them out in a real way," Cami shared.

4. Joy Harjo and Native American members of the Native Organizers Alliance Action Fund, the Native American Rights Fund, the American Indian

Movement, Eastern Navajo Diné Against Uranium Mining (ENDAUM), and other advocacy groups

They will hold a workshop on How White People Can Avoid Land Acknowledgments as Performative Virtue Signaling and Actively Support Indigenous People.

Derrick told us, "Man, we brought in a bunch of great leaders, some from the past, on this panel. I'm on it too, about Afrofuturism and imagining how things could and should be. Cami's excited—she's read Octavia Butler and now gets to meet her."

5. Marva Williams, Derrick, Martin Luther King Jr., Isabel Wilkerson, Heather McGee, Octavia Butler, and Robin D.G. Kelley

Their workshop will be on The Black Radical Imagination, Afrofuturism, and Surrealism.

The mountaintop that Dr. King spoke about does not exist in this universe. It's an imaginary construct of what the future could be. —John Jennings

Juxtaposing surrealism and Black conceptions of liberation is no mere academic exercise; it is an injunction, a proposition, perhaps even a declaration of war. I am suggesting that the Black freedom movement take a long, hard look at our own surreality as well as surrealist thought and practice in order to build new movements, new possibilities, new conceptions of liberation. —Robin D.G. Kelley

The panel describes what a visionary Afrofuturist and surrealist society looks like. It includes community building toward a culture of hope, peace, healing, and the arts. All are invited and welcome to share their dreams.

Billy spoke about the next panel. "Hey, these are the guys I told you all about who created comic superheroes who also save Brooklyn! They're happy to be a part of this."

6. New Brooklyn Superheroes in Graphic Comics Introduced by their Creators

Dean Haspiel: *Red Hook*
Seth Kushner, Shamus Beyale, Jason Goungor: *The Brooklynite*
Vito Delsante and Ricardo Venancio: *The Purple Heart*

Arielle then shared, "We all came up with this one, Mr. T., people can talk to their favorite ancestors. We've all picked the ones we want to meet."

I had to try this one out right away.

7. Talk to your favorite Ancestors! Better than Ancestry.com!

I was thrilled to meet my grandfather, Vigdor, the democratic socialist from Sheepshead Bay, whom I never knew and who worked with Xen Kohen. He told me how as a young Bundist militant he escaped the Polish region of the czarist empire after the failure of the revolution of 1905. He went to Manchester, England, where he met my grandmother, then moved to New York where he was active in the Amalgamated Clothing Workers Union. He said that Xen Kohen kept showing up in his dreams. Sometimes he looked like his hero, Karl Marx; other times he appeared as a Yiddisheh mameh who kept noodging him about being a good father to my own father and his other kids. We ate some herring and potato kugel and had a beer together. "Keep fighting for the oppressed!" he told me.

Dina told us, "Our new friend Marva, who helped us defeat the rats, offered to help lead a workshop on Double Dutch with a bunch of young women she knows from Bed-Stuy."

8. Double Dutch Lessons and Demonstrations— Ropes Provided

Marva Williams and friends. Astounding embodiment of timing and athleticism.

"Great!" I was thrilled with that one and planned to try it with Maya.

Tiresias, although a mere spectator and not indeed a "character," is yet the most important personage in the poem, uniting all the rest. —T.S. Eliot, Notes on The Waste Land

"So, listen, Mr. T.," May May then said. "This kinda strange old person, Tiresias, came up to us and said they wanted to do a workshop. We didn't know them, but they say they know you, so we figured okay, let them do one. They're a showboat, though."

"We Googled them and checked them out with our goggles too," Arielle said. She looked down at her notes. "They say they're intersex and have witnessed and foresuffered all of human history and even the future with compassion. They're gonna give some examples of cosmic works of art that transcend time and show compassion for everyone who ever lived, without judging them."

"One cosmic bisexy human, awright," Derrick added.

I suspected it was Xen Kohen but couldn't be sure. Was Xen Kohen—that *meshugeneh* character with genders that haven't even been created yet, who can witness the past, present, and future— Tiresias? Or just cosplaying? I had to check out this person's shtick.

9. Tiresias Presents: Fierce Compassionate Cosmic Witnessing of the Heaven and Hell of Everyday Life

"Here's the deal," Tiresias said with a voice that sounded suspiciously like Xen Kohen trying to sound like Harvey Firestein. "I, Tiresias—an old man with wrinkled dugs, as T.S. Eliot likes to say about me—am a seer, a visionary, a prophet. I got an overarching cosmic viewpoint on all of humanity. I'm gonna introduce you to some works of art that take a fierce compassionate and dispassionate perspective on everyone and everything that people do, the way I do."

You could see or hear the artworks Tiresias presented via the XK AI Anti-Google Goggles. Here are a few and what Tiresias said about them. I was even more suspicious when he chose some of my favorites. Yeah okay, these artists are white guys, but you know, I feel they transcend their so-called identity and take a universalist, timeless view that includes everybody.

"Frans Masereel's *The City*. This is a gem of a wordless book by a great progressive Belgian artist from the 1920s whose character witnesses with compassion love, injustice, mean bosses, labor strikes, poverty, families, prostitutes and johns, everyone.

"The song 'Passing Through' by Richard Blakeslee. The narrator goes on a historical trip through time, like me, and talks with Adam, Jesus, George Washington, and FDR, each of whom tells him, well, I'm just passing through, but glad that I ran into you, I do what I gotta do for everyone's sake, just tell everyone you saw me passing through.

"*Time*, by Lorado Taft in Washington Park, on the South Side of Chicago, near the university, is a massive 1922 statue of Father Time witnessing the parade of humanity. It was inspired by an 1883 poem, "Paradox of Time," by Henry Austin Dobson:

Time goes, you say? Ah no!
Alas, Time stays, we go

He sees them all, accepts them all. He stays; the people go. Yeah, like me. You oughta see it when you're in Chicago.

"Terrence Malick's flicks, especially *The Tree of Life*. Listen, you have to see he takes a cosmic view of everything. He looks at all of life and time, even the whole universe, and accepts and forgives all. He often has beautiful shots of *komorebi* right in the middle of his movie. That's a Japanese word for when you see the play of sunlight through leaves, those beams of light that shine through trees when they fall on grass or anywhere, the light and the dark. It's a feeling of peace and tranquility you get from the transient beauty of experiencing it.

Help each other. Love everyone. Every leaf. Every ray of light. Forgive—The Tree of Life

"*Raintree County* by Ross Lockridge Jr. meets my standard of weaving a cosmic vision within a particular historical time, in this case nineteenth-century America. Oh, and the movie, with the terrific Montgomery Clift, is unfortunately terrible. Here is a fragment from the book:

The wall between himself and the world dissolved. He seemed suddenly lost from himself, plucked out of time and space, being both time and space himself, an inclusive being in which all other beings had their being. A vast unrest was in the earth. The Valley of Humanity was turbulent with changing forms. The immense dream trembled on a point of night and nothingness and threatened explosion.

"And of course there's Whitman, Blake, Baldwin, others.... But hey, listening to the music we love often gives us the same transcendent, timeless yet embodied experience. Music of course depends on time. Yet when you're locked in, time also stops...."

Suddenly Tiresias froze and their eyes rolled up into their head. "Time is also history," Tiresias intoned in a loud, slow voice. "Here is a glimpse of your future, if you want it: The racist, sexist, system based on greed, profit, competition, and violence will burn itself out. No more self-blame, self-harm. No more exploitation of others and the Earth. People care for and support and respect each other. They see themselves as connected with everyone and everything...."

Tiresias came out of the trance, looked around, and resumed their previous voice. "Okay, back to the music. Choose your favorites and enjoy!" After that prophecy I was even more suspicious it was Xen Kohen cosplaying Tiresias.

Dina shook her head and after a long pause spoke. "As you see, Mr. T.," Dina explained, "Tiresias agreed to plug the music venues scene. In the music venues each musician sings and plays for as long as people want to hear them. We got some of your favorite singers and songs here, Mr. T. You get to pick the keynote song and singer too."

Cami said, "Your tastes are kinda, like old, though, Mr. T...."

I couldn't argue with that.

"... So later we're gonna add our own favorite singers and the music kids listen to today—rap, reggaton, hip hop, you know. But when people come, they can ask for their own! The performers will show up!"

"You saying Taylor Swift and Beyoncé and Bad Bunny are gonna be there?"

"Yup!"

10. The Music Venues: Climbin' Up the Ladder of Time to Hear a Fragment of Song

I chose Paul Simon to provide the keynote song, the one sung and paraphrased by the accountability coordinator in Hell Inc.— "The Afterlife."

Simon hits all the main themes: You ascend the ladder of time! You get to meet God! You're in infinite space, beyond words! You're swimming in a sea of love! But when you try to figure out the answer to the mystery, you're just left with a puzzling fragment from one rock song or another. Simon poses a deep xen kohen: is it *Be Bop A Lu La or Ooh Poppa Do?*

Meditate on that.

You'll have to ask the kids who they want; by the time I write them down they could be out of date. Here are some of my faves. Common themes are the ladder to heaven, mystery, love, time, and utopian futuristic visions and dreams.:

Leonard Cohen sings "Hallelujah"; Bob Dylan, "Forever Young"; John Lennon, "Imagine"; Van Morrison, "Days Like This"; Laura Nyro, "Save the Country"; John Prine, "The Tree of Forgiveness"; and Esther Satterfield, "Land of Make Believe."

This world is full of conflicts and full of things that cannot be reconciled. But there are moments when we can ... reconcile and embrace the whole mess, and that's what I mean by 'Hallelujah.' Leonard Cohen

Patti Smith conducts everyone in the chorus of "People Have the Power."

I also had to have Cindi Lauper, who leads a line of dancing people all around the Botanic Garden while singing "Girls Just Wanna Have Fun."

The dream that gets acted out in [the video of] Girls Just Want to Have Fun is a dream of bringing together our private and public lives, of uniting the rights of man [sic] and the rights of a citizen. By fulfilling the first commandment of liberal individualism— Express Yourself, Have Fun— we can create a beloved community, a community so radiant that even our parents will want to join. — Marshall Berman, "Take It to the Streets: Conflict and Community in Public Space" in *Modernism in the Streets*

I wanted to bring in some Brooklyn-born or resident singers/song writers: Richard Farina, "Reflections in a Crystal Wind"; Mos Def, "Brooklyn"; Talib Kweli, "Beautiful Struggle"; B.I.G.'s "A Dream"; Richie Havens, "Follow"; Woody Guthrie's "Heaven" and "This Land is Your Land," with its last radical verse (look it up). David Byrne performs

"One Fine Day" with the Brooklyn Youth Choir: *Then a peace of mind fell over me/In these troubled times, I still can see…*

Festival Highlight: Paul Robeson and Bruce Springsteen sing the Cosmic Gospel Song "Jacob's Ladder."

Everyone is invited to sing along. First, Paul sings his elegiac version. Bruce joins in. Then Bruce sings his celebratory rendition with a large, ebullient, raucous band. Paul joins in. Everyone can dance or enjoy the music as they wish.

"Jacob's Ladder"

*We are climbing
Jacob's Ladder…
We are climbing higher and higher…
We are brothers, sisters all…*

The Rats Are Still Here

I told the Dream Team I felt we needed to provide our enemies, Pete, Ratty, and Ayn, a venue, one that would be monitored and regulated by a panel of Brooklyn citizens.

"No way," Cami said.

"I know, but here's the thing. I now remember what Pete said when I was down there, they're not such bad creatures. It's what uncaring people do, like leave garbage around, that gets them to act the way they do."

"They're still bad dudes," Derrick said.

"True, though they did pay their debt and went to an intensive rehab program," Arielle said.

"More than that," I said, "I learned that in some way they're an aspect of all of us, kind of our lower, earlier evolved selves, and we're connected to them."

"Yeah, I get that," May May said. "They're never gonna go away, we have to learn to live with that part of us, with them too."

"Okay, Mr. T.," Dina chimed in, "as long as they behave themselves!"

Here's a bit of background:

In the early days, New York was able to limit the rats from over-running the city and kept them under relative control. Some city council members called themselves the Rat Pack and formed a "Rat Action Plan" with an aggressive package of bills aimed at reducing street trash. As one of them said, "Our icon should not be a rat dragging a pizza through the subway."

The city created a new position, a director of rodent mitigation, popularly known as the Rat Czar, that required the final candidate to have a "swashbuckling attitude, a general aura of badassery, and a somewhat bloodthirsty" nature. They waged a campaign to kill rats through traps, drowning, and poison and starve them by mandating early garbage pickup and in sealed containers.

Alongside the Rat Czar, the new sanitation commissioner launched the attack with a quote that became a viral meme: *The rats don't run this city, we do.* It was posted on the sides of sanitation trucks and on T-shirts above an image of a frightened, nervous rat. The new Rat Czar, like the Rat Pack, also took on Pete the Pizza Rat in her message to New Yorkers: *Pizza Rat may live in infamy, but rats and the conditions that support their thriving will no longer be tolerated in New York City.*

The three rats, Pete, Ratty, and Ayn, like many politicians and celebrities, were determined to rehabilitate their reputations as victims of an unjust system.

Pete continued to crave publicity and was often sought out for soundbites on the media. He was not impressed with the Rat Pack, the new sanitation commissioner, or the new Rat Czar.

"The Rat Pack with a Rat Action Plan—wadda joke—they're proud to call themselves rats but they don't like real rats. Then the sanitation commissioner and this Rat Czar, whatever that is, they insult *me,* the pizza rat, and tink they can stop us with earlier garbage collections. We like to eat at night anyway, that makes no diffrince to us!"

Ratty was also interviewed on the media and pointed out the mayor, himself a sworn enemy of rats, was fined for rat infestation on his own property. "How's that for a hypocrite mayor, hah?"

11. The Venue of the Three Rats—Pete, Ratty, and Ayn

"We are living in a time of failing social structures and a literal rat problem across major cities.... Rats are resilient and able to scurry for basic necessities...." "Rat Girl Summer trend is exactly about not doing something because capitalism told us to do it, and only doing things you genuinely want to" ... "Coming out of the pandemic, society wants us to go back to the old normal, but young people are saying they don't want to meet society's expectations anymore" ..." Don't overthink. If rats don't think twice before stealing a slice of pizza and escaping across the subway platform...." —Maham Javaid, Washington Post

We allowed Pete, Ratty, and Ayn, on probation and under strict supervision after an intensive mandatory rehabilitation, to staff their own venue at the festival, which proved highly popular.

Pete had learned to make pizza in the rehab facility. In their venue he had his own outdoor oven and handed out free slices of New York style and artisanal pizza, for which there were long queues.

The three rats found they could capitalize on some people's lingering RatocRatic sympathies. As a nostalgic shtick they gave out old RatocRat paraphernalia like the Pizza Rat berets, Ghouliani hair dye, and Ayn Ratnd autographed books and cigarette holders.

As part of their community service they were required to hand out posters and T-shirts that said: *New York: Stop Feeding Your Inner and Outer Rats!* The Codgers, the Dream Team, Marva, Maya, and I wore ours with pride.

The three provided pamphlets that explained their grievances and claimed they were misunderstood. If you give us what we need, take care of our mutual environment, they argued, we're not a problem.

The rats asked people who stopped by to sign a petition started by the animal activist group PETA, People for the Ethical Treatment of Animals. The group was incensed by the mayor's fixation on killing rats, whom a PETA spokesperson described as "intelligent and sensitive creatures" and said the city should stop leaving garbage on the streets. "As long as the garbage is there and being littered across the city, rats will be there … it's human beings' disgusting behavior that has led to the rat population explosion in NYC," a spokesperson for the group said.

Pete, Ratty, and Ayn also provided articles on how they're indeed sensitive, intelligent, good guys, and cool—even anti-capitalist—and they loved to argue their case with anyone. They cited articles from the *New York Post, Scientific American, National Geographic*, and the *Washington Post*:

"Rats can help earthquake survivors!"

"Rats have the power of imagination!"

"Rats can sniff out tuberculosis!"

"Hip Rat Girls have a Rat Girl Summer! It's a worldwide TikTok movement! They embrace rodent energy—live like a rat: run around all day and night, snack on whatever and whenever, go to places you have no business going to!"

12. Hell Residents Restitution Group and Workshop

I also convinced the Dream Team to practice fierce compassion toward some of the bad dudes from Hell Inc. We arranged with the bureaucrats from below to offer motivated and sincere residents short-term visas to Heaven for a chance to redeem themselves from their hellish conditions.

The applicants were sent upstairs, where a panel of Brooklyn citizens interviewed and evaluated them for their level of genuine remorse and potential for rehabilitation. Those selected could remain in the Botanic Garden Festival. They engaged in therapy and studied the harsh injustices of the capitalist system and their role in it. They could practice personal restitution and community service with others to create a decent post-capitalist world. Many applied, though few were found to be eligible.

***

Moving On

We live in a world that is not perfectible, a world that always presents you with a sense of something undone, something missing, something hurting, something irritating...there is a certain wisdom of no exit: this is our human predicament and the only consolation is embracing it. —Leonard Cohen

The Dream Team and I celebrated our victory and being together. We had a huge feast at one of Dina's cousin's Palestinian restaurants in Bay Ridge and exchanged toasts and gifts, laughter and tears into the night.

"You won't see as much of me," I told them. I was both sad and happy to see they had come into their own. We all knew it.

"We'll miss you, Mr. T."

"I'll miss you too. But I'm always here for you."

The BK Dream Team stayed together and would go on to become a renowned and trusted team of superheroes within Brooklyn, New York City, the United States, and the rest of the world. They collaborated with many communities and became leaders and consultants in Radical Contemplative Bullshit Busting, Community Connecting, and Defensive Disarming. They began to find and work with members of the next generation of future contemplative and radical surrealist visionaries.

CHAPTER TWENTY-SIX

The End and Beginning of Time. XK Returns and Departs

"Brother," he replied, "thy great desire
in the last sphere above shall be fulfilled,
where all thine others are, and mine as well.
Every desire is perfect there, mature
and whole; in that sphere only is each part
where it has always been; for it is not
in space, nor turns on poles, and up to it
our Ladder reaches; and because of this
it steals itself away beyond thy ken.
Jacob, the patriarch, beheld it stretch
thus far its upper portion, when of old
laden with Angels it appeared to him.
—Canto XXII, Paradiso, trans. Courtney Langdon

To become the species that the earth needs—creatures who are not only self-conscious but conscious that we are how the earth becomes self-conscious—we need to embrace the new bodhisattva path, which unites individual and social transformation. That involves contemplative practices deconstructing and reconstructing one's sense of self, in service of social and ecological engagement. — David R. Loy

Maya and I had an exit interview with Xen Kohen. One night we both had the same dream at the same time in which XK appeared as the person whom I first met in the sub-subway station. How about that? It was mostly for me, but Maya got to meet the mighty XK in another form.

Xen Kohen was all mega-watt smiles. "You've reached the last sphere, dude, the top of the Ladder Jacob saw! Like Benedict told Dante, you can see the temporal and the eternal together! You can see the boundlessness of time and space! You're back with Maya, your own Beatrice!

"And … you're free of debt, it's all paid…. Well, not quite. You're required to continue as a mensch on the new bodhisattva path. You gotta keep deconstructing and reconstructing yourself and your relationships, especially with Maya, for the sake of everyone, for the sake of the Earth. As someone who's becoming even more aware of yourself, you and other similar people need to know you are the way the Earth becomes conscious of *itself.* Breathe and Push!" Xen Kohen laughed. "It's how we move up the Divine Ladder!

"Your legacy is the BK Dream Team," XK told us. "They carry on your dreams, and their own, for a beautiful future. And hey, happy to see the other night you had the Codgers and Marva over for dinner." Maya had made us a terrific meal. XK didn't miss a note.

"Do we get to see you again?" Maya and I both asked in the dream. Xen Kohen smiled and said, "In one form, look to the Dream Team. They are me, I am them. You can be with me through them whenever you want."

Was XK the kids? I finally realized at different times XK had taken on each of their backgrounds in a crazy way to help me out.

In the dream, Maya said, "I just remembered, I never told Jacob, but right after I left for Jill's I dreamt I was flying around with him, like in a Chagall painting, all around Brooklyn, and we saw the Camperdown Elm and I pointed it out to him."

I was stunned and turned to Maya. "So that person next to me whom I couldn't see, that wasn't Xen Kohen, it was you?"

XK just smiled and said, "Now you both can do that, like Chagall flying around with Bella, the love of his life—you can fly out beyond time and space." Then XK disappeared in a rainbow flash.

In the morning, we found a note on the kitchen counter:

"As promised, here's Dogen's answer to Dylan's xen kohen: Are birds free from the chains of the skyway?

A fish swims in the ocean, and no matter how far it swims there is no end to the water.
A bird flies in the sky, and no matter how far it flies there is no end to the air.
However, the fish and the bird have never left their elements.
When their activity is large their field is large.
When their need is small their field is small.
Thus, each of them totally covers its full range, and each of them totally experiences its realm…. Know that water is life and air is life.
The bird is life and the fish is life.
Life must be the bird and life must be the fish.

Bonus: *The butterfly counts not months but moments, and has time enough.* —Rabindranath Tagore"

After discussing it Maya and I interpreted it this way:

For the bird, the skyway is its entire life, the bird is the sky, the sky is the bird. The sky expands and shrinks depending on what the bird does, on what it needs. So, there is no separation between the bird and the sky, there is no problem of whether it is free. The larger meaning is that you (the bird) can and should fully, freely live your relative, historical life (which includes fighting for a less broken, better world for all) and at the same time fully participate in and experience the absolute beauty and harmony of the universe (the sky).

As for time, same with the butterfly. It has all the time it needs!

We still couldn't get enough of Xen Kohen. XK must have read our minds and in the next part of the note, they addressed our longing:

"Walt, the Brooklyn godparent of all cosmic dreams, and I, both send you this message he wrote (the end of "Song of Myself," which always makes me cry)—and with it all our love. XK"

I bequeath myself to the dirt to grow from the grass I love,
If you want me again look for me under your boot-soles.
You will hardly know who I am or what I mean,
But I shall be good health to you nevertheless,
And filter and fibre your blood.
Failing to fetch me at first keep encouraged,
Missing me one place search another,
I stop somewhere waiting for you.

***

Sometime later, we read Katy Waldman's *New Yorker* review (June 17, 2024) of novels written during COVID. She concluded,

... pandemic novels, for all their inability to transform the past or undo millions of deaths, can mark that a real and irreversible metamorphosis has taken place.... Rather than narrating the pandemic, [the best writing] *drives home the fact that the pandemic happened: that something broke apart, dispersed, and remains to be reconstituted. By resisting closure, books ... refuse to rush readers into an understanding that the world has not yet achieved. They don't fake an equilibrium that is likely months or years away.*

I laughed. "She hasn't read my book yet."

Maya wasn't laughing. She shook her head and looked me in the eye. "She's right. An unalterable change has occurred. Nothing is final. Some broken things still need to be made whole. For now, most of the world doesn't get what you've written about."

As usual, Maya was right too. I put on my *New York: Stop Feeding Your Inner and Outer Rats!* T-shirt and crossed Eastern Parkway into the Botanic Garden, the jewel of the Terminal Moraine, onto the sun-dappled, *komorebi* grass of the Cherry Tree Esplanade, in search of Xen Kohen, who has stopped somewhere, waiting for me, waiting for you.

Coda

The End and Beginning of Time

On the Waste Land's edge
On the Terminal Moraine
We hold each other
Then let go
We dwell within
Our words
Our dreams
Our imaginings
Our longings

We become them

May we heal
The fragmented earth
May we transform
The Broken Land
Together
May we ascend
The Divine
Ladder of Time
Toward the
One
Universal
Love

Acknowledgements

I am most grateful to my wise editor, Julie Friesner, who believed in this project, and to Jenn Harris of Lucid Pulp for her brilliant copyediting and suggestions. Many thanks to Jeanne V. of epublishinghelp.com for her patience and helpful expertise.

Many thanks to my colleagues and friends, professors emeriti of English Peter Taubman and Geraldine DeLuca, and Barbara Winslow, emerita, of Brooklyn College, who have given me invaluable feedback on the manuscript.

Thanks to Eleanor Bader, an intrepid journalist, for her help and encouragement, and Nomi Naeem, a former student and a knowledgeable librarian at the Brooklyn Grand Army Plaza Library, who has provided guidance in my research of challenging topics. Thanks to my nephew, Joshua Cohen, for his terrific technical assistance.

Friends and colleagues Judith Bejot, Larry Lockridge, Eliott Lopez, José Sanchez, Luchi Sanchez, Ben Susswein, Aimee Telsey, Suzanne Telsey, Donna Glee Williams, Barbara Winslow, Michael Yonchenko, cousins Warren Friesner and Richard Friesner, and sister Vicki Forbes have been encouraging and supportive of this project. Most of all, my wife, Iris Lopez, has been a source of unwavering support and love for which I am forever grateful.

Permissions

Poems, First Edition, edited by Robert Bly, ©1997; permission conveyed through Copyright Clearance Center, Inc.

Ursula Le Guin, excerpt from "Hymn to Time" from *Late in the Day: 2010-2014.* © 2015. Reprinted by permission of PM Press.

Excerpt from THE LEFT HAND OF DARKNESS: 50TH ANNIVERSARY EDITION by Ursula K. Le Guin, © 1969 by Ursula K. Le Guin. Used by permission of Ace, an imprint of Penguin Publishing Group, a division of Penguin Random House LLC. All rights reserved.

"Invitation" by Mary Oliver. Reprinted by the permission of The Charlotte Sheedy Literary Agency as agent for the author. Copyright © 2008, 2017 by Mary Oliver with permission of Bill Reichblum.

"When I am Among the Trees" by Mary Oliver. Reprinted by the permission of The Charlotte Sheedy Literary Agency as agent for the author. Copyright © 2006, 2010, 2017 by Mary Oliver with permission of Bill Reichblum.

Excerpts from SLAUGHTERHOUSE-FIVE: A NOVEL: 50TH ANNIVERSARY EDITION BY Kurt Vonnegut, copyright © 1968, 1969 and copyright renewed ©1996, 1997 by Kurt Vonnegut, Jr. Used by permission of Dell Publishing, an imprint of Random House, a division of Penguin Random House LLC. All rights reserved.

Excerpt from "Sacred Trees" from the book *On the Imperial Highway: New and Selected Poems* by Jayne Cortez used with grateful permission by Mark Pawlak of Hanging Loose Press.

Excerpt from the movie script, "Repo Man" used with grateful permission by writer and director Alex Cox.

Author Bio

David Forbes is an emeritus professor, the Graduate Center of the City University of New York and author of *Mindfulness and Its Discontents: Education, Self, and Social Transformation*. He taught school counseling at Brooklyn College for nineteen years. He lives in Brooklyn with his wife, Iris Lopez, a professor at City College/CUNY.